# Rev. Dr. Megalo Maniac's Supernatural Salvation Spectacle and Marvelous Mega-Church Meeting

Jerry Faught II

**Parson's Porch Books**

*Rev. Dr. Megalo Maniac's Supernatural Salvation Spectacle and Marvelous Mega-Church Meeting*

**To order additional copies of this book, contact:**

**Parson's Porch & Company**
**1-423-475-7308**
**www.parsonsporchbooks.com**

# Rev. Dr. Megalo Maniac's Supernatural Salvation Spectacle and Marvelous Mega-Church Meeting

Jerry Faught II

# Table of Contents

# Introduction:

# The Greatest Show on Earth

Reverend Megalo Maniac stood gazing out the large window of his plush office overlooking the college and seminary campus that bore his name. He pondered his many great accomplishments and wondered how he would be remembered when he passed from this life to live in his heavenly mansion in the sky. He knew that Jesus, not Peter, would greet him in heaven with open arms, hug him tightly and say,

"Well done good and faithful servant."

Homosexuals, atheists, Jews, Mormons, Muslims, and Catholics, in that order, were far from the kingdom of heaven. Yet, heaven would gladly welcome him and Jesus would show great appreciation to Megalo for all of his significant contributions on earth. Megalo had no uncertainty when it came to the hereafter. In fact, there were only a handful of questions to which Megalo did not have ready answers. One of his biggest uncertainties, however, had to do with his legacy. Which of his important achievements would be most celebrated by the world? Everywhere he traveled to preach the host pastor would introduce him as an important man who knew many important men. After all, Megalo claimed that he had held weekly meetings with the past three U.S. presidents in order to give them spiritual guidance and encouragement.

"G.W. had me in his phone as a favorite," Megalo boasted on many occasions.

Most hosts who introduced Megalo spent a lot of time detailing Megalo's many accomplishments primarily because Megalo had informed his secretary, Ima Dormat, to request that this be done. Ima did not have much of a life of her own because Megalo required her to be available twenty-four hours a day every day to do whatever Megalo demanded. Megalo asked much of Ima but never acknowledged what she did except that he had her phone up the florist on secretary's day to have them deliver roses to her office.

Based on his own evaluation and what his pastor friends had said about him, Megalo made a list in his head of his most significant

7

contributions while he leaned back in his plush red, white, and blue leather office chair emblazoned with small white stars and gazed at all of the animal heads he had mounted on his office walls. Megalo had killed the animals during his many African safaris over the years. He was especially proud of the mounted giraffe that towered above all the other animals. When a local reporter, Skip Scoop, visited Megalo's office one day and saw the giraffe he went back to the office and asked his colleagues,

"Who the hell would kill an innocent giraffe and mount the poor animal upon his office wall?"

One of Skip's fellow reporters responded, "This is the same guy who goes around the country putting on "Fin, Feather, and Faith Festivals. Anyway, he claims the giraffe was old and needed to be put down."

"Seriously," added Skip, "Who even kills an old giraffe?"

Megalo loved his special meetings with brawny hunters all decked out in camouflage attire eating wild game and sharing with them his favorite hunting sermon entitled, "Shooting Straight in a Crooked World." On one occasion Megalo held one of his festivals in Bullshoe, Texas where the only thing on the menu was calf fries and freedom (not French) fries. Bullshoe men refused to use the word "French" because they hated the French insisting that the French had in the past refused to assist the U.S. effectively in its war on terror. Unaware that French Fries have nothing to do with France, the inhabitants of Bullshoe joined other conservative Christians from across the U.S. in boycotting anything that might come from France or might be remotely related to the country.

The Bullshoe Fun with Guns Club along with the First Baptist Church of Bullshoe sponsored Megalo's festival and invited all the men of the town to the "Freedom Fried Testicle Festival and Salvation Camp Meeting." After consuming a bucket load of calf fries, a plate full of freedom fries, and numerous RC Cola's Megalo gave an evangelistic sermon and invited all the "lost" men of Bullshoe to have the "cajones" to receive Christ.

"The calf gave his little bit, but Christ gave his all for you," Megalo shouted.

Twenty men came forward to receive Christ and to join the Bullshoe Fun with Guns Club. The First Baptist pastor met with the men and invited them to a pheasant hunt the next Saturday if they promised to let him baptize them on Sunday morning.

"Perhaps I will be known as a great charismatic evangelistic preacher," Megalo mused.

He had started out with a congregation of only thirty persons but over the years had moved to bigger and bigger churches until finally he made it to Houston where he established himself as the world's premier mega-church pastor. Megalo had left a mega-church in the Dallas-Ft. Worth

Metroplex to become pastor of the Third Baptist Church of Houston, an even bigger church. Meanwhile, Second Baptist Church of Houston had experienced some troubles and fired their pastor so Megalo asked struggling Second Baptist to merge with Third Baptist and the merger happened. Finally, Megalo asked the dwindling First Baptist Church to join Second and Third Baptist and they gladly did so. Megalo's church grew so large he had to buy a giant downtown arena that once housed a professional basketball team to house all the members. The church became known in Houston as Arena Church.

"Megalo bragged to a group of Houston area reporters, "I hit a home run in the Arena by combining First, Second, and Third!"

The reporters responded, "But it's a basketball arena, it's not big enough for a baseball team. Your analogy doesn't make sense."

Megalo smiled and remarked, "Guys, you are right, I should have said, I hit a slam dunk. Who cares anyway. All that matters is that I am a winner in Christ."

Needless to say Megalo's church became the largest evangelical church in the world. Of course, Megalo's primary method of judging success was in counting numbers of persons in the arena who had come to hear him preach and the numbers who tuned in to his radio and TV broadcasts. His second method of evaluating his success had to do with counting the money in his bank account that had grown impressively over the years primarily due to the large offerings taken up every Sunday.

Megalo even found the time to carry on a robust ministry as a traveling evangelist. For years Megalo had been highly sought after as a speaker at pastor's conferences and revivals all over the world. He could thunder from the pulpit better than any preacher he had ever heard. His followers told him that he had made the world forget Billy Graham. One of his devoted fans sent Megalo a bumper sticker that read, "Billy Who?" Megalo proudly displayed the sticker on his customized Rolls Royce even though no one knew what it meant. In fact, most people who pulled up behind Megalo in traffic had confused looks on their faces. The sticker did not only stymie them, they could not understand Megalo's personalized license plate. It read WWMD? (What Would Megalo Do?)

"I might be remembered as a great denominational statesman," Megalo continued.

Megalo had served as president of his denomination on two separate occasions and had served on various committees. He had been one of the chief figures who had carried out a doctrinal cleansing in his denomination. Some of his pals claimed that he single handedly "deliberalized" the denomination by kicking out churches and individuals who did not adhere to the fundamentals of the faith. Megalo's opponents referred to him as the "Frenetic Fundamentalist," but his cronies called him

"God's Appointed Guardian of the Faith." After all, Megalo had been instrumental in banning books, firing seminary presidents and faculty members all because they disagreed with his religious and political ideas. For Megalo, anyone who wanted to be in his denomination had to pass the VIP test. They must adhere to a belief in the Virgin birth of Christ, the Inerrancy of Scripture, and the Pre-millennial return of Christ. For Megalo, if you weren't a VIP believer then you were not one at all. And of course, you had to be a right wing Republican. Megalo didn't believe one could be a Christian and also be a member of the Democratic party.

As Megalo continued to ponder his greatness suddenly he remembered his schools.

"Founder of elite Christian schools, that is how people will remember me," Megalo said aloud as he popped his red, white, and blue suspenders that stretched over his protruding gut.

After his church had become enormous and the money flowed freely into the offering plates then into his pockets, Megalo built a K-12 Christian school so that his congregants would not have to send their children to the godless public schools to receive an education. Megalo often ranted how the public schools had taken prayer and Bible reading out of the schools and these actions had led to the disintegration of public education. Megalo believed the public schools to be dens of iniquity and the peddlers of secular ideology. Although he served several terms on the Texas School Board with a view toward reforming public schools, Megalo promoted the home school movement and even founded a K-12 Christian school called Patriot Bible Academy where young evangelicals could train to become the leaders of the nation. Megalo founded a college that he and his buddies referred to as a world class university but the college folded after only a few years so Megalo orchestrated a planned takeover of an existing Baptist University and turned it into Absolute Truth College.

Megalo believed that Christian universities had largely become poor imitations of prestigious secular universities. He planned and carried out the takeover of Mainstream Baptist University in Waco, Texas in order to demonstrate to other fundamentalist Christians how they could save their schools and turn them back on the right path.

Megalo immediately began assembling what he considered to be the best scholars in the world at Absolute Truth College. Everyone Megalo hired was "world-renowned," "the most respected scholar in the field," and a "professor that all the best schools in the country wanted." Megalo constantly reminded trustees and donors that one who possesses greatness recognizes it in others. When Megalo introduced his newly assembled faculty to his handpicked board of trustees he exclaimed,

"Mark this day. These men, who represent the brightest theological minds today, will lead ATC to outdistance all other schools in the world."

He also told his board of trustees that since he possessed the truth his teachers would inculcate that same truth to the students.

"Our students will come to ATC not to ask questions, but to receive answers and then go out in the world and share those answers with the confused people of the world who have only questions." Megalo boasted.

When a local newspaper ran a story calling the school an indoctrination center and questioning the reputation and the credentials of Megalo's faculty, Megalo responded by thundering from the pulpit and on his daily radio program that he despised the secular media who hated him because of his courageous stands for the truth and that he loathed the relativistic postmodern world that refused to acknowledge that one could reach absolute certainty on all important matters if one simply adopted the worldview of the Bible.

"We will teach the absolute truth absolutely," Megalo told his audience who cheered enthusiastically.

Megalo wondered too if he might be known as America's most prolific religious author.

"Dr. Publish A Lot they will call me," Megalo muttered to himself.

Megalo had written Sunday School lessons for his denomination, the Southwide Baptist Confederation, and a number of books for various evangelical publishers many of which were essentially collections of his sermons. Megalo wrote on a variety of subjects including biblical hermeneutics and eschatology. When he first solicited the Southwide Sunday School Board to write a book dealing with end times events he informed the executive director of the Sunday School Board, Censor N. Bowdlerize, that he wanted to write a book on scatology. This request alarmed Censor until he figured out that Megalo meant eschatology. Megalo enjoyed impressing people by using theological words such as exegesis and eisegesis but he often used theological terms incorrectly or imprecisely. As a young pastor Megalo once informed his congregation that he could "execrate" a passage of Scripture better than any living pastor. Megalo could churn out a book after just an afternoon of researching and writing amazing members of his congregation who took him at his word and agreed that he must be the most brilliant man in the nation. Cutting and pasting articles written by others that he discovered on internet web sites and incorporating them into his own books along with employing ghost writers, primarily former ATC students who admired Megalo, made it quite easy to reach his goal of publishing six books a year. Several of his books won awards in the evangelical publishing world. His books always sold well to evangelical audiences who longed for their daily doses of theological pablum.

Finally, Megalo considered that he might be known for his

prodigious political activity. In the 1980s Megalo spearheaded the Reclaiming America for Christ movement that had as its primary goal to either abolish or significantly blur the lines between the separation of church and state in America. Megalo believed that the state had become hostile to the church when it should favor the Christian church. Megalo believed the United States had been founded upon the teachings of Christ and that the nation had been chosen by God to proclaim the gospel to the rest of the world. Yet, God's chosen nation had in recent years abandoned its mission as secularists and theological liberals had gained control of the country and had advanced their agenda. Now, the nation stood under the judgment of God until the U.S. turned back to God. Megalo believed that God had called him to clean up God's chosen nation and wrest it from control of liberals and secularists so that the country might once again blow a sure sounding trumpet for God that the rest of the world needed to hear.

All of this reflection concerning his legacy gave Megalo an idea for his weekly TV show entitled "Megalo's Supernatural Salvation Spectacle and Marvelous Mega-Church Meeting." For five weeks he would invite his protégé, Natu Bright, to share with Megalo's vast audience the great contributions Megalo had made to the global religious scene. Several years earlier Natu had stumbled into Megalo's office in Houston requesting to interview his pastor whom he admired greatly. Megalo's secretary informed the pastor that a young man in a dark blue suit who looked to be about twenty years old wanted to visit with him.

"Allow him entrance from the Court of Well Dressed Young Men into the Holy Place," Megalo piously instructed his secretary.

Natu entered the office and marveled at not only the size of the office but the many wild animals and framed certificates that hung on the wall.

"Tell me about all the things on your wall pastor," said Natu.

"Tell me who you are first," demanded Megalo.

"I'm sorry I did not introduce myself. My name is Natu, Natu Bright. I admire you so much and I want to be like you and I want everything you have. So, I just wanted to interview you to discover the secret to your success."

"Nice to meet you Natu. I know we will be good friends. You have many things to learn but I will teach you," Megalo answered.

Megalo and Natu had a long conversation and Megalo told Natu about all the animals and certificates on his walls and how he had become the most well known mega-church pastor in the world. Megalo told Natu how God had blessed him with the gift of only needing five hours of sleep a night.

"Natu, my abundant productivity would not have been possible without this God given gift. I hope God has given it to you or you will become frustrated just like so many others who have tried to emulate me but have failed because they are weak and need a full eight hours of rest each night," bragged Megalo.

Natu perked up and inquired, "By the way, what is your salary? I know it must be pretty good because I have seen your wife driving a BMW and I heard through the grapevine that you live in a 2 million dollar home. I could sleep for only five hours a night for all that. Maybe even less."

Megalo chuckled, "I make enough to get by but I do pay a lot in taxes and tithes. It is a burden that I must bear but I do it gladly because God has blessed me richly."

"Tell me about your house, I've heard it's amazing. Don't leave out any details!" Natu said excitedly.

"Yes, it is a blessing from God. My wife calls it our little parsonage. It is a modest 6-bed, 6 bath, 5-fireplace, 4-car garage, 4 acre vicarage. Of course, I do receive a modest $500,000 parsonage allowance. We have decorated the home with the finest mahogany furniture and a small lake house sits behind the home so I have easy access to my 161 foot Trinity luxury yacht I purchased for small family outings."

After the interview Natu exclaimed, "I believe God has called me to preach. I just feel so inspired after seeing all this and listening to you speak. Megalo took Natu under his wing and spent the next few years teaching him how to be a mega-church pastor. Natu also served as Megalo's personal chauffeur, driving Megalo to all his speaking engagements so Megalo could read his Bible and pray while in the car on the way. Now, years later, he would call upon his young friend to tell the great story of the life of Megalo Maniac to the entire world. After all Megalo did not want to host the shows himself because he did not want to appear self-indulgent. Megalo would be on stage during the series but would allow Natu to be host and spokesman. After each show, Megalo would allow his sponsors to present a five-minute infomercial advertising their special evangelical products. After the final program but before the final infomercial Natu the Narrator would ask Megalo's congregation and the vast television audience to vote on what they considered as Megalo's most important contribution.

"Why try to make such an important determination alone when others in the community of faith could be involved in the decision?" Megalo told Natu.

After the final infomercial the results would be shared with viewers and then a huge party would be held in Megalo's honor. Megalo loved it when he was the subject of conversation and the center of attention. He knew deep in his heart that his followers loved hearing about him too. He held the chief seat in the church of me, my, and I and basked in his own glory. Megalo prepared for what he believed would be the greatest show ever to be viewed by humans. Not only would millions be tuning in but even God himself would take time from His busy schedule to catch this program. In fact, the idea for the show had come from God.

Megalo told Natu, "God told me recently He needed some quality religious entertainment because He had become bored watching all the other hackneyed religious TV programs featuring slick haired, smooth tongued, self-promoting evangelists. And he also told me that contrary to popular opinion he is not a fan of Southern Gospel Music. He finds it monotonous. He said something about it being a big bunch of piffle. Now, I like the Gaither Vocal Band especially, but God told me he couldn't stand Gaither music. He thought it to be sappy, sentimental, and way too Southern. I like that kind of music ok, but evidently it's not God's cup of tea at all. You know, Natu, I'm beginning to think that God may not be a Southerner despite popular opinion. I always imagined God's voice to sound like old George Wallace from Alabama but now I'm not so sure. I know God is no Yankee for sure. I believe he might be a Southwesterner, you know, an Oklahoman or a Texan."

Megalo continued, "Natu, I am certain that God, the Ultimate Man's Man who created Man first because He is most definitely Male, and who created woman as sort of an afterthought so that men could have a way to get much needed sexual release and to bring children into the world— This God has impressed upon my Manly heart that such a spectacular show must take place because it would cause many people to honor me which would in turn lead them to glorify the Ultimate Guy's Guy better known to the Jews as YHWH or 'I Am a Man, I Am, I Am' and known to most people as the Lord of the Universe."

Chapter One

# Charismatic Evangelistic Preacher and Master of the Mega-Church: From Ding Dong to the Superdome

What do you say out there folks? Is Megalo's greatest achievement his role as charismatic evangelistic preacher? Asked Natu Bright.

"Let me tell you how he came to be called the Master of the Mega-Church, the king of charisma, the emperor of evangelism. You will stand in wonder and awe at the gift that God has given us in Megalo" Natu added.

Then Natu began telling the audience Megalo's wonderful, marvelous, spectacular story.

Megalo did not start out as a Mega-Church pastor. At the age of nineteen he entered his first pastorate at the Ding Dong Baptist Church in Ding Dong, Texas. At Ding Dong the people loved Megalo's simple "bumper-sticker" sermons. The congregation found Megalo's preaching a refreshing alternative to that of their former pastor, A.C.A. Demic. A.C.A. preached intellectually challenging as well as practical sermons but in the minds of many he tried to make them think and reflect upon their faith too much instead of simply telling the people every Sunday that God loves them and has a plan for their lives even if they don't pray enough, witness enough, or read their Bibles enough. Pastor Demic had recently graduated with a Religion major from Thinkfree University and while most of the church members liked him they thought he spent too much time reading and studying books besides the Bible. One night in a Wednesday Business Meeting Deacon Troll stood and out of the blue said,

"Pastor Demic your schoolbook preaching ain't working for us. Your learnin' has made you too smart to preach. You don't preach like a real preacher but a professor and it's not working here. You haven't pounded the pulpit even once since you have been here. You haven't yelled at all. You haven't stepped on anyone's toes. You ain't never said nothing about hell being reserved for all the people who ain't here on Sunday morning. We want the pulpit pounded, toes trounced, and we want to hear about a fiery hell reserved for the lost."

Pastor Demic stood speechless and in the next few months began a series of sermons in which he challenged the congregation to confess their sins of racism, sexism, ageism, and many other "isms." Pastor Demic asked the congregation one Sunday morning,

"Why are all the members of this congregation white? Why don't we make a conscious decision to reach out to the minority population in our community?"

Pastor Demic earlier in the year had actually baptized a young black male that he had befriended but the congregation made him feel so unwelcome that he stopped coming to church although he had coffee with Pastor Demic once a week.

Pastor Demic continued for weeks to preach thoughtful and challenging sermons until finally Deacon Troll stood up one Sunday morning and interrupted Pastor Demic's sermon about selfishness and shouted,

"For weeks now you been criticizing us preacher. And I'm tired of it."

Demic remarked, "But you told me to step on your toes. So, I am simply doing what you asked me to do."

Deacon Troll responded angrily, "But you done stepped on the wrong toes. I mean, we don't want our toes stepped on the way you are doing it. We want it done our way. You know, make us weep cause we don't witness enough or read our Bibles every day or give enough money to the church. You are a pouncing and a trouncing us on the wrong issues and you furthermore you haven't talked about hell one bit. There's a lot of people out here in our community going to hell and you are not saying a word about it. Because you haven't pounced like we want you to pounce we're gonna give you the bounce."

Right then and there Deacon Troll made a motion that the church enter a special business meeting. The members, most of who nodded in agreement as Deacon Troll spoke to Pastor Demic, voted overwhelmingly to remove Pastor Demic from his Ding Dong pastorate. During the meeting Deacon Troll had addressed the members by stating pointedly,

"We need a new pastor folks. I recommend that we dismiss Pastor Demic and look for a simple preacher who does not have three initials in his name. Anyone who has three initials is an intellectual snob and we don't need academics in the church."

Deacon Form backed Deacon Troll's recommendation. Deacon Fuse knew something was not right about what was happening but he couldn't put his finger on it so he did nothing. Deacon Front supported Pastor Demic and refused to support Deacon Troll but he had only a few supporters. He left the meeting and the Baptists and joined the Methodists. Deacon Genial simply kept repeating,

"Now, we should just all get along and not fight with each other. Let's just be nice."

Deacon Niver stood up and shouted,

"I have talked to almost everyone in the church and they agree that Pastor Demic needs to go or the church will become apostate and die."

Of course, under Pastor Demic's leadership the church had enjoyed some numerical growth but the Ding Dongers were not satisfied. In the end, the church took the vote and tossed Demic to the curb.

After a period of unemployment Demic went back to school and eventually graduated with his Ph.D. in Religion and landed a job as a Religion professor at OpenMind University. In a few months the pastor search committee found what they wanted. Megalo Maniac became the pastor of Ding Dong Baptist Church in Ding Dong, Texas.

Although the Ding Dong congregation only consisted of ninety members, Megalo convinced them to televise the morning worship service so that his preaching could reach beyond the Ding Dong church walls. Megalo's program was broadcast throughout central Texas. His show quickly became the most popular regional religious program on television despite the fact that he had to compete with the Lawrence Welk show each Saturday night at 7:00. Megalo hated Norma Zimmer and the Lennon Sisters and their "sappy, silly songs that had no substance at all." He actually wrote a scathing letter to Welk when he saw a Welk rerun and two of the singers belted "One Toke Over the Line Sweet Jesus" in big band style. Megalo's letter read in part,

"While most people watching your show Lawrence would think it to be harmless entertainment, this sacrilegious song you allowed on your show demonstrates that your show is a tool of Satan. The devil disguises himself as an angel of light, this we know. But who would have thought the devil would disguise himself as Lawrence Welk? Satan, masquerading as an ethnic German accordionist from North Dakota! Who would have thought? Satan is a clever one indeed."

One of Megalo's most dedicated viewers, Loyola Fanbase, handed out flyers all over central Texas nearly every day for Megalo. Her fliers read,

"If Jesus came back to earth would you want him to find you watching Welk, whose music promotes the drinking of champagne, or Megalo, whose sermons promote the loving of Jesus?"

Loyola persuaded many folks to tune in to Megalo's broadcast. She even convinced the elderly gentlemen who spent all day every day playing dominoes down at the Bluebonnet Hotel to watch Megalo's preaching.

They became supporters of Megalo because they liked his boot stomping, hair raising, high pitched squealing, heart melting, head spinning, walk on water, raise the dead, holy whine preaching. They also liked it that Megalo gave the Invocation before all the Ding Dong Ringers football and basketball games and that he never preached against domino playing.

Megalo initially referred to the program as "Megalo's Musings" but that seemed far too dull so he eventually came up with the name "Megalo Maniac's Supernatural Salvation Spectacle and Marvelous Mega-Church Meeting." Even though he had not reached the big time yet he used the term Mega-Church in the name of his show because he knew it was only a matter of time until he had his own huge congregation. To Megalo the size of a pastor's congregation did indeed matter. Megalo felt he was destined to become a Mega-Church pastor. He claimed that when in his teens that a nine hundred feet tall Jesus had appeared to him in a vision and said,

"Megalo, you will soon be the pastor of the largest church in the world and millions will watch you preach on your own television show."

Several years later a smaller Jesus, only two hundred feet tall, appeared to Megalo and told him he would become the wealthiest preacher in the world. Megalo said that he asked both the large and the small Jesus,

"Why would you choose to give me a big church and great riches?"

Both the big and the small Jesus appeared together and thundered from on high in unison,

"So, we will be glorified and so you can be rich and famous."

Megalo responded to the two Lords, "And so it must be."

Inspired by these visions Megalo worked to make his name great in all the earth. All the while Megalo pastored in Ding Dong he longed for God to call him to a bigger church where his talents could be better utilized. After two years in Ding Dong he sent his resume to the First Baptist Church of Many People but the church called Pastor Waterlog. Pastor Waterlog had impressed the Church of Many People because he had recently been named chairperson of the Frequent Dunkers Assocation (FDA). This elite group of pastors had distinguished themselves by baptizing at least one thousand persons in the first ten years of their ministry. Most of the members of the FDA had gone on to become mega-church pastors. Megalo realized that if he wanted to achieve his dream of pastoring a mega-church he would have to become a member of the FDA and he would need it to happen soon. He realized that if he stayed in Ding Dong he would never make it into the elite club. Megalo pondered his future,

"There are just not enough people here in Ding Dong. When I preach the folks here stream down the aisles to get saved but there are simply not enough people here to get me into the FDA. Besides, I have to pay my own health insurance here and on this salary I will never get that

BMW that I want God to give me."

After baptizing and rebaptizing most everyone in the church and many in the community Megalo left Ding Dong. Megalo would be missed but few persons hated to see Megalo leave Ding Dong more than Steve Grebel. Steve, a twenty something man who made and sold pastry items at the Ding Dong Doughroom had been baptized so many times that folks in town called him Scuba Steve. Steve sought grace but Megalo's sermons always made him feel guilty about his life choices. Only Megalo could preach about the grace of the Lord and make everyone feel an enormous load of guilt. Like a priest who sought out confessions, in Ding Dong Megalo thumped his listeners on the head by preaching about all the ways they did not measure up to God's standards. Then he offered them the opportunity to receive salvation. Then the next Sunday he would repeat the process so that everyone who had accepted God's salvation the week before would need to receive it again or at least run to the altar to rededicate their lives to Christ. During one revival Steve came down the aisle all five nights to be saved and baptized. On the second night Steve told Megalo,

"I've been saved. Remember me. Last night I was saved. So, I just want to rededicate my life cause I did some bad stuff today. I looked at some porn and had bad thoughts."

"Yes, I remember you," replied Megalo, "but if you looked at porn the day after you were saved then you don't simply need to rededicate your life to God you need to really get saved because you weren't really saved last night."

Megalo then turned to the congregation and announced, "Steve has come to be saved."

Steve protested loudly, "No, Megalo, I've come to rededicate my life. I think I really was saved last night."

Megalo quickly replied aloud, "No, Steve, as I just said privately to you a minute ago, you weren't really saved."

Steve relented and agreed to get saved and baptized again and again and again. On the final night of the revival Megalo asked Steve,

"Do you realize you have been saved and baptized five times this week?"

Steve blubbered, "Yes, Megalo, but I've got problems and they won't go away. I know I wouldn't be struggling so much in life if I were right with Jesus."

Megalo grabbed Steve by the arm and said, "Steve, when you are right with Jesus you may visit sin you just won't live there anymore."

Steve shot back, "But preacher, I am living there. Every day I'm living there. I am neck deep into sin every day."

Megalo replied, "Well Steve, I guess you should go get your robe on and get ready to get baptized again. You definitely aren't saved yet. Maybe tonight will be the night salvation will come to your house."

Deacon Troll was by far Megalo's biggest fan in Ding Dong. Megalo offered a weekly buffet of guilt followed by emotional release that Deacon Troll found satisfying. In fact, he tried to convince his teenaged daughter to stop going to her psychologist believing that Megalo could help her deal with her depression and suicidal thoughts. Anna went to hear Megalo's sermon in which he repeated an often-used phrase,

"Jesus is the answer to all your problems. Get Jesus and you will be well."

Anna Troll Downs had been through a failed marriage, had no job, and lived with her parents despite the fact that her psychologist recommended that Anna not live with her domineering father who had a history of abusing her. When Megalo offered the evangelistic invitation, Deacon Troll grabbed Anna and rushed down the aisle so she could get saved and baptized. Megalo had Anna repeat a prayer of repentance of sin, sign a Ding Dong Baptist membership card, then he baptized her right then and there. Megalo announced to the congregation,

"Many of you are aware of Anna's mental and emotional problems and how desperate she is to find peace of mind. This baptism cannot delay. We are going to fill the baptistery right now and put Anna under the healing and cleansing baptismal waters."

After her baptism Anna felt a warm rush of emotion within. She felt her depression lift. For at least two weeks week the Ding Dong folks saw a changed Anna. About a month after her baptism though, the dark clouds returned and Anna had to be taken to the emergency room after having taken an overdose of sleeping pills. Jesus had not cured her and deep inside Anna knew it. She felt even more hopeless than ever. Deacon Troll believed that Anna just needed to have more faith and she would be healed.

Meanwhile Megalo moved from Ding Dong when God called him to pastor the Broomville Baptist Church in the county seat town of Broomville, Texas. Actually, Megalo's Uncle Anthony, the evangelism director at denominational headquarters who served as the interim pastor, recommended Megalo to Broomville. After Megalo accepted the call to Broomville he prayed,

"Lord, I claim your promise that he that is faithful in little will be given more responsibility. Yes, Lord, you always call your choicest servants to larger fields of service."

Megalo enjoyed the first year at Broomville happy to have access to more people whom he could baptize and thrilled with his bigger salary. After his first month in town Megalo told his Uncle Anthony,

"I'm into some serious lost people now and the church not only pays my health insurance but retirement benefits as well."

Megalo baptized as many people as he could in Broomville and became a leader in the local association of churches. In his first year at Broomville Megalo delivered the keynote sermon at the associational meeting. In the audience sat Pastor Markis Territory the former pastor of Broomville who now pastored at nearby Lickskillet Baptist Church. Broomville had been Markis's first church and the people loved him. Markis had helped the church regain stability after suffering through several years under the ministry of Pastor Jackas who was eventually fired because all he did was sit and drink coffee and chat all day with his buddies down at the Sunnyside Up Diner. Megalo did not like Markis because he felt Markis still tried to act as the pastor at Broomville. Marquis still attended many of the Broomville Sweepers football and basketball games and visited elderly church members as well. Megalo became angry when he visited an elderly woman with health problems who thanked him for coming but admitted,

"I wish Brother Markis would come see me. He was a special person. I'll never get over his leaving the church."

The chairman of the deacons once told Megalo, "You will never be able to replace Markis."

Megalo determined in his heart that he would make the Broomville folks forget Pastor Markis. Now, Megalo stood in front of the area pastors and Pastor Markis ready to deliver a major blow to the reputation of Pastor Markis while enhancing his own status.

Megalo began, "Fellow pastors, we need to win souls for Jesus. That is the main thing we are to do. And that is what I have done. Before I came to Broomville attendance had been declining for several years. After my first year at Broomvillle church attendance has increased 110 percent and baptistms are at an all-time high. And there is no recession in sight. Currently, I am fiftieth, all-time, on the list of baptism leaders in the state. I am getting ever so close to being eligible to join the FDA. Of course, one day I will be the number one dunker in the state and the nation. I will eventually surpass even the legendary Pastor I.B. Dunkenem who founded the FDA and holds the record for most persons baptized."

Megalo continued, "Before I came to Broomville, the members lacked excitement and focus. Since I have been the pastor the church has a renewed passion for winning souls."

Megalo continued his "Before I came, Since I came" routine for forty minutes. The pastors applauded Megalo, everyone that is except Pastor Markis Territory who slinked out the door and back to Lickskillet. Megalo never heard another peep from Markis who decided to stick to Lickskillet and make a name for himself there. He just couldn't compete with Megalo and he knew it.

Megalo's reputation as a soul winning full body dunker having been established in Broomville in only a few years he ultimately became restless and began to pray that the Lord would move him to a larger church. God answered Megalo's prayer and he accepted God's unmistakable call to the Little Bigger Baptist Church in Little Bigger, Texas. At Little Bigger, a suburb of the Dallas-Ft. Worth Metroplex, Megalo discovered a church on the make located in an upper class community growing by leaps and bounds. To help him grow the church Megalo brought in consultants from California, organizers from Orlando, promoters from Philadelphia, and developers from Disney World. Megalo convinced the Little Bigger members that they could become the Really Big Baptist Church if they built a state of the art auditorium that would seat thousands. The people agreed and they built the grandest church in the land. The members called it a Mallatorium. In addition to a spacious worship center and space for Sunday School classes the Little Bigger Mallatorium housed a hair salon, several upscale clothing and shoe stores, a food court, a Christian bookstore, an ice cream shop, a fitness center, and, of course, a Starbucks.

When visitors entered the church a giant bronze statue of Jesus with arms spread open welcomed them to the Mallatorium. Above Jesus hung a sign with the church's motto, "God is Huge and So Are We, Join us Now It's All Free." The church grew and grew and all the people at Little Bigger looked around at what they had accomplished and said to themselves,

"We must change our name to reflect our hugeness."

The church voted to change the name to the Enormous Church of God in Christ. While serving as pastor of the Enormous Church of God in Christ Megalo not only made it into the FDA he shredded all the baptism records and replaced Pastor Waterlog as chairman of the FDA.

"What sweet revenge. He may have won the first battle by beating me out and becoming the pastor of the First Church of Many People but I am going to win the war," Megalo thought to himself as he assumed leadership of the FDA.

Megalo eventually became known across the nation as a leading mega-church pastor. He had made it to the big time but Megalo still believed God had bigger plans for him.

After five years God called Megalo to pastor the even larger Third Baptist Church in Houston. Megalo believed here he could build an even bigger church and become the undisputed leading mega-church pastor in the world. On his first Sunday in Houston Megalo told his congregation,

"I am here because I answered God's call. God has always called me to lead a church bigger than the one I led before. That's God's way. He also told me he wants to do something extraordinary in my life here and that is good news for you too."

When he first arrived in Houston Third Baptist Church met in a spacious warehouse once used to manufacture Elmer Fudd Root Beer but the brand never caught on so Third Baptist had bought the building to house the growing congregation. Eventually as the mergers took place between First, Second, and Third Baptist the church outgrew the warehouse so Megalo bought a huge thirty thousand seat basketball arena once home to the Lameville Crash. Although the Crash had not had a winning season in ten years the city built the team a new, state of the art forty thousand seat stadium. Usually only half the seats were filled. Yet, in the old Lameville arena Megalo preached two services every Sunday to a packed house. ArenaChurch, as Megalo called it, became a big hit in Houston and became the place to be on Sunday morning.

Megalo's sphere of influence reached far beyond the walls of ArenaChurch. No other preacher in America enjoyed the success that Megalo did. Back in Ding Dong he used to eat at The Sizzler after church on Sundays but now Megalo enjoyed fine dining every day at exclusive restaurants. He joined several elite clubs open only to powerful Houston businessmen. He played squash every Tuesday with local and state politicians. He became the spiritual advisor to the governor of Texas and held a weekly Bible Study with the governor and his staff. He started a blog at MegaloManiac.com and before long had many followers. Thousands tuned into his daily live radio program called the Megalo Maniac Hour where he preached, answered theological questions from listeners, and excoriated liberals. Megalo also continued his weekly TV show although his audience had grown considerably as the show now reached beyond the nation.

Megalo had already changed his preaching style by the time he landed in Houston. Although in Ding Dong he had established a reputation around the area as the Ding Dong Screamer and the people responded favorably to that style, the screaming did not work in Dallas or Houston and Megalo realized this right away. He noticed that other mega church pastors had done away with the pulpit, dressed casually, and preached very practical sermons and Megalo followed suit. Although he continued to be animated while preaching in Dallas he began to preach in a more personable style. A Houston religion reporter upon hearing Megalo commented,

"In the pulpit he becomes an actor on a stage. Although he preached to a large crowd I had the feeling that while he was speaking he was shaking hands with everyone in the audience. He essentially preaches the same sermon Sunday after Sunday but he does so with such gravitas and flare that no one seems to notice or care."

Megalo loved showing off to the congregation his knowledge of Greek and Hebrew. Each time he read Scripture he reminded his congregants that they might have some difficulty following along because he was reading from the "original" Greek or Hebrew and not an English translation. Megalo spat out Greek and Hebrew words during his sermons in machine gun fashion. His congregation believed him to be the foremost Greek and Hebrew scholar in the nation. Of course, Megalo told his congregation that he was the leading Greek and Hebrew scholar in the nation.

On occasion Megalo amazed his congregation by reading from Dead Sea Scrolls he claimed he had collected over the years. As Megalo told it he traveled to Bethlehem and visited the family of Muhammad Ahmed al-Hamed, nicknamed "The Wolf," who had discovered the Dead Sea Scrolls, and asked if they had any scrolls they had not turned over to the authorities. The family members grinned at Megalo and said they had been expecting him. Muhammad's grandson said to Megalo,

"The Lord appeared to me while I was out tending my sheep and a host of angels appeared with him singing 'Great is the Lord' and then the Lord said to me, 'A great man from America will come and ask a favor of you. Do what he asks. He is my servant."

The family handed over jars with several scrolls inside to Megalo who took them back home and kept them in his office. When Megalo read from the scrolls he would tell his congregation the story about how he had procured the scrolls and would give thanks to God for choosing him to receive the scrolls.

Above all, Megalo's congregants loved hearing his stories. His stories had always been his bread and butter going back to Ding Dong days. Megalo captivated his hearers with astonishing stories of his heroic feats for the cause of Christ. He especially loved telling stories about people he had won to Christ. Megalo's congregation could not believe the number of persons Megalo had won to Christ. One of Megalo's favorite stories had to do with the witch he had won to Christ. Megalo told his congregation,

"I got a call from a guy who told me he was a witch. You know, a Wiccan. He told me his Wiccan girlfriend had put a curse on him and he was scared. I went over to his house and frankly it scared me to death. This man had gargoyles at the entrance of his home. I didn't want to go in but the prophet Ezekiel appeared to me told me that if I did not go in that I would have blood on my hands. I asked Ezekiel what he meant. He told me that if the watchman of a city does not warn the inhabitants of an approaching enemy then the watchman will have blood on his hands if the enemy sacks the city. Ezekiel told me that I needed to warn this man that he would go to hell unless he received Christ. Then suddenly Ezekiel disappeared. With a fresh sense of boldness I marched into this guy's house and told him to accept Jesus and he would not have to worry about any curse and he wouldn't have to worry about going to hell. That man prayed and accepted Christ and is now a staunch member of the Enormous

Church of God in Christ. Jesus 1, Wiccans 0. Jesus always wins over the Wiccans."

Megalo loved telling of how he had traveled years ago to Indonesia and had preached at a Muslim school there. Afterward a young Muslim boy came up to him in secret and said he had received Christ but he did not want anyone at the school to know it or they would hurt him or even kill him.

"I told that young boy I would pray for him every day and I did. Just the other day after the Sunday service a young man came up to me and introduced himself to me as the young boy who I had led to Christ years earlier at the Muslim school and that over the years he had led many other Muslims to the Lord. See how God used me and I didn't even know it for many years."

Always the hero of his stories, Megalo could take the most mundane of daily occurrences and turn it into a spectacular event. For example, Megalo loved telling about his flat tire revival. According to Megalo he had a flat on his car and he took it into Discount Tire and Lube to have it fixed. The place was busy as could be and the manager told Megalo he would have to wait for hours to have his flat fixed. Megalo almost lost his cool but as he tells it,

"Instead of getting frustrated and angry I went out into the garage and began sharing the gospel with the workers. They listened to me intently as they worked. As I concluded my message they all put down their tire tools in unison and got down on their knees and prayed to receive Christ. When the customers in the waiting area witnessed this they also came out into the bay area and knelt with the workers and accepted Christ."

Megalo told his congregation that 27 people had come to know the Lord that day because he had turned his back on anger and frustration and decided to let the Lord use him to change the lives of many lost people. Megalo's congregation stood and applauded him for five minutes after he told that story.

Megalo used his blog, his radio and TV program to hawk his sermon and Bible study DVD's which all sold well to evangelicals and increased his fame. His biggest seller was the Genesis Pack that sold for two easy payments of $19.99. This pack included several items all related to the book of Genesis. The pack contained two sermons on DVD. Megalo entitled the first sermon, "Galapagos Has No Apes," in which he argued against the theory of evolution and claimed that the book of Genesis teaches that God created the universe in six days and that Adam & Eve were the first humans on the earth and they looked just like humans today and in no way resembled monkeys or lower life forms. To underscore his point he held a live monkey in his arms while he preached the sermon. The monkey kept slapping Megalo on the face, however, making Megalo extremely angry. Megalo knew he couldn't choke or slap the monkey in front of his congregation, so he just stood there preaching while the monkey slapped him repeatedly. This episode merely endeared Megalo to his congregation even more.

Even though he did not care for the slapping monkey Megalo loved animals. When Megalo pastored in Broomville a nearby Cowboy Church invited him to speak. Megalo donned his Ostrich Skin Boots and his Stetson Cowboy Hat and prepared to rope some lost people for Jesus. Megalo preached his sermon while doing some rope tricks he had learned as a youth. He talked about how God had roped him and wrestled him to the ground back when he was a rebellious young steer and had captured his heart.

"God corralled me for Christ— roped me for the redeemer— lassoed me for the Lord." Megalo declared.

In the middle of Megalo's sermon an old rodeo clown ran down the aisle crying asking Jesus to save his soul. The clown then asked Megalo to baptize him but he requested that his horse be allowed to watch the baptism. Megalo agreed and the clown brought his horse in through the back door of the church and down the aisle near the baptistery. When the congregation applauded after the baptism the horse got spooked and started running up and down the aisles. The horse laid a big pile of crap on Megalo's boots and trampled an elderly woman who jumped in front of the horse after crying out,

"Jesus has come back for us on his white horse."

Never mind that the horse was black as coal. In the meantime, someone called the fire department. Fire fighters arrived quickly and evacuated the church and took the old woman to the hospital. On the way to the hospital one of the firefighters exclaimed that he saw a naked clown with big red lips wearing a bright yellow wig riding a black horse down Main Street cursing and shouting,

"Dunk me again you damn preacher, the first time didn't take."

After the rodeo clown fiasco Megalo would never bring a large animal into the church again although he had been tempted to bring an elephant into the church when he invited Republican presidential candidate Mickey Shuckbut to preach to his congregation. Megalo thought that preceding Shuckbut the elephant should come out on stage with a banner across its back that read "Shuckbut for President." Shuckbut congratulated Megalo for coming up with a grand idea but warned that elephants were mercurial creatures that might get spooked and injure members of the congregation. Remembering the rodeo clown horse incident from earlier years Megalo decided against bringing an elephant into the church.

Megalo especially loved his pet monkey, Mr. Bim. He had not held Mr. Bim during his anti-evolution sermon but another monkey that he had borrowed from a friend who worked at the local zoo. Megalo had not wanted Mr. Bim to become fatigued during the lengthy sermon. Some members of the Little Bigger congregation had started rumors that Megalo slept in the same bed with Mr. Bim and that they took baths together. Tolly Snoopenly, Megalo's neighbor in Dallas, told her friends that she had peaked in the bathroom window and saw Megalo feeding Mr. Bim oranges while they sat in the bathtub together. Even with these rumors no one seemed to care about Megalo's relationship with his monkey because they thought it was cute that he had a monkey as a special friend.

Megalo only brought Mr. Bim on his show one time and only for a few brief moments. Megalo's wife Sue said he became livid when he received a letter from a listener who after seeing Mr. Bim's appearance said he wished the monkey alone would host all future shows. Yet, most folks who tuned into his show loved Megalo, especially his second and most popular sermon he entitled, "Adam & Eve, White and Straight." Here he argued against gender ambiguity, homosexuality and interracial marriage. He received a standing ovation when he preached that sermon to his congregation for the first time. The folks at WhitesRight Baptist Church especially loved his lines, "God does not deal in ambiguity and uncertainty" and "You can't mix and match the human race," and "Hate the sin and if necessary loathe the sinner."

Along with the two sermons contained in the Genesis Pack the wife in the family received a white apron imprinted with red apples. As she cooked family meals the white color reminded her to cultivate purity by submitting to her husband daily. The apples helped her remember that she caused the fall of humanity by eating the fruit in the Garden of Eden and manipulating her husband to do the same. The apron also doubled as a head covering for the woman when she attended church. On the back row she would sit silently covered by her cloth. She should not be seen nor heard. That is, unless her name happened to be Sue B. Maniac.

Megalo had bought one of these aprons for his wife, Sue B., and she wore it all the time at home. He had met and married his wife while they attended Billy Sunday Baptist Bible College in Buloxi, Mississippi. One day while Sue prayed and read her Bible God gave her a "Bible Promise" that she would marry Megalo. Reading from the Psalms, she came upon Psalms 45:10:

"Hear O daughter, consider, and incline your ear; forget your people and your father's house; and the king will desire your beauty. Since he is your lord, bow to him."

At the moment that Sue finished reading that verse Megalo called her and asked her out on a date. When he arrived to pick her up, she bowed when she saw him. Two years later when Megalo asked Sue to marry him she told him of her "Bible Promise" and how God had set him apart for her to be her king. An astounded Megalo informed Sue that about the same time God gave her the "Bible Promise" that God had given him one too. As Megalo described it, he had read Psalms 45 one day in his "Quiet Time" with God when he came upon Psalms 45:13:

"The king's daughter is all glorious within: her clothing is wrought of gold."

He suddenly remembered seeing Sue earlier that day wearing a gold colored dress and decided to call her and ask her out on a date believing that God had set her apart for him to marry. According to Megalo, God told him that if Sue bowed when they met that she was indeed the one he should marry. The couple agreed that God used the message of the Bible to bring them together. Many years later Megalo read an article by a seminary professor who criticized the use of subjective Bible promises calling it a "magic book" approach to the Bible, Megalo became angry and wrote him a letter stating,

"Obviously, you don't trust God's inerrant word. The Bible is better than any magic book. Through it God teaches, reproves, and instructs and he used it to bring Sue and me together. And since we're still together, it must have been God's will. Sue and I married certain that we were fulfilling the perfect will of God and we still feel that way. You should stop questioning God! I can't believe you're a seminary professor. You're obviously not a Godly teacher."

Megalo and Sue had been married for thirty years when he wrote that letter. Earlier in their marriage Megalo had enjoyed a few secret dalliances while traveling alone as a revival evangelist and his guilt eventually overwhelmed him that he vowed never to be alone with a woman for any reason. Even Megalo's secretary had to bring in a friend if she wanted to speak to Megalo in his office. On one occasion Megalo traveled to a Bible conference with two men and one woman. Megalo had known these friends for many years. Megalo drove to the conference because he had the nicest and biggest vehicle. After the conference Megalo dropped his riders off in the parking lot in a pouring rain. The men exited the vehicle and ran to their cars. The woman did not get out informing Megalo that she didn't have a car in the lot because she only lived two blocks away. She asked Megalo to drop her off at home.

Megalo refused, and said to her, "I make it a policy never to be alone with a woman who is not my wife. I can't give you a ride home."

Megalo forced the woman to walk home in the rain because he couldn't trust himself. For Megalo, a woman was a beautiful temptress unless she happened to be unattractive. Megalo paid no attention at all to women he did not consider to be beautiful.

Megalo loved Sue especially because Sue would do whatever Megalo demanded.

"God made Sue just for me," Megalo often said.

When Sue B. Missive, for that was her maiden name, became Sue B. Maniac she had not wanted to change her name. Sue B. Maniac didn't did not ring clearly in the ear like Sue B. Missive but Megalo insisted that her last name become Maniac. She asked Megalo if she could hyphenate and become Sue B. Missive-Maniac. Megalo told his new wife that only liberal feminists hyphenated and that the hyphen itself was a liberal punctuation mark. In fact, Megalo refused to use hyphens in any of his writings. Sue relented and became Mrs. Maniac. At the age of thirty she became the president of Submitters United for Christ the King and Savior. SUCKS, the acronym by which the organization became widely known, sought to convert women to submit graciously to their husbands in all things.

Sue became a distinguished speaker at the annual Lane Bryant Women of Large Faith Conference. Once Megalo made it to Houston he thought it would be a great idea of Sue could become a well-known leader among evangelical women to help enhance his own status. Sue loved throwing off her apron and getting out from behind the stove to speak in front of big crowds of women. In fact, Sue loved talking in general to anyone about anything. Her beautician in Houston told the other customers,

"Sue is pretty nice but what a terrible case of logorrhea that woman has."

Sue and Megalo often appeared together on stage at conferences throughout the country. He even had several special sermons he preached over and over at the conferences. "Be Quiet and Follow," became an instant classic that the women loved. Megalo told them exactly what God expected of them as Christian wives and the women loved knowing for sure God's requirements.

After Megalo finished preaching Sue would come and stand behind him and wave to the audience. Then Megalo and Sue would call on everyone to join hands and sing a special hymn Megalo had written especially for the women's conference. Many news reporters who covered the conferences were surprised when they discovered that the women liked the song and that they sang it with such gusto. One woman in a post conference interview stated that she found it difficult but satisfying to follow God's laws and that worldly people would not understand the complementarian position but that God's ways were different than the ways of man. Then she began to sing Megalo's song.

> Little women, we know our place
> Second class citizens in the human race
> We know we cannot be president or priest?

If women take the lead then get prepared
for the mark of the beast

Megalo also led a men's only conference that he started in Houston called the Order of the Studs. The Order grew into a major national movement when the Biblical Council of Studhood and the Evangelical Defenders of God Conference decided to merge. The Defenders of God were convinced that "lost" people could be won to Christ via apologetics.

"We must argue persons into the kingdom of God," wrote Paul Emics in his bestselling book, *The Indisputable, Irrefutable, Unquestionable, Undeniable, Incontestable Case for Christ.*

Megalo thought some sermon topics would be better suited to a crowd of men so that is why he founded the Order of the Studs. In his sermon on Ephesians 5:21-32, Megalo told the men that their wives should always be ready and willing to meet their every need, especially their sexual needs, at all times. If the woman does not comply, Megalo told the men **to** sit down with their wives, read Ephesians 5:21-32 to them, and command them to do the laundry or perform their sexual duty or do whatever the situation demanded. The men always applauded Megalo profusely for his Ephesians 5 sermon and after he delivered the sermon they would circle up and raise their hands together and shout, "Here's a High Five for Ephesians 5." Megalo then closed his men's conferences in the same way as the women's conferences, with a hymn. All the men would stay in the circle and hold hands and sing Megalo's hymn that he had written especially for the Order of the Studs.

You know that I love you, temptress so fair
With your soft skin and silky brown hair
God made the rule that you must submit
To male authority, it's in Holy Writ
Although the liberals may call me extreme
I'll gladly stand up and yell and scream
That I'm not a bad guy, I'm lots of fun
I'm simply a complementarian.

Sue occasionally attended the Order of the Studs Convention. She loved to appear on stage with Megalo and wave to all the men who hooted and hollered at her. Sue had some interest in spiritual matters although she thought theology was a man's domain, but she attended the men's conferences primarily to market her products. She sold her products to the women as well but found that the men were her best customers because they wanted to take a gift home to their wives after they left the conference and returned home. In the early years of her ministry conference attendees had frequently questioned how Sue could get her hair to be so tall and stiff. Although possessing a rather portly figure due to her love for fine European chocolate, Sue's tall hair made her appear taller and thinner. Of course, the multi-colored muumuu she wore emblazoned with three huge white crosses across the front helped conceal her girth. Even during outdoor conferences Sue's hair withstood a brisk wind. At the God and Country convention sponsored by Megalo and held on the capitol steps in Washington D.C., her hair did not move even though forty mile an hour winds turned over chairs.

Over the years many women tried to copy her hair style but to no avail. Sue had concocted her own secret Mega-hold hair spray. When she realized that her female admirers were saddened by their inability to imitate her, Sue marketed her hair spray calling it SueBee's Mega-grip Hair Stiffener and Reinforcer. Her customers simply referred to it as Evangihold. Sue made a handsome profit from sales of her product. Sue also adorned her face with large quantities of make-up. Her signature look included a thick-caked base, purple eye shadow, and bright red lipstick. She had thought about developing her own line of make-up but Megalo had forbidden her to go forward because he believed that she had too many projects going on already.

Sue traveled across the country visiting Christian stores to try to get them to stock Evangihold and had a great deal of success convincing the stores to sell her product. On one occasion Sue boarded a plane at the Dallas-Ft. Worth airport in order to fly to Phoenix, Arizona to market Evangihold and the flight attendant asked Sue if she would give up her first class seat and move to coach.

The flight attendant explained, "We have just had a last minute boarding. A family has a young child who is ill and needs to get to the Children's Hospital in Phoenix immediately."

Sue snapped at the flight attendant, "Do you know who I am? Why are you asking me to give up my seat instead of asking that black nobody in the seat in front of me? No, I paid for this seat and I refuse to move."

The flight attendant became incensed and said sharply, "No, I don't know who you are and I don't care. All I know is that you have an empty seat next to you so it would be easiest if you would give up your seat so this family could sit together. But since you won't be kind enough to move I will indeed ask this man in front of you if he will give up his seat. Senator, would you be willing to give up your seat?"

Senator Key Ullison of Minnesota, who had made headlines because of his Muslim faith and his being sworn into office while placing his hand on the Qur'an, gladly gave up his seat and moved to coach. Sue sat steaming all the way to Phoenix.

"When I get home I'm going to write a letter of complaint against you," Sue told the flight attendant when she brought Sue her hot fudge sundae with nuts.

Megalo not only marketed his Genesis Pack he was especially proud of the Dogma Pack which included something for the ruler of the household. The husband received a camouflage vest with the initials WWJS plastered on the front and back. When buying new guns to keep around the house, in the car, to give as gifts to friends, and to use on hunting trips the man should wear this vest to help him make a purchase that would please the Lord Jesus. The initials stood for "What Would Jesus Shoot?" Not only did the initials inquire as to what type of gun the hunter would use, it also referred to the kind of animal the hunter would kill. The "What Would Jesus Shoot?" vest became a best seller and could be found at all Big Crappie Pro Shops around the country.

For every Dogma Pack sold Megalo also threw in a free copy of his version of the Bible that he had worked on for twenty years. Although he argued extensively with Imprudent Publishing Company about the form and name of the Bible Megalo got his way. He wrote copious commentary notes that he placed in the body of the biblical text. Even a seasoned Bible reader had difficulty distinguishing between the biblical text and the commentary notes. Another distinctive of Megalo's Bible was that he placed Jesus' words in blue, Peter's words in purple, Paul's words in pink, and his own notes in red. Also, Megalo's notes appear in parentheses within the text. For example, Genesis 1 begins,

"In the beginning God created the heavens and the earth, (about five thousand years ago). Now the earth was formless and empty (but it was flatter than a pancake and all the people had flat heads, and Eve was flat too).

Yes, Megalo founded the Intercontinental Flat Earth Society, a group dedicated to debunking ideas such as evolutionary theory, the law of gravitation, and a spherically shaped earth. Megalo believed that Muslim insurgents who wanted to destroy America's confidence in the inerrant Bible had promulgated these ideas. Megalo did believe in microevolution in some sense.

"The original Eve did not have breasts until she had children because she had no use of breasts before then. The second after she birthed her first child God gave her the gift of breasts." Megalo wrote in his commentary notes.

Megalo added, "Men have nipples so that every time they take off their shirts they can thank the Lord that only women have to breast feed and that women no longer are flat chested like them."

As for the name of Megalo's Bible, it is no surprise that the Bible hit the market as, *Megalo Maniac's Inerrant, Infallible, Seamless, Ultimate Version.* The *M&M, Double I, SUV Bible* became an immediate bestseller and replaced the New International Version as the Bible of choice for evangelicals. Megalo's Bible came to be simply known as the *Ultimater*. Megalo simply referred to it as the "true word-a-God."

Megalo claimed in his commentary notes that although a man named Freer had discovered the Codex Washingtonensis located in the Freer Gallery of Art in Washington D.C., it was he, Megalo Maniac who first discovered a copyist insertion between Mark 16:14 and 16:15. The so-called Freer Logion, which Megalo claims should be called the Megalo Logion, describes a conversation between Jesus and his disciples in which Jesus implies that Satan no longer had any power even though bad things will continue to occur. Megalo called the inserted text a forgery made by a liberal Christian who wanted to convince the church that Satan was not a real supernatural entity who continually tries to thwart the purposes of God on earth.

Megalo wrote, "If I had not pointed out that this text is a forgery then I am convinced that many Christians today would believe that Satan is no longer at work in the world and that would be a grave error."

Barney Baptist from Bowlegs, Oklahoma wrote to Megalo claiming that Megalo's Bible had become his Bible of choice because of the notes.

Barney wrote, "I've been waiting for the Bible with a commentary that shows the one true way to understand the Bible. And thank you so much for your great discoveries. I am humbled as I read your explanation of how you became an expert in Greek, Hebrew, Aramaic, and other Semitic languages."

Barney pumped gas during the week down at the Sinclair station and preached at the Bowlegs Blazing Balls Bowling Alley on Sundays to a small group of disaffected church members who had separated from several other Baptist churches in town due to an argument over the Lord's Supper. This group initially became offended when the pastor started using Tropical flavored Hi-C punch instead of Welch's Grape Juice during the Lord's Supper. The Welchers complained in business meeting but were outvoted by the Punchers. The angry Welchers realized they could not have communion with the Punchers and so the Welchers left to form a church that used only Welch's grape juice during the Lord's Supper. The Welchers split again when an argument arose over whether to use frozen concentrate or bottled grape juice. The Bottlers left their frozen friends behind and began meeting at the local Blazing Balls Bowling Alley. The Bottlers accused the Frozen Welchers of being moderate compromisers and the Punchers of being liberal. Billy and the Blazing Balls Bowling Alley Bottlers could not fellowship with any group who embraced error. Billy and the Bottlers warned their erring brothers and sisters that they had started down a slippery, juicy slope and that in the end God would judge them for their unwise actions.

"First, Hi-C creeps in, then next it will be Capri-Sun, then Juicy Juice. Where will it end, with church members drinking Boone's Farm Wine?" Barney surmised.

Unlike Barney, Megalo claimed he never had experienced a church split. He had his share of controversies of course but he always won the battles. In Dallas Megalo became aware that Larry the church organist had a gay partner he lived with.

Megalo told the deacons, "You men know that I am against homosexuality but on the other hand I have been told that the only good organists are the gay ones. I hate doing this but I'm going to have to fire Larry and obtain a non-gay organist which means that the quality of our music problem will suffer."

The deacons backed Megalo and Larry received his walking papers but found a gig playing in the Lutheran church. Some people were unhappy with Larry's departure and stepped forward to challenge Megalo but Megalo simply preached a sermon rebuking certain troublemakers in the church who compromised the clear teaching of Scripture on the issue of homosexuality. Eventually Larry attended a Lutheran seminary and became a well-respected pastor of a church in Philadelphia. Due to his eloquence and his thoughtful sermons Larry became known in Philadelphia as The Gay Pulpiteer. When Megalo heard this he scoffed at the news and preached a sermon to his congregation against gay preachers entitled, "Homo Preachers: Erecting a House on the Sand."

Megalo's biggest controversy concerned an activity in the Family Life Center at his Dallas congregation. Some of the women met together on Tuesday nights to study the Bible and practice yoga. Megalo discovered this and marched into the yoga class and informed the women that no more yoga classes would be held at the church. The women told Megalo to go away but he would not go.

"Tell us why you won't let us have our yoga class. It renews my spirituality" remarked the leader of the class, Lakshmi Karma.

Megalo told the women that yoga and Christianity are not compatible.

Megalo continued, "Biblical Christianity is not about enhancing a person's spirituality with no reference to the Christian gospel and the meditation and inward concentration associated with yoga is not Gospel centered. Yoga as a spiritual practice is not consistent with the teaching of the Bible."

The women left angry and hurt. Yet, later Lakshmi returned to Megalo and asked if the women could simply have Bible study and do stretching without meditating. Megalo agreed and told the women to call the class, Dynamic Stretching with Jesus. Megalo's compromise appeased the women who continued their Tuesday night class. Megalo asked his associate pastor's wife to attend the sessions to make sure that the women were simply stretching and not engaging in eastern meditation.

Megalo always preached to his congregations that they must submit to their pastor in all things just like a wife submits to her husband. Megalo would excoriate anyone who challenged him and encourage them to move on to another church. He would cultivate members who would be loyal to him in everything. In Houston Megalo surrounded himself with handpicked advisors called the Endorsers. Only the Endorsers knew the financial business of the church including Megalo's salary and benefits. When Megalo bought a 2 million dollar, 10,000 square foot sprawling estate home on Lake Decadent and claimed a $500,000 tax free ministerial housing allowance only the Endorsers approved it. When Megalo purchased an $8 million dollar Falcon 50 private jet so that he could travel easily to his many speaking engagements and take family vacations the only church members who approved it were the Endorsers. Megalo and the Endorsers even listed the home and the jet as church property so that Megalo's tax burden would not be so great. When a Houston reporter asked Megalo why he did not reveal his salary or the purchase of the home and the plane to the church members who provided it through their tithes and offerings Megalo answered,

"I have people in the church that keep me accountable. I don't need to answer your questions because you did not call me into ministry, God did. And I am ultimately accountable only to Him. And besides, I am one of the lowest paid mega-church pastors in the nation."

When the reporter discovered Megalo's $2.4 million yearly salary and his lavish lifestyle and wrote a story about it in the Houston Daily Gazette a group of Megalo's church members called the Enablers immediately came to his defense. The Enablers wrote on Megalo's blog about how his ministry had changed their lives and how he should just ignore these attacks upon him that were obviously from the devil who wanted to destroy Megalo's influence. The Sunday after the article appeared Megalo received a standing ovation from his members as he walked upon the stage.

Megalo thanked his congregation for their unwavering support and then spoke to his congregation. "God has blessed me. Where does it say in the Bible that I should feel guilty if I am blessed by God? And I want to help you get blessed. Now hopefully you understand when I say 'get blessed' I don't mean you begin to bring your portion to the storehouse and you will become a multi-squillionaire. I'm not saying that, but some of you will. I said 'some of you will.' He's gonna make a lot of us a lotta money - I'm talking about God - because He knows if he can get it through us, he'll get it to us. But the problem is, God wants to bless a lot of you, but you're in the Jordan River, in your floaties, splashing around thinking a mission trip will do it, thinking another Bible study will do it, thinking that serving the church will do it, thinking prayer will do it. It's all about the money. It's all about the money. Show me the money people. Show me the money!"

Megalo then announced that in a month the church would be holding a Raffle for Jesus. He encouraged everyone to buy a $5 ticket that would enable each person entered into a drawing to win a new Hummer.

Megalo told his congregation, "Obviously, we will not receive enough money from ticket sales to buy a Hummer so I am pitching in and purchasing the Hummer using my own funds."

Again, the congregation stood and applauded Megalo.

Shouts of "Amen!" and "You are so generous!" could be heard reverberating across the massive worship center.

Megalo not only claimed he had never experienced a church schism, according to Megalo, he had never led a church that he didn't singlehandedly revive. Only once did he have a close call and Megalo did not count the time he had preached at the African-American Missionary Baptist Church in Marshall, Texas. In Marshall Megalo preached from Deuteronomy about the slave who would drive an awl through his or her ear in order to become a slave for life to a beloved master. Without repudiating the horror of slavery, Megalo simply told the congregation to become life long slaves for Jesus.

Megalo explained later, "I can't understand why the congregation didn't receive me and my message with open arms but I guess it's the Lord telling me He hasn't called me to preach to the blacks."

According to Megalo, the close call came when he, in his early twenties, preached in Monkstown, Texas and the revival meetings had not produced any conversions by Thursday night. During the day on Friday, the last night of the revival, he canvassed the neighborhoods handing out flyers advertising a corn dog feast for children and youth. That evening children from all over the county poured into the little Monkstown church. After the corn dog party the children were packed into the front rows of the church where Megalo told them of a young girl who had refused to accept Christ at a revival service and had been burned alive in a car accident just after leaving the revival services. Megalo told the children how he and the rescue workers had heard the girl screaming in agony in the flames as she burned to death without Christ. Megalo moved closer to the children, leaned in while looking at them intently and shouted,

"Oh, how I wish I would have accepted Jesus into my heart, but now it's too late! Help me! I'm burning! Help me!"

Megalo told the children that he could smell the stench of burning flesh.

"This girl will actually suffer a far worse punishment than burning up in a car fire. She will suffer an eternity of burning and you will burn in an eternal car fire if you do not accept Jesus immediately!"

The terrified children certainly did not want to burn for all eternity. During the evangelistic invitation the children ran toward Megalo in a single wave begging to receive Christ. One frightened child began heaving so terribly that he threw up his corn dog and red Kool-Aid all over the other children. Megalo suggested that he baptize them right away to remove the taint of sin and supper. The parents agreed and Megalo stirred the baptistery waters like never before in the small Monkstown church. All sorts of yuck floated in the waters but Megalo convinced the children that being immersed in a bit of throw up in no way compares to the sacrifice upon the cross that Jesus made in their behalf. Megalo left town the next morning thrilled to report to his evangelist friends that he had won forty converts to Christ in the little town of Monkstown, Texas. News of the Monkstown Miracle as Megalo called it spread throughout Texas and he began receiving so many preaching invitations that he had to turn many requests down.

Several weeks later Megalo found himself at the Paradise Baptist Church where the revival had not been going as well as he had hoped. Megalo convinced the pastor at Paradise to contact the local superintendent of schools and ask if Megalo and the pastor could visit each classroom at the local school and invite all the school children to the revival. The superintendent, who served as a deacon at Paradise Baptist Church, agreed to Megalo's request. Megalo knew he could not offer a simple invitation to the children and expect them to come. He would have to come up with an award-winning gimmick. Before he left to visit the school he saw a popular television commercial with the Frito Bandito hawking Frito Lays Corn Chips. Megalo had a brilliant idea. He would invite all the children to the revival to meet the Frito Bandito. He would preach to them and then feed them Frito Chili Pies. After Megalo visited the local school and made his invitation the school children were excited. That evening every child in town showed up to see the Frito Bandito. Megalo did not expect the many African-American children who showed up because Paradise Baptist consisted of all white members. Megalo arranged for them to eat their Frito Pies outside and told them the church could not hold them due to the large crowd inside.

Some of the older children protested and asked, "But we want to see the Frito Bandito."

Megalo told them, "There is no Frito Bandito. I made it up. Now go home to your own church."

Megalo turned to the pastor and said, "Ain't that the funniest thing. Black kids came to church to see a Mexican bandit. Who would have thought?"

Megalo went back inside the church where he put on a huge

mustache and a sombrero and a gun belt that held two six shooters on each hip.

With a southern styled Spanish accent Megalo roared, "Who is trying to steal my Fritos? I will shoot them with my Mexican pistols."

Megalo then pointed the pistols in the air. Bang! Bang! The church fellowship hall became suddenly silent at the sound of gunfire ringing out. Floydella Vinetrap, who had been in the kitchen putting chili on Fritos fainted and dropped the bowl of chili she had been carrying.

A frightened young boy shouted, "My God, he's shot Grandma Floydella with his Mexican pistols."

Megalo quickly explained to the boy that he only had toy cap guns and that Grandma Floydella had probably just fainted unless of course she had suffered a heart attack and if that were the case she was in real trouble and might not make it. The little boy ran off to the kitchen, crying hysterically all the way, to check on his grandma. After the kitchen staff revived Floydella she cleaned the chili spill and went back to work while Megalo sang the Frito Bandito song to all the children. They laughed politely but most of them were sad because they had expected to see the real Frito Bandito. Jenny Verificaccion, a Hispanic girl who had been adopted by the youth pastor and his wife, cried out,

"You are a fake bandit, not real at all."

Megalo felt the tide turning against him so he did some quick thinking.

"You are correct. I am not the real Frito Bandito. I wanted to show you something important. The world claims that it will offer you real things but only offers you fake things that do not satisfy. I simply wanted to drive that point home to you."

Megalo saved the day. The young people bought his story and came pouring down the aisles later when Megalo gave an emotion laden invitation telling the children that they might die tonight and go to a hot burning hell forever unless they turned their backs on the fake world and accepted the real life only Jesus could provide.

Although Megalo had developed powerful persuasive skills, and became a master of gauche gimmicks, he credited his revival success with his ability to bring the Spirit of God with him wherever he traveled. After he struck gold with the Frito Bandito bit he really began to believe that the Spirit works best through what he called "creative tactics." When Megalo finally established his Arena Church in Houston his gimmicks or tactics became all the more impressive. For example, he brought in a muscular group of men from the Christian Power Wrestling Association to put on a show before he preached to the crowd. The wrestlers not only put on wrestling exhibitions but would perform feats of strength such as driving nails through a block of wood using only an open palm, breaking bricks over each other's heads, lifting tables with people sitting on them, and kicking one another in the crotch repeatedly. Then the wrestlers would give a talk on abstinence telling the students that every time they were tempted to have premarital sex they should think of how the wrestlers had suffered vicariously during the reciprocal crotch kicking exercise so that the students might remain pure. After the exhibition many of the young men in the audience would rock back and forth and cry out,

"You did it for us, so we won't do it with them. Thank you Jesus."

Megalo brought a tank on stage along with a slew of automatic weapons when he preached a sermon on spiritual warfare.

Megalo popped out of the tank shouting, "We're gonna take this hill. Yes, folks, just like Sam Houston beat the pants off of Santa Anna at the Battle of San Jacinto we are going to win the victory in the city named after that great American warrior."

Megalo's congregation stood in unison and applauded approvingly. Megalo then handed out cards with targets on them and asked the audience to write down the names of persons in the target areas who needed to be "targeted" with the gospel.

"The person's name in the middle of the target should be the one you go to first. Then you should aim your gospel guns at the other targets," Megalo pleaded.

Megalo drove a corvette out on the ArenaChurch stage on another occasion and preached a sermon from the driver's seat entitled, "The God of the American Dream." Megalo informed the audience that he prayed to God for the corvette and God gave it to him as a sign of prosperity.

"Others will see my obedience to God and how that brings me wealth and prestige, and that will convince them to follow God so they can get a sweet piece of the American dream," Megalo told his followers while adjusting the rear view mirror.

Megalo then prayed, "God and author of the American dream. I thank you that you made me an American, not an Albanian or an African or a Cuban or some other weird ethnicity. I thank you for making my American dream come true. Thank you Lord for not keeping your riches from me but giving them to me freely so that the poor may see my abundance and be encouraged to work harder to achieve their American dream."

After the prayer Megalo concluded the meeting by informing the congregation that he was going to exit the stage and drive his corvette to Brahman's Ice Cream Shoppe and buy a triple dip ice cream cone. He invited everyone to come and join him but entertained his congregants with a parting story.

"When I was a child I went down to the local Dairy King and bought me a double dip of chocolate chip ice cream. The town bully Juvi

Bound came up and knocked it out of my hands after I had only taken a bite. I did not cry but I walked home and told my father what had happened. My father, who sold Kirby Vacuum cleaners for a living, walked with me back to the Dairy King and went over and smacked Juvi across the back of the head and said, 'Mess with me punk ass and I'll put a PowerSuck 1000 Kirby Deluxe up your ass and suck your organs out one at a time.' Then my father bought me a triple dip chocolate ice cream cone. He sat with me outside the Dairy King while I ate it all in front of Juvi taunting him the whole time. Juvi dared not say a word with my father there. He just glared at me with tears in his eyes. The lesson here folks is that if you lose something you love then God will give it back to you with more added to it. If you lose your double dip cone all you have to do is go to your Heavenly Father and he will provide you with a triple dip cone. And He will smack around the bullies in your life too! He will give Satan a royal butt kickin' in your behalf. Yes, my friends, God wants all of you to have a triple dip ice cream cone, not just a single or even a double dip. So, let's go get it."

With that Megalo sped off the stage in his red corvette and flew out the back door toward the ice cream shop. Many of his followers were not far behind in pursuit of a triple dip cone their new symbol of the American dream.

Megalo refuted the charge that some pastors made against him that he only catered to the upper classes and ignored the poor. Megalo claimed he did not neglect the poor although he admitted that he had no fondness in his heart for immigrants, especially immigrants whose skin was brown or black. In one sermon entitled, "Migration for the Migrants," Megalo called for all recent illegal immigrants to be rounded up by government officials and taken to Panama so that they would not be able to find their way back to America again.

"Don't send these people back to Mexico where they will come back again and again. Send them far away," Megalo declared.

Nevertheless, to demonstrate concern for the poor Megalo sponsored a well-publicized annual event called Super Surplus Sunday. Megalo invited poor people from all across the Houston metroplex area to buy a Super Surplus Sunday ticket for $1 and then come to ArenaChurch where on Super Surplus Sunday there would be a drawing for valuable prizes. Ten lucky persons would get their electric bill paid for a year and another ten would receive free gas for a year for their automobile. On Super Surplus Sunday visitors from all over Houston showed up at ArenaChurch with their tickets. Blacks and Browns showed up as well as whites but Megalo tolerated it because each one represented another $1 into Megalo's pockets. Megalo preached an evangelistic sermon to the crowd who had assembled on Super Surplus Sunday.

Megalo told the people, "Jesus gave salvation away for free just like

I am giving away free prizes. It cost you a dollar to buy a ticket to Super Surplus Sunday but it won't cost you a thing to receive salvation in Christ. Come now and receive the free gift of salvation."

Megalo also intimated that the chances of winning would be improved for those who would come down the aisle and make a decision for Christ and be willing to be baptized immediately. Sally Balks came hesitantly down the aisle during the evangelistic invitation and received Jesus and Megalo slipped her a few additional tickets to improve her chances of winning. Megalo baptized her and many others then held the grand drawing. Megalo's Super Surplus Sunday brought to ArenaChurch many new members who were willing to give their money to God in order that God might give them back a lot more than they had given. The Sunday after the drawing Megalo would preach his famous sermon on tithing entitled, "Thou Shalt Not Steal: Cheating on God." Megalo wanted his new members to know what God expected of them.

Megalo told his congregants, "Now people you may think you are pretty good folks because you don't steal. You think you keep the 8th commandment but if you refuse to give to God 10% of your income then you are stealing from God. If you steal from God he won't bless you. The reason many of you people, especially you younger people, are poor is because you are cheating on God. If you cheat on God he can't bless you but if you do give your 10% he will bless you. God puts a curse on anyone who comes to church and doesn't tithe 10% of his or her income. God's message is clear. Tithe big or stay home. When I was fifteen I made a deal with God, although I don't believe in making deals with God anymore, that if he would give me places to preach that I would give him 20% the rest of my life. Well, God has provided me a place to preach every Sunday of my life since I made that deal and I have given him 20% of my income. When I was young at times I had to borrow money from my daddy to pay God, but I kept my promise. I'm not bragging, of course. I'm just telling you that God has blessed me with wealth and fame because I have been a generous giver and he will bless you in the same way when you bring your money to ArenaChurch where God can use it mightily to expand His kingdom."

When Megalo preached his tithing sermon the Sunday after Sally Balks had joined ArenaChurch she marched down the aisle during the invitation and asked Megalo,

"I thought you said salvation was free? Now, you are telling me that it's going to cost me 10% of my income to be a Christian. So, salvation is about believing in Jesus and tithing too?"

Megalo told Sally, "You are just a new believer and have so much to understand. Don't ask questions Sally. Just listen to what I say and do it. Jesus asks us to be blindly obedient to Him and since I am His representative you must be blindly obedient to me. Besides, I have been a

Christian and a pastor for many years and I know better than you what God wants of His children."

Sally went back to her seat and took out her checkbook and wrote out a $30 check. She didn't know who to make it out to so she made the checkout to "God." Later that afternoon, when Megalo and the Endorsers were counting the offering Megalo chuckled when he saw the check made out to "God." He put it in his wallet and went to the bank the next morning and cashed it without hesitation and then used the money later to pay for his lunch.

In one of his boldest moves Megalo brought a bed on stage and while sitting on the bed challenged all married heterosexual couples in the audience to have sex once a day for seven days. He warned that God hated premarital and homosexual sex and that if anyone in the audience engaged in unnatural sexual acts that God would bring judgment upon them in the form of disease or some catastrophic event. Megalo crowed that God loved only heterosexual sex between married couples and bragged that if the couples followed his "Seven Days of Heaven" plan they would spice up their boring sex lives and their marriage would be affair proof.

"Christian couples are getting too many divorces because of one reason. The men are not having good sex often enough," Megalo proclaimed boldly. "You don't need counseling to help you with issues you have about intimacy or sex. Even if you have had sexual abuse in your past, you just need to leave it in the past and have more sex with your spouse. That is the cure. And please understand that I'm basically talking to the women at this point," Megalo continued.

Megalo admitted later to the men in his small group Bible study, made up of local businessmen and celebrities and who called themselves Bigwigs for Christ, that his many duties for the Lord had made him too tired to have sex for seven straight days. He confessed that after three days he had become too worn out to complete the program. He hated to disappoint his wife by not giving her what she needed and so very much wanted but Megalo admitted that he had simply set his aim too high.

"Next year, I'll scale things down to a three day event and call it Spree for Three."

One of Megalo's greatest gimmicks was his Zeitgeist Zinger. This sermon had helped turn a boring church meeting into a Cane Ridge replication on a number of occasions but it worked wonders in the giant arena. Megalo preached the Zeitgeist Zinger when the congregation would not respond to his message. This sermon would provoke even the feeblest of folks to stream down the church aisles in order to get baptized or re-baptized. Megalo would tell the congregation about persons in previous churches he pastored who were indifferent or who had opposed him and had suffered dire consequences. He loved telling the story about a woman who had constantly criticized him during his first pastorate at the Ding Dong Baptist Church. He prayed one night before going to sleep that God would revive her or remove her. The night after his prayer the woman died of a heart attack. Megalo called this a back door revival.

Megalo warned his audience, "God might just bring a back door revival your way if you are criticizing me or if you are not excited about me and what the Lord is doing through me in this church. Come now. Get up out of that seat. March down that aisle and publicly repent of your sins. Do not delay. The Lord is waiting but He may not wait much longer for you."

Another special sermon brought the parishioners streaming down the aisles. Megalo's, "Are You Sure That You Are Sure For Sure?" sermon made even the most seasoned veteran Christian doubt whether he or she had received salvation. In this sermon Megalo informed his listeners that they probably had never been saved because their lives were chaotic and fruitless. Megalo pleaded with the congregants to come down the aisle and settle their salvation once and for all. To everyone who responded Megalo advised to take a wooden stake, write the date of one's conversion on the stake, and then drive the stake in the ground.

"Every time you doubt your salvation," intoned Megalo, "go in your back yard and let that stake be a reminder of the date of your salvation."

When Megalo preached this sermon early on in his career at the Toad Suck #7 Baptist church in Toad Suck, Texas, Fanny Beauchamp declared to the congregation that she had placed five stakes in her back yard, just to be on the safe side. Years earlier when she just had one stake in the ground she went to her back yard when struggling with doubts about her relationship to God only to find that the stake had been stolen. Fanny was terrified that God had removed the stake from the ground because He had become unhappy with her. She was relieved later to find that her neighbor, Radbertus Rinkus, had taken the stake to put in his back yard.

Fanny told the congregants that Radbertus had once inquired as to why she had small wooden stakes in her yard. She told him that the stake was her proof that God loved her. Radbertus took her stake so God would love him too. Fanny did not have the heart to take it back so she simply went down to Sinblot Lumber and bought five stakes to put in her yard. Fanny added that Radbertus had once told her that he had never said a mumbling word to God and he had never heard God say anything to him, and he had never even attended church, but he heard TV preacher Angus Huxter say that putting a stake in your yard not only helped a person put away all doubts about salvation but the stake also guarded against a future world plague that God would soon send upon the earth when He came to punish the world and set up a new ideal world where there would be no pain nor constant doubts. Fanny warned the spellbound congregation to go home immediately and drive stakes in the ground in their back yards.

"When God brings a plague on this world, the plague will skip the houses that have wooden stakes in the back yard," Fanny warned.

The next day after Fanny's testimony small wooden stakes could be found all over town in every yard and even at the post office too. Thanks to Radbertus and Fanny the town of Toadsuck had become plague proof.

Megalo's Zinger and his "Are You Sure?" sermons were his gold medal winners. These sermons alone had netted Megalo more baptisms than all of his other sermons put together. Even his popular sermons, "Don't Do Porn," "Don't Be Gay," and "Sow Your Seed in My Ministry," did not come close to Megalo's Zinger and his "Are You Sure" sermons in bringing people down the aisles. In third place stood Megalo's Vacation Bible School sermon entitled, "Those Queer Teletubbies." This sermon netted lots of baptisms among children. In this sermon Megalo warned children not to watch Barney the Dinosaur and the Teletubbies and other "secular" educational programming because these shows sent subliminal messages to them encouraging them to engage in aberrant sexual behavior.

"You need to repent and be baptized and stop watching junk on TV. God will punish you if you disobey Him. God will not punish you if you get baptized and stop watching these awful shows," Megalo warned the VBS kids.

Megalo had always loved baptizing people and his passion for baptizing people never waned even after he became a member of the FDA. While at ArenaChurch he continued to set all kinds of records for numbers of persons baptized. At five consecutive statewide annual convention meetings he received the prestigious "Dunker of the Year" award given to the pastor whose church has the most baptisms during the year. Some of his pastor friends began to refer to Megalo as "The Immaculate Immerser." Megalo especially loved baptizing children. In fact, the vast majority of people he baptized were children between the ages of 5-8 who had come to Vacation Bible School. Besides his Teletubbies sermon Megalo had other successful ways of convincing children that they needed to be baptized. He began using these methods on Children's Night during a revival or on the final night of VBS. Megalo offered free pony rides and a petting zoo for all children under the age of ten who would agree to get baptized. To further entice the children Megalo set up a baptistery outside the church that looked like a miniature fire truck. Megalo dressed up like a fireman and baptized the children one by one. The front of his helmet read, "Sir Dunkalot." On his jacket one could read the phrase, "Sprinkling is for Lawns." Megalo despised the denominations that sprinkled rather than immersed converts. He referred to Episcopalian and Methodist pastors as "Sprinkly Tinklies." Of course, Megalo became enraged when an Episcopal priest once called him a "Flunky Dunky."

Megalo dunked thousands of children over the course of his ministry although on one occasion he had to turn the hose on one unruly fifth grade boy who refused to be dunked. The boy, who lived in Nowata, Oklahoma, did not like getting wet. Nonetheless, Megalo turned the hose on full blast and the force of the spray tossed the boy around like a rag doll convincing him that getting dunked would be much better than getting hosed. Of course Megalo baptized some adults as well. He not only baptized Scuba Steve five consecutive nights during that revival in Ding Dong Megalo, he baptized Large Marge Meskowitz five consecutive years at the Lotawatah Road Baptist Church in Lotawatah, Texas where he was a frequent evangelist.

The first year Large Marge walked the aisle during the evangelistic invitation she explained to Megalo that she had made a decision as a teenager to become a Christian but that she had fallen into sin by working as a stripper at the Fancy Cats Club down near the Red River. She also confessed to gluttony that caused her to lose her job at Fancy Cats because she put on too much weight and broke several of the poles at the club. She also confessed to living in an unmarried state with her second cousin Bo Needem in a doublewide trailer that sat in the pasture behind her mother's house not far from the river. Marge and Bo had upgraded to the doublewide with the insurance money they received after the F4 tornado of 1994 tore their old trailer to pieces. Because of the insurance money she received Marge looked back fondly upon the "F4 of 94." Nonetheless, Marge did not know if she should simply rededicate her life to God or get saved all over again. Megalo assured her that her sins were so egregious that no mere rededication would suffice. Marge would have to come again to Jesus for salvation and be re-baptized.

"Only a really good dunking in the water can wash your sins away," Megalo remarked.

The first time that Megalo baptized Marge the baptistery had been filled to the brim. When Marge went under the water the choir received quite a surprise when the water sloshed out all over them and doused them all. When Marge emerged from the water and saw the wet choir members she cried out,

"Preacher, I think I know now how the Methodist church began."

One of the elderly choir members cried out, "That felt refreshing just like the log ride at Six Flags."

An elderly woman in the congregation shouted, "Hey, they just took the Nestea Plunge!"

Of course, when Megalo reported to the district office the number of baptisms he had administered at Lotawatah he counted all the choir members as well as Marge. Every time Megalo visited Lotawatah thereafter Marge walked the aisle and confessed some great sin that she had committed during the course of the year. Usually her iniquity had to do with eating too many Twinkies or Ho Ho's or spreading gossip about someone in town. Whatever the sin it didn't matter to Megalo, He dunked her again and again thinking that at some point her salvation might take. Until that time, Megalo informed the Lotawatah congregation that they should keep the baptistery half full at all times.

Megalo also brought in the crowds with Mike the Midget Music Man. When Megalo took his show on the road he would put up fliers all over town a week before the revival announcing that the great Megalo Maniac would be preaching an old fashioned, Bible based, God honoring, Holy Spirit empowered revival and that he would be accompanied by the charismatic and talented Mike the Midget Music Man who would serve as the song leader. The fliers worked their magic bringing in all sorts of curious townspeople who wanted to hear Mike the Midget Music Man sing,

"I'm 3 ft. 11 and I'm going to heaven and that makes me feel ten feet tall."

Mike the Midget Music Man also had a unique talent. He could sing and whistle simultaneously. Although to the average person the noise Mike made sounded like a wild turkey running headlong into a wild boar while pursued closely by a pack of rabid raccoons being chased by a pack of hounds, the church crowds hooped and hollered with delight marveling at such a rare ability. Cankle Crabtree the pianist at the Baptist church in Riverby, Texas thought Mike to be the most uniquely gifted musician she had ever known.

Mike the Midget Music Man could pack the crowds into the church house or the arena even better than Harlow the Heavy Healer. Megalo did not hold spectacular healing services like the Charismatics that he so despised. He hated the popular Kenny Richman and Benny Hiney and thought what they did was fake. On the contrary, Megalo's healing services were low key because he did not want anyone in the Southwide Baptist Confederation to think he had Charismatic tendencies. Usually, Megalo would dismiss everyone except for the infirmed and their loved ones and he would lay hands on them and pray for God to heal them. Then he would preach his trademark healing sermon entitled, "Liquidating the Lepers." In this sermon Megalo preached that just as Jesus eliminated leprosy in his day, He wants to exterminate all illness and disease today.

"We must have faith. If we have faith and believe that we will be healed then we will be healed. If we don't have faith and don't believe we will be healed then we won't be healed," proclaimed Megalo.

Epiphany Magi, a deaf young woman, came to Megalo's revival and asked him to heal her. Megalo anointed her with oil while quoting verses from James 5:14-15. These verses guarantee that anointing a sick person with oil while praying a prayer of faith will restore the health to the sick person. Yet, after Megalo anointed Epiphany with oil and prayed over her she did not receive her healing. Megalo repeated the process for two weeks straight but Epiphany remained deaf. After the last session Megalo scolded Epiphany for not having enough faith and told her that when she decided to believe in the power of God to heal her that she would be healed. Epiphany walked away sad and feeling very alone. Unlike Benny Hiney Megalo did not guarantee a healing and didn't think healing to be an entitlement. Sometimes Megalo failed to heal but he always blamed it on the sick person's lack of faith. Still, Megalo bragged to his friends that he had an 85 percent healing rate.

"Not a bad percentage for a non-charismatic Baptist," Megalo bragged to his friends.

While Megalo's healing services tended to be subdued and rather quiet Harlow the Heavy Healer liked to push the envelope. If Megalo preached at a place where there were lots of sick people or the revival had become stale because none of his tricks were working he would call in Harlow to help him stir things up. Megalo only rarely called upon Harlow's services because Harlow's unorthodox methods tended to alienate some persons. Also, the Southwide Baptist Confederation had Harlow on their Charismatic Watch List. The Confederation approved him as an official denominational evangelist but some in the denomination feared that the nature of Harlow's healing services could lead to his allowing the infiltration of Charismatic practices in the denomination.

Harlow denied the charge of being a Benny Hiney tongue speaking, forehead smacking, money grabbing, holy healer, but he did have unconventional ways. First, Harlow would cast all the demons of disease out of the church. Then he would call all the sick and diseased to come up to the front of the church and stand in a line. Harlow would then slap each person on the right cheek then the left cheek then kick them in the shins then turn them around and kick them in the butt and then throw them down on the floor and sit on them while crying out,

"You are healed in the name of Jesus."

The congregation stood in awe. Megalo teamed up with Harlow, who tipped the scales at about four hundred pounds, because Megalo believed that bringing in a four hundred pound miraculous healer who slapped, kicked, and sat on people would definitely bring in the crowds. And it did.

Harlow expressed no concern about being morbidly obese and repeated often that God had given him perfect health even with all the extra pounds in order to demonstrate to the world that God much more than doctors should be trusted when it comes to health and healing matters. Once when a representative from Subway sandwich restaurants approached Harlow about going on a Subway diet in order to become their new spokesperson to replace a now bulimic Jared, Harlow responded by eating five, five-dollar footlongs, in five minutes. He then drove to Sonic Drive-In and ate five footlong cheese coneys, five large orders of cheese tots, and a Route 44 Coke easy ice. Harlow then attended a revival service later in the evening and bragged not only about what he had eaten but that he had perfect cholesterol levels and an ideal heart rate.

Usually Harlow held healing services by himself in which folks with all sorts of ailments would come to him to receive his healing touch. He had healed so many people that later in his ministry people began to refer to him not only as Harlow the Heavy Healer but Harlow the Wonderworker. Ida Bea Polly of Tigertown, Texas claimed that Harlow healed her of cancer. Even on her deathbed a year later she told her family members that Harlow's touch had given her a few more months of life. Wherever Harlow went he claimed that he could document a significant drop off in doctor's visits and surgeries.

Harlow healed everything from knee and back problems to heart conditions. Harlow claimed that he had emptied a hospital in Paris, Texas on one occasion by simply placing his hands on the hospital sign and praying that God would heal everyone inside. As Harlow described it, a sea of men, women, and children dressed only in hospital gowns walked single file out of the front of the hospital and into the parking lot where they lifted up their hands and praised God in unison for delivering them from disease, death and hospital food. Harlow then preached to the assembled crowd and won them all to Christ.

At other times Megalo filled the pews and arena seats by inviting Wild Wally Amos the Knife Thrower to entertain the congregation. Wild Wally threw knives at a volunteer from the congregation while he recited Scripture and preached a brief sermon. Megalo never volunteered to have knives thrown at him but when he preached for other congregations he often encouraged the local pastor to do so. Megalo told the pastors that the act of getting on top of the roof of the church to sing a hymn for the congregation if the church reached its goal for high attendance Sunday had been way overdone.

"Your people are tired of silly little gimmicks. They want to see you do something daring," Megalo informed every pastor he knew.

"Having Wild Wally Amos fling knives your way will amaze your people and gain their respect," he added.

Although Wild Wally Amos claimed he never hit anyone with a knife, on one occasion he did nick Pastor Wigglesworth on the cheek while reciting the words of Jesus about turning the other cheek. Although he found it ironic, Wild Wally Amos did not accept the blame for that mistake claiming,

"Wigglesworth just would not stop fidgeting."

Because of Megalo's success over the years but especially in Houston the *Baptist Blowhard,* the national paper of the Southwide Baptist Confederation, named Megalo as one of the top ten pastors to watch. Megalo was pleased with this recognition as the paper listed him as the top pastor in the field of ten. After all Megalo was first in number of baptisms and rebaptisms and no one in the Southwide Confederation had a church as big as Megalo's.

## Commercial Break

"Well folks," said Natu the Narrator, "that about does it for our first program. I hope you enjoyed hearing about Megalo's numerous adventures that has sealed his status as America's greatest preacher and evangelist. We know you will want to tune in next week as we examine Megalo's extensive contributions to his denomination. You will be even more amazed than you are right now. But please don't touch that remote just yet. Sit back and enjoy this five-minute commercial about natural foods found in the Bible brought to you by one of our beloved sponsors Bible Fare Incorporated."

Hey everyone, my name is Daniel Shadrach the founder of Bible Fare Incorporated. When I was a boy I used to eat lots of junk food and I became obese. In my late teens I went with a friend to a Vacation Bible School designed for all ages and during the week I accepted Jesus as my Savior and began reading the Bible seriously. I noticed that in the Bible many different foods are mentioned. I thought to myself, if God wrote the Bible then the foods mentioned there must be godly foods that he wants us to eat. Of course I know God prohibits certain foods but besides those there are many delicious foods that are mentioned in the Bible that are healthy too. So, for a year I decided to eat biblically. For one year I ate God's way. I only ate approved foods mentioned in the Old and New Testaments. And, by the way, I don't include Apocryphal books in my Bible. God doesn't want us eating deutero-canonical dishes. Down with foods of the Apocrypha!

Anyway, I started out eating a big helping of Ezekiel's Bread but I did not cook it over dung. I then ate some lamb that I cooked in olive oil, some unleavened bread, some grapes, dates, figs, and pomegranates. I ate these super foods and other great foodstuffs mentioned in the Bible and after a year I was perfectly fit. I didn't even exercise that much. After the year of eating I biblically, of course I decided to stick with it. I then began marketing products so that other could people could join me. All my products are natural and I will ship them to you as soon as you place your order.

Let me introduce you to some of my most recent products. The

Bible Bar contains bits and pieces of various foods mentioned in both Testaments. The Deuteronomy Delight is a nutritious bar that contains the seven foods mentioned in Deuteronomy 8:8. King David's Treat is an extraordinary fruitcake designed for kings. For those of you who are morbidly obese let me suggest the Garden of Eden Meal Replacement System. You can enjoy a low calorie drink fresh from God's biblical garden and burn away those unwanted pounds. King Solomon's Seed Bar is recommended in case you happen to get off your biblical diet and start eating processed foods again. King Solomon's Seed Bar will cleanse your digestive system and relieve bloating and constipation. King Solomon's Seed Bar is a honey flavored grain bar that is so delicious.

And I cannot forget one of my best selling products, Noah's Nuggets. This is a delicious peanut and honey flavored bar that is a dessert substitute. If Noah had eaten this he would never have gotten drunk and naked and he would have never cursed Canaan and we would have never had to put up with slavery. Oh, and I almost forgot. I developed something especially for the kids. Crosspops are frozen popsicles in the shape of a cross and are made with only biblical ingredients. Kids love them. They can suck on these red colored pops and not only enjoy a tasty treat but also ponder how the spilled red blood of Jesus and his death on the cross has given them abundant and eternal life. I have so many more foods I could tell you about but I am out of time. So, please place your order at BibleFare.com and I will send it to you right away. Here's to biblical and healthy eating! Good night and God bless.

# Chapter Two

# The Greatest Show on Earth:
# Premier Denominational Statesman

"Welcome back friends to our second Megalo show. Tonight we will demonstrate to you why Megalo is not only the most famous pulpiteer in America, but America's premier denominational statesman. Megalo, although so busy with preaching responsibilities, has served his denomination faithfully and selflessly for so many years. Tonight we will explore how Megalo has distinguished himself as a servant to his denomination." Natu Bright the Narrator then began telling Megalo's story to the audience while Megalo sat on stage beaming with pride.

Megalo's ties to the Southwide Baptist Confederation go back to his childhood days. He grew up in the Flippin Baptist Church in Flippin, Arkansas. His parents did not attend a Flippin church.

Megalo's dad told his son, "You'll never get me to go to that Flippin Church or any Flippin church." With no parental support Megalo used to hitch a ride on his cousin Tyrone McCoy's riding lawnmower that he had converted into a racing mower. Tyrone had won the Arkansas state champion riding lawnmower championship three years straight. He credited his success to God and to Barnard Phipps who gave him his first lawn-mowing job and taught him about small engine repair. On one occasion Tyrone found a nickel in Barnard's yard. Instead of putting it in his pocket he gave it to Barnard. Barnard, so impressed with Tyrone's honesty, continued to trust Tyrone and recommended him to all the neighbors for lawn mowing services. Tyrone told anyone who would listen that the "nickel decision" set him on his path of greatness. Before lawn mower racers Tyrone would give motivational speeches to the young people. He would tell them to be sure and make "nickel decisions" in life now and they would become great. During one of Tyrone's speeches Little Jimmy Smartas pulled a nickel out of his pocket and threw it on the ground and yelled out,

"Tyrone, I found your nickel. I'm on the path to greatness."

Tyrone did not like Little Jimmy's sarcasm and replied, "Little Jimmy Smartas, you are a penny brain who will never be able to make a "nickel decision.'"

Jimmy just laughed and yelled, "Hey, nickel head, my dad is gonna beat your ass in the race tonight."

Tyrone not only made a name for himself as a driver and motivational speaker on the lawn mowing racing circuit, he also built a road worthy recliner that could go up to twenty-five miles an hour. Equipped with cup holders, headlights, a radio and CD player, and chrome rims, Tyrone could be found riding about town in the recliner when his wife had borrowed the lawnmower to go to get groceries. Tyrone's wife refused to drive the recliner because it had a manual transmission that she did not know how to operate.

Megalo's father, Hypo Maniac, traveled a great deal selling Kirby vacuum cleaners. Fast talking Hypo bragged that he could sell an expensive vacuum cleaner to an elderly widow on a fixed income whose home did not even have a stitch of carpet in it and never even feel a twinge of guilt.

"The old woman will leave it to her kids and they can use it later," Hypo rationalized.

Hypo made a great deal of money sucking people dry but he seldom stayed at home. Megalo's mother, Euphoria, did not have the emotional stability or the desire to take proper care of Megalo. She allowed him to roam the neighborhood while she sat home in her polyester saffron nightgown smoking Camels, drinking Jim Beam, watching the soaps, and making purchases from QVC. All My Children and the Bold and the Beautiful were her favorite soaps. She fantasized about having the plush and exciting life of Erica Kane and even tried to by some of Kane's cosmetics on QVC but could only find Susan Lucci peddling her hair care products on the channel. Euphoria bought the hair products and hoped she might be able to have hair as beautiful as Erica Kane's.

Tyrone started bringing Megalo to church when the Flippin pastor encouraged him to get Megalo off the streets and into church. Not long after Megalo started attending the Flippin Baptist Church he got saved.

In a sermon on hell Pastor Hokum yelled, "There's no stop, drop, and roll in hell! Without Jesus you'll burn and just keep on burning! Turn or Burn! Get your fire insurance now, trust Jesus!"

Finally he added, "Exposure to the Son, prevents burning!"

Scared to death and wanting to avoid the awful scenario of eternal immolation Megalo raced down the aisle during the invitation and said to the pastor,

"I want to go to heaven. This is such a no brainer preacher. This is like making a choice between getting a whippin' from dad or gettin' to go to town to buy a pair of new cowboy boots."

A week later the pastor baptized ten-year old Megalo. He became a member of the Flippin Baptist Church. Neither of his parents attended the baptism. An angry Megalo rushed home afterward, took a small gas can and poured out some gas on the front lawn, threw a match on the front lawn and set it on fire.

His parents rushed out to try and put the fire out while Megalo yelled at them.

"You are going to split hell wide open and burn eternally if you all don't come to church and get saved."

It took his parents and the volunteer fire department an hour to put the fire out and it came dangerously close to burning the family's house down. Megalo's parents never did come to church despite this warning and their son's constant pleading. The greatest disappointment of Megalo's career is that despite all the converts he had made he never converted his parents who died in a car accident when they broadsided an Angus bull on FM 273 a few years before Megalo turned forty. The thought of his parents burning for eternity haunted Megalo and fueled his evangelistic zeal. In fact, Megalo had a recurring dream in which he heard his parents screaming that the devil's hell was hotter than a thousand fires. This dream haunted Megalo and as much as he tried he could never make the dream disappear.

Although his parents never did come around to Megalo's viewpoints they did at least help support him when he went off to Billy Sunday Bible College. At the college Megalo learned to hate sin and love sinners except for liberals, communists, Roman Catholics, and blacks, and any other strange people who had immigrated to the United States. Just like Billy Sunday Megalo believed that America would be better if folks like that would be lined up and executed by rifle fire because they had become reprobate and would never accept the gospel. Although he did not like any Jews he had ever met he did at least think they should not be lined up and shot because they were God's people even if they were in error. Megalo held out hope that in the last days of this earth some Jews would believe in Jesus even though most Jews would throughout history would go so quickly to hell when they died they wouldn't even have time to adjust their kippahs. For Megalo the Holocaust was horrible primarily because millions of Jews went to hell because they rejected Jesus as Savior. Megalo often mocked Jewish traditions and wondered why Jews had such odd customs.

"Why do these people wear those silly little hats, refuse to eat ham and worship God on Saturday?" Megalo had asked himself more than once.

He concluded, "These people read their Bible too literally and that leads them to follow ancient and outdated customs."

Megalo especially wondered why Jews wore prayer shawls. After all, if Jews did not believe in Jesus God would not even hear their prayers. At least, that's what his Billy Sunday Bible College Hebrew professor, Barley Schmitz, had told Megalo in class one day.

"God does not hear the prayer of the Jew that is without a doubt. Just read Isaiah 1:15; Psalms 66:18; and Proverbs 28:9. Jews are unrepentant nonbelievers; therefore, God does not hear their prayers. Any questions?"

Megalo's Flippin church gave him a scholarship and since the church belonged to the Southwide Baptist Confederation, this national organization provided tuition funds for Megalo as well. His church and his denominational leaders were proud to send Megalo off to receive a fine Bible College education. Unlike those Christian liberal arts universities that destroyed the faith of many innocent and well-meaning Christian kids, the Bible College could be trusted to deepen the faith of students instead of challenging them intellectually. Megalo's favorite professor at Billy Sunday Bible College, Al Moldya, taught Megalo his most important lessons about understanding the Bible. Moldya told Megalo, "Don't lean on your own understanding. Don't think for yourself too much. Just read the books I tell you to read and listen to me and adopt the ideology I impose upon you and then go and impose that upon others. This, Megalo, is authentic Bible college education."

Megalo, grateful to his local church, to Al Moldya, and to Southwide for their generosity, remained loyal to his church and denomination to the end.

Megalo would later adopt as his mantra, "I pledge allegiance to institutionalism above radical individualism and to the conforming priest above the reforming prophet and to a rigid pietism protected by the community of faith."

Once Megalo had become a star of the denomination through his success as a pastor and evangelist, Confederation leaders invited him to appear before the Council on Establishing Brilliance. Wally Amos Crissick, pastor of the First Baptist Church of Dallas, Texas, had founded the Council as well as an inner circle of denominational leaders known as the Virtuous Circle. Most Southwide members referred to Crissick as the Father of Fundamentalism, The Southwide Baptist Pope or simply as Papa Crissick because he spearheaded the fledgling fundamentalist movement in the Southwide Baptist Confederation in the early 1960s. Crissick took a small group of men under his wing and mentored them to become the Friars of Fundamentalism. Papa Crissick often told his friars,

"Men, a remnant of cloth must be exactly like the original cloth or it is not a true remnant. God's remnant church today must look just like the original New Testament church. It must be pure. A church that sprinkles and doesn't dunk can't be the true remnant. A church that doesn't believe all the things we in the Southwide Baptist Confederation believe cannot be God's remnant church. Men, we are God's last and only hope for this sick and dying world. It is up to you to keep the church doctrinally pure. You must safeguard it against the forces of liberalism that assault it constantly. Be on your guard and hold that line."

After Crissick's death the mantle passed to Crissick's protégé Grandeur Pompous who now headed the Virtuous Circle whose members served as an unofficial Baptist Cardinalate for the Southwide Baptist Confederation. Under Grandeur's leadership the Council on Establishing Brilliance checked Megalo's Inerrancy Quotient (IQ) and found that indeed Megalo had put his faith and trust in an absolutely Inerrant Bible. The Council realized that Megalo would adopt the party line at all times and be a Southwide Company Man so they deemed him brilliant and invited him to join the Virtuous Circle. Megalo took a vow to protect the interests of the Virtuous Circle at all costs and never cease from protecting the denomination from the evils of liberalism. The Council even gave Megalo a certificate to hang on the wall of his office so that all visitors would see that they were in the presence of brilliance.

The certificate read, "Megalo Maniac: Highest IQ in the Southwide Confederation."

After establishing Megalo's brilliance the Council recommended that Megalo be recruited to write Sunday School lessons for the Southwide Sunday School Board in order to enhance his reputation. Megalo wrote the best Sunday School lessons because he followed the Board's guidelines carefully. The Board demanded that its writers use the Fog Index to determine that they were not writing above a second grade level.

"You write above a second grade level and you have lost the vast majority of Southwide members," Dr. Mellifluous, the executive director of the Sunday School Board, informed the writers at the annual conference for Sunday School Lesson Writers.

Board guidelines also stipulated that no writer could challenge traditional and historic Southwide beliefs and certainly could not write anything that would cause Southwide readers to think too much.

At every conference Dr. Mellifluous, who had been the executive director of the Sunday School Board for over thirty years reminded writers,

"Not only are you writing for persons with below second grade reading ability but these almost second graders are mean as hell when you challenge their folk theology. If you are writing lessons from Isaiah you better say that the Suffering Servant in Isaiah is Jesus or they will hunt you down and tar and feather you. I remember the time when we had a host of letters come in criticizing one of our lessons because it had a picture of Adam and Eve with the garden with a monkey and writers thought we were promoting the theory of evolution with that picture. On another occasion critics lambasted us because our picture of Jesus on the cross did not show any blood. They wanted to know why we did not show a bloody Christ since it was by His blood that persons are saved. One of the letter writers wrote rather pointedly, 'When Jesus is depicted on the cross Baptists want him to bloody. Baptists want blood!' And of course, I will never forget the Job incident. One of our lesson writers suggested that the biblical Job was not such a patient man and that the Satan figure in the book of Job was a friend of God and not the adversary depicted in the New Testament. Wow, did the mean letters ever fly in after people read that lesson. One of our biggest controversies had to do with a picture that we put on the cover of one of our lesson books. We put a picture of a young black male talking to two young blonde women outside of a school. The Southwiders went crazy over that one. We received so many letters that we had to pull the lesson from circulation. The secular media caught wind of it and had a field day and excoriated us publicly but we weathered the storm in the end. So, what I'm saying is we are writing for rather simple folks. Many of them are probably a bit racist and some are just plain crazy asses. But of course, we love them all in the name of Jesus Christ our Lord and our happy that they are buying our literature and not literature from some other publishing house."

Southwide leaders also recruited Megalo to serve on numerous denominational committees hoping that his service would further engender loyal to the group. Confederation leaders also knew that Megalo had access to lots of donors who could help support a denomination that had been suffering financial setbacks in recent years. In all of its publicity Southwide reported financial gains but in reality the Confederation had been losing members and money at a fast pace over the last twenty years. In one closed-door session Grandeur Pompous, who had been elected as the executive director of the Confederation by the Council on Establishing Brilliance, exclaimed,

"We must encourage our members to have more babies. If we want to increase our members and the uninterrupted flow of money into our coffers, we must plead with the couples in our denomination to have more children and to adopt more children."

This seemed like a golden idea to every man in the room.

Confederation leaders had been meeting in closed-door sessions for many years. Although they received tithe monies from many different churches and individuals, the leaders did not believe that supporters of the denomination should be aware of much of Confederation business. Years ago some disaffected Confederation members and a couple of independent local journalists had tried to enter an executive session but they were kicked out immediately. The Confederation hired armed guards to stand outside the locked doors of the meeting while the members who had been booted out sang gospel hymns and a lovely *Te Deum*. The two reporters, who were members of local Confederation churches, having been expelled were then excommunicated from the denomination the next day. The day after that the reporters were anathematized— this is the equivalent of being denominationally vaporized.

"We can't afford to put our guns on stun when we need to take care of the opposition," intoned Pompous.

"The people only need to know what we need for them to know, and we don't need a couple of unbiased journalists to report on our meetings. We need journalists who are biased in support of our denomination and who will only write positive things about the denomination." Grandeur said to Confederation leaders as they voted to boot the reporters from the denomination.

Everyone in the room agreed. From that point on Grandeur, by virtue of his position as executive director, controlled the denominational press. Since he controlled what the rank and file members knew about the inner workings of the denomination, Grandeur controlled the denomination. The Confederation had been moving toward a more highly centralized structure for years even though publicly Confederation leaders spouted that they affirmed and respected the autonomy of each local church. Most members of local churches, however, did not have the slightest idea that precious ideals such as freedom of individual conscience and local church autonomy were in danger. They just wanted everyone in the denomination to get along and not fight and serve Jesus by being nice and going to church on Sunday morning, Sunday evening, and Wednesday evening.

Since Megalo and Grandeur shared the same views on virtually every theological and political matter, Grandeur knew he could trust Megalo to do his bidding. No one was surprised when Grandeur appointed Megalo to serve on the Investigation of Names Committee. Grandeur formed the committee when he discovered a widespread problem in the churches with regard to pastors' names. Some men who had women's names or gender ambiguous names were preaching. The denomination years ago had settled the issue of women preachers. Motion # 333 had passed handily at the 1987 convention meeting. It stated that any church that calls a woman to be pastor has committed a "grave crime" against God and the Southwide Baptist Confederation.

"The woman will be banished from the denomination and the church will be censored and perhaps ejected from the Confederation," read motion # 333.

Megalo's Uncle Anthony brought the motion to the floor and Bully Beaumont, a pastor from Truth or Consequences, New Mexico, seconded the motion. In his closing remarks to convention delegates Uncle Anthony added that the convention would not allow churches to call pedophile pastors so they should not allow female pastors either. Earlier in the year Anthony and Bully had garnered national attention when both of them carried out a well-orchestrated public condemnation of Holly Parson, one of the few female preachers in the convention at the time. In the *Southside Searchlight*, the official newspaper of the convention, Anthony, stated that the Scripture made it clear that only men were called to be senior pastors therefore Holly must be mistaken about her call to ministry.

Bully wrote that he would rather never attend church again than have to listen to a woman preach.

"Who wants to listen to a high pitched whiny squeal on Sunday morning when I have had to listen to it all week at home!"

Bully had also become disturbed earlier in the year when his friend Carl Complementarian had changed his name to Ethan Egalitarian and had turned his back on his authoritarian views. Carl's transformation had occurred after he had a marvelous experience in Jerusalem. Carl received a sudden afflatus and in an instant realized that complementarianism was just a polite word for sexism. After Carl arrived home from his trip to Jerusalem he explained to Bully what had happened to him on his tour of the Western Wall Tunnels.

"While listening to the Israeli guide drone on about the massive size of the Temple stones, I leaned up against one of the huge stones. Suddenly the stone moved revealing hidden documents. Evidently, Temple builders had assembled an ancient hydraulic system and when I touched the stone in a particular place I activated the system and the stone moved. I quickly grabbed the documents and discovered that they were ancient letters written by Paul. The first letter was entitled the *Letter to the Laodiceans*. Another letter was called the *Real First Corinthians*, another letter to Corinth was called the *Sorrowful Letter*, and the final letter was entitled the *Polished Uterus*. The last letter caught my attention. I took pictures of the pages of the letter with my camera phone before Jewish authorities grabbed the documents from my hands and whisked them away. When I reached my hotel room I printed off the pictures of the documents from my camera phone and read them carefully. Paul gave his usual grace and peace greeting but then offered the following astounding instruction:"

> *Dear friends, one day this letter will be discovered long after I am gone. I hid it in the Temple stone on the day that I was almost beaten with rods by Claudius Lysias. I told Claudius that I needed to finish performing a Jewish vow then I hid this and other letters in the stone that my teacher Gamaliel had rigged up during Herod's remodeling project. Please know that one day teachers will arrive and say that I do not want women to teach men, that I do not want*

*women to speak in the church, and that I want wives to be submissive to their husbands. They will say that only men can lead the church. All of you who have a uterus and those of you who are uterus friendly will be happy to know that the risen Christ appeared to me during my three years in the wilderness and gave to me not only the gospel of salvation by grace through faith, he also told me that having a uterus does not indicate inferiority. Really, one day I was eating some berries down by the river Jordan and I saw a vision of a polished uterus and a voice from heaven said, "Blessed are those with a uterus, for they shall inherit the earth. Be uterus friendly, as I am uterus friendly." I recognized the voice as the same one that had earlier said "Saul, Saul, why are you persecuting me?" Then above the polished uterus I saw a sign that read, "In the name of this sign, go forth and conquer." I could not believe what I had seen and heard. I treasured this experience in my heart and when it came time to go on missionary journeys I remembered the vision. That is why I commended Phoebe to the Romans and recognized Mary as one who labored diligently. Hey, I even referred to my good friend Junia as an apostle. Her parents were very proud of her. And of course, no one can forget my fellow laborer and tent-making friend Priscilla. And should I mention Euodia and Syntyche who struggled beside me in the work for many years? Should I mention the four daughters of Philip who had the gift of prophecy? I stayed in their home on my third missionary journey on my way back to Jerusalem. I sat up all night and listened to these women prophesy. Therefore, if some among you begin to teach that I was not uterus friendly and that I treated women as second-class citizens then please set them straight. And those who want to proof text my letters and fail to read them contextually and attribute to me letters that I did not write, well just know that they are preaching another gospel, which is not a gospel. I opposed the Anti-Uterites in Philippi, Rome, Ephesus, and in Galatia. These dogs and evil workers have tried to distort my teaching but I have resisted them. So, must you. Go ye therefore and remember what I have taught you. Follow my example. Remember the vision of the polished uterus and embrace all of those who are called to do the work of the Lord— both female and male. I Paul, write this greeting with my own hand with very large letters, not because I have bad eyesight, but simply because I had a lot of empty space on the papyrus that I needed to fill. See these large letters I am using to sign my name. This is my signature. This is how I write. PAUL*

"After I had finished reading this letter I leaned back against the pillows on my bed, looked to the ceiling, and fell asleep. While asleep I had a dream of a large sheet that was filled with many uteri. A voice spoke,

'Of course women can be leaders in the church, Carl. Just because you have a penis doesn't make you special.'

I woke up and I could not see and for a moment I could not feel my penis. I grabbed it and thank God, it was still there. I'm so grateful that visions from God make you go blind sometimes but never cause you to lose your package. I am into immaculate visions, but not emasculating visions. That would have totally destroyed the vision for me if I had become a eunuch for the sake of the kingdom of God. Surely you can see where wooden literalism leads? Nevertheless, I asked a hotel worker named Annie Nias to guide me to the Western Wall. I stood against the wall praying for God to forgive me for my sexist orientation. Annie patted my approvingly on the shoulder. Suddenly, scales fell from my eyes and I saw things clearly. I saw Annie smiling at me. God forgave me and although I had been blind now I could see. For the first time, I could really see."

When Bully heard his friend Carl tell this amazing story he discounted it completely.

"Surely, you cannot accept this letter as being authentic? Carl, we must only accept the authority of canonical Scripture."

"Well, Bully, first of all please call me Ethan from now on. And furthermore it makes more sense to me to accept Paul's Western Wall Letters as authentic as it does to accept some of his canonical letters as authentic, especially the so-called Pastoral Epistles. Further, I can't simply ignore the vision I had which served to confirm the Western Wall Letters. Now I know that if Holly Parson believes that God called her to be a minister then I should not question her experience nor is it my place or yours to stand in judgment on the experience of another."

Despite Ethan Egalitarian's experience Bully, Anthony and other denominational leaders continued to demand that women could not become pastors on the grounds that they were not men and did not have a penis.

Bully and Anthony also told Grandeur, "Just to be on the safe side, we should also restrict from the pastorate any woman who claims to have a penis."

Grandeur and his pro-penile friends led the denomination to adopt a confession of faith stipulating that women could never be senior pastors. Although normally a confession describes the belief of a group at a particular time in history, denominational leaders demanded that the churches adhere to the confession. Sarah Lovelady, an elderly widow who had served her local church faithfully and without fanfare for many years, wrote to Megalo, who at the time served as convention president, indicating that this action had essentially transformed the confession into a creed; that is, something that everyone must believe. Megalo wrote to Sarah scolding her for questioning him. He pontificated that credalism is sometimes necessary to ensure doctrinal conformity and that doctrinal uniformity was the key to a healthy, tranquil denomination.

"Those who have abundant knowledge and wisdom have a sacred duty to impose their beliefs and practices upon the unsophisticated commoners in the denomination who would fall into grave theological error otherwise," Megalo wrote.

When Sarah received Megalo's response she became overwhelmed with sadness.

Sarah wrote back to Megalo and asked, "Don't you think that using a confession of faith as an instrument of doctrinal accountability is an admission by the Southwide Confederation that we are losing the culture wars and that we are becoming increasingly irrelevant to mainstream culture?"

She added, "If we have to enforce uniformity of belief and practice then our denomination has lost its voice in society."

Sarah believed that any effort to enforce uniformity could only be disastrous for the Confederation in the end. Besides, she knew that uniformity would never be approximated despite the best efforts of Confederation leaders.

Megalo's only response to Sarah's second letter was to send her an invitation to Southwide's annual Symposium on Cultural Irrelevance. Megalo, the keynote speaker at the next meeting, thought Sarah would benefit from hearing his sermon entitled, "How to Enforce Doctrinal Uniformity in a Secular World." Along with the letter, Megalo also sent Sarah a booklet he had published entitled, "Catechism: A Sure Cure for Secularitis." A bewildered Sarah wrote no more letters telling her friends that there was nothing more that she could say or do because she had been relegated to second-class status in her denomination. She had no theological training and she was a woman.

"Two strikes and you're out in the Southwide Baptist Confederation," Sarah muttered to herself as she threw Megalo's letter on top of some used coffee grounds that lay in the trash.

In a few moments the letter became completely soaked and no longer readable. Megalo did not like anyone, much less an old woman, criticizing the "Confession that is used as a Creed" because he had served as chair of the committee that had written the articles. In fact, Megalo had written most of the "Confession that is used as a Creed" himself. Megalo referred to his document as **The Code**. The preamble of **The Code**, written by Megalo and other denominational leaders, spelled out clearly how the document should be utilized.

We believe that we can discern the mind of God so clearly that our understanding of Scripture is absolute. We are not interpreters of Scripture but simply conduits through which God reveals his perfect will to us through Scripture. Therefore, we are able to indicate to others whether or not the Holy Spirit has spoken to them or guided them accurately. We bear this responsibility with all humility. Finally, please note that all churches associated with the Southwide Baptist Confederation must abide by **The Code** or be excommunicated *confestim* (For all you rank and file commoners in the convention that last word is Latin and means "without delay.").

Delegates at the annual convention meeting gladly accepted **The Code** with only a few persons voting against it. Query Battlequam stood to question **The Code** but delegates shouted him down as he tried to ask,

"Couldn't you be wrong?"

Megalo called for silence and said to Query, "Sit down. Do not question us. Do you not understand that the close relationship we have with the Lord insures our orthodoxy? Had you attended the "Affirming the Bible According to Our Own Interpretation Conference" in Denver last year or had you attended this year's "Consortium on a Non-Contextual Understanding of the Bible" you would not dare ask such an absurd question. At the two conferences, which by the way was sponsored by the prestigious National Association of Proof Texters (NAPT), you would have heard from the learned leaders in our denomination how to ignore liberal hermeneutical principles such as giving attention to the context of a passage of Scripture and you would have learned how to follow official denominationally approved interpretations of the Bible. Yes, denominational leaders would have taught you how to view the Inerrant Bible through the lens of the flawless **Code**. These speakers would have destroyed all your doubts and would have helped you to see that theology should never be left up to the despised herd of humanity. The untrained always get it wrong. Only qualified and denominationally approved theologians should delve into the deep waters of theological inquiry. They never get it wrong.

Query refused to sit down.

He shouted out, "I don't have the time or the money to attend these conferences of which you speak. I work all year round except for two weeks out of the year. During those two weeks I spend time with my family. Besides, it all sounds like a bunch of bureaucratic boondoggle to me."

Query then gathered his things and left the convention hall and the Southwide Baptist Confederation and organized religion altogether for good. His wife, Histrionic, had hated the restrictive nature of the Southwide Confederation for years. When Query left she left with him but found a home among the Pentecostals.

She told Query, "I love the unrestrained worship and that as a woman I am affirmed and valued."

Query asked, "But how can you stand the simplistic, naive, repetitive sermons?"

"Oh, I don't pay much attention to that part of the service. I just go for the music and dancing," Histrionic responded. "Of all the Christian denominations, no one busts a move better than the Pentecostals."

Eventually Histrionic became disenchanted with the Pentecostals and joined the Holy Laughers of Toronto. This group believes that the primary manifestation of being filled with the Holy Spirit is a feeling of joy that leads incessant laughter and even barking and trembling. The adherents gather in large auditoriums and listen to sermons and music but most of the time they spend simply laughing in the Spirit. Histrionic felt the laughing to be satisfying for a time but she began having uncontrollable crying episodes following her laughing attacks so the Holy Laughers asked her to stop crying or leave their group. Histrionic left and founded her own organization she called the International House of Prayer, Praise, and Yelling (IHOPPY). IHOPPY Christians believed that the primary expression of being filled with the Holy Spirit was yelling praises to God in prayer. They also believed that God would eventually save all humans and that no one would be damned. The opponents of IHOPPY called them the No-Heller Yellers. Histrionic's IHOPPY group grew exponentially as many disenfranchised young evangelicals joined the ranks.

Grandeur and Megalo had feared that some men and women such as Query and Histrionic would be offended by **The Code.** That is why they encouraged Fupa Paunch to join Sue B. Missive in leading the now floundering Submitters United in Christ the King and Savior organization (SUCKS). In her younger days Fupa had been sought after as a speaker at women's conferences all over the country. Fupa traveled continuously hardly spending anytime at home leaving her husband to take care of the home by himself. All the while she exhorted women to be good wives and take care of their husbands and obey them in all things. Fupa's husband, Papi, really didn't complain much about her absence from home because he enjoyed his freedom and the time away from Fupa. When she was home she criticized him constantly and complained about the way he kept the house. She also criticized Papi's cooking and would throw her meal into the trash and heat up a frozen dinner for the evening meal. Fupa really loved the Super-Sized Hungry Man Fried Chicken Dinner the best.

Papi tolerated Fupa's intermittent outbursts of anger because he liked the money that she brought home from her speaking engagements and book signings. Fupa had several bestsellers that both won an award for Best Evangelical Book of the Year in the Women's Category. Her first book, *Gracious Submission*, exhorts women to stop following the secular program that seeks to advance the cause of women's rights and simply follow the biblical model of surrendering their rights to the proper authorities that God has placed over them. Her second book, *If You Want Him to Commit, Then You Must Submit*, informed young women that they could snag a husband by simply repeating one simple phrase while in their presence,

"Whatever you want, I'll do it. Lead Me On, O King Eternal."

When Fupa first met with Sue to reorganize SUCKS she they decided to expand the organization by enlisting women of any age above sixteen who were willing to conform to the aims of the organization. Fupa and Sue also involved the women in new and exciting activities. The women in SUCKS began holding bake sales to raise money for missions and leading charm schools to teach younger women how to make tea and knit and most importantly how to obey their husbands in all things. The women made a video that all initiates were required to watch entitled, "Girls Gone Submissive." The movie highlighted the lives of prominent women in the organization who explained the joys of submissive living. Shortly after the founding the women of SUCKS began holding regular local meetings across the Confederation once a month on Elaborate Hat Day. On the first Thursday of every month the women don their favorite ornamented hat that they call a "Protector." Fupa made and sold the hats to the women. Sue B. had encouraged her to get into the hat making business as a way to have some "mad" money that she could spend however she wanted. The women of SUCKS loved Fupa's hats and soon the hats began appearing in small boutiques across the country. The demand for hats became so great that Fupa had to outsource the hatmaking to sweatshops in Indonesia where young women worked long hours at low wages to make the hats that Fupa would sell for a handsome profit.

Fupa's elaborate hats symbolize for the women that their husbands have authority over them and that they will be protected from the evils of the world by submitting to their husbands. At the meetings the women pray, play Yahtzee, and have a unique sort of communion service that involves drinking a small glass of milk and eating little chocolate filled cookies that resemble fortune cookies that they call "Overseers." The women eat the Overseer then chase it down with the milk. Then they recite in unison the SUCKS motto,

"We eat this Overseer in remembrance of our solemn duty to submit to our God appointed overseers, our husbands. Amen"

SUCKS members were thrilled when the Confederation had appointed the Investigation of Names Committee along with the committee's subsequent recommendations to kick out several churches from the Confederation, not because the churches had women pastors, but because their male pastors had feminine names such as Lesley and Pat. Denominational leaders in many cases failed to recognize the ordination of these pastors unless they changed their names to masculine ones.

Megalo agreed that not only could a woman not be a pastor neither could any man with a feminine name. When a church member pointed out that Megalo had once gone by the nickname Pastor Meg, Megalo insisted that nicknames did not count. Last year when Megalo brought his committee's report to the annual meeting of the Confederation he made a motion that **The Code** or the "Confession which is used like a Creed" be amended indicating that not only can a woman not serve as pastor; a man with a feminine sounding name cannot be pastor. The motion passed unanimously.

Confusion reigned in the churches after this decision. Pastor Lesley was fired but not Pastor Pat. Pastor Jerry thought he was safe until someone mentioned that his name had feminine spellings such as Jeri and Gerri. Finally, the executive committee of the denomination stepped in and unilaterally set the following process into motion. Any ordained pastor who has a disputed name shall appear before the executive committee and shall apply for a name change. The committee will give him a new masculine name. The pastor will also be quizzed regarding his beliefs about the Bible just to be on the safe side. In the case of an un-ordained person with a feminine or ambiguous name, the candidate will appear before the executive committee of the Confederation to receive his new masculine name. After a day of investigating his doctrinal positions the committee will approve the candidate for ordination if he is found to be doctrinally pure and is thoroughly mannish. If the candidate exhibits even the slightest of feminine qualities he shall not be approved for ordination.

Megalo also served on the Confederation Seminary Oversight Committee. Grandeur Pompous developed this committee after he and Megalo met and decided that Southwide Baptist seminaries had become too liberal and that the trustees were allowing it to happen. Since Megalo served as chair of the Seminary Oversight Committee he and Grandeur worked together to appoint trustees who would do their bidding and to replace any who would not comply.

All of the agencies and schools owned and operated by the Southwide Baptist Confederation had a Board of Trustees to oversee the operations of each agency and school. A typical Megalo appointed Board consisted of mostly Southwide pastors, a few overextended and theologically naïve businessmen, and a few subservient pastor's wives. The Board members only met several times a year, had no idea what really transpired daily at an agency or on a campus, and believed that their primary responsibility was to keep liberalism from infiltrating Southwide's entities.

Megalo and Grandeur referred privately to their handpicked trustees as Lackeys. Some members of the Confederation thought it strange that Grandeur appointed Megalo as the head of the committee that would oversee Confederation seminaries since Megalo had founded a college of his own that did not fall under the authority of the Confederation. Nevertheless, no one publicly challenged the great Megalo. Megalo saw his primary responsibility on the Seminary Oversight Committee as ensuring doctrinal uniformity in the Confederation's six seminaries and the way to do that was to appoint trustees who shared his outlook and that he could trust to throw out the liberals. In only a few years Megalo had his trustees in place.

Megalo believed that education did not involve exploration, but indoctrination. And he wanted seminary students to be immersed in the doctrines of the Southwide Baptist Confederation, or at least the doctrines he believed were most important.

"If you allow students to think for themselves too much, then you begin to have diversity of thought and that undermines the health of the denomination," Megalo often stated.

Megalo's effort to prevent education from occurring at the seminaries was no easy task. In his very first attempt to take over one of the Confederation seminaries he found himself in the fight of his life. President Russ Clearday, of the largest Confederation Seminary, Southwest Seminary, had not only served as president of the school but for years had taught a hermeneutics course and had introduced different theological ideas to the students. Clearday also encouraged the professors at Southwest to familiarize the students with various ideologies and interpretations of the Bible and to do it as objectively as possible. The president even suggested in a chapel address that he was open not only to men with feminine sounding names serving in the pastorate, he was open to women serving as senior pastors. Megalo knew that Clearday had to be the first president of a Confederation seminary to be fired.

"This is how liberalism is trying to gain a foothold in the denomination once again," Megalo told Grandeur. "You know how we marginalized many liberals years ago and many of them left our denomination yet we never were able to take over our seminaries or many of our Baptist colleges. This is where liberals have been hiding and this is where liberalism continues to show its ugly face. In our seminaries and colleges liberalism is making another run at us to try and ruin our denomination in a very subtle way. You know how? It's the women's issue. Our administration, faculty, and students are studying many false ideologies and aberrant interpretations of Scripture and that is a problem. But the biggest problem is many of them believe that women can serve in leadership positions in the church. Many of the faculty members teach that women can serve as pastors. Yes, liberalism is trying to sneak in the back door via this issue. If we allow women to become leaders in our churches and in our denomination then the next thing we know liberalism will have a stranglehold on us. If women begin to be leaders our denomination is doomed because women are the weaker sex. They were the first ones to sin in the Garden of Eden. If not for Eve, we would all be living in paradise right now. Also, if we allow women ministers that will open the door to gay ministers. If we have gay ministers, the next thing you know we will have transgendered pastors. Down in Tupelo, Mississippi a few years ago a church hired a pastor thinking he was a man. When he took the young people to church camp the boys saw him in the shower and he didn't even have a penis. When the deacons heard about it they held a meeting and fired him for not having a penis. The pastor concocted some story about being born with ambiguous genitalia and that the doctor had decided that he was female and should be raised as a girl. He said his family tried to raise him as a girl but the pastor said he always felt he was a boy. When he became eighteen he left home and started living as a boy. Can you believe it, a boy without a penis? What kind of nonsense is that? A pastor has to have a penis. If a pastor goes into the pulpit without a penis, he might as well go to the pulpit without his Bible. Yes, the two keys to pastoral success are a penis and a proof text. Besides, the Bible says that God made males and then he made females. He never made a man with a vagina or a woman with a penis. God doesn't deal in ambiguities. His creation is perfect. God never makes mistakes. No sir, we must fix this now or our denomination will be ruined soon enough."

Megalo called Ralph Pushey, chairman of the Board of Trustees at Southwest Seminary and Chief Lackey, and requested a special meeting of the Board and the president.

When Ralph Pushey received Megalo's call he could not have been more pleased.

"Megalo, I am so glad you are taking action. This president is unfit. We thought he was conservative but he has been hiding his true orientation. In his hermeneutics class he would not call the Bible inerrant. He mentioned something about the necessity of reading the Bible contextually and with humility, whatever that means, and would only say that the Bible is infallible. The word "infallible" is a code word liberals use to conceal their disdain for the Bible. The president also told the students that even devout Christians have differences of interpretation on Scripture. He even taught them that higher criticism crap and told his students that there are other preaching methods besides the expository model. Yes, Megalo, he must go. And, I'm willing to make the motion and get my buddy Ollie Collie to second the motion."

Megalo called the board meeting and in the closed meeting, Megalo informed the Board that this president was an advocate of education instead of indoctrination and that the board had a duty to vote him out of office. Pushey made the motion, and Ollie seconded it. During the time of the discussion Ollie asked President Clearday what had caused him to adopt unhealthy viewpoints.

President Clearday simply responded, "I just did a lot of reading."

Ollie asked Clearday, "Did you read books that offered viewpoints that differed from your own?"

"Yes," replied Clearday. "I read a lot of theological books that represented different perspectives."

Ollie chided Clearday, "Well, that's your problem, Clearday. Don't you remember that the denomination has an approved book list for seminary students?"

Clearday retorted, "Yes, but there were so many good books that were not on the approved list. Some I had read but some I had not read. One day I found myself in a bookstore downtown and I just pulled a Paul Tillich book off the shelf because I had not yet read this particular book and my intellectual curiosity got the best of me. The next thing you know I was reading more Barth and Pannenburg than I ever had before."

"Heretic," shouted Ralph Pushey. "All the books from those authors are on the list of forbidden books."

Clearday shot back, "But the list is only for the students. Professors can read some books not on the list as long as they are approved by the Committee on Doctrinal Correctness."

Pulley asked, "Yes, but not only must you gain approval you must sign a waiver that you will read such books only with the intent of refuting them. Otherwise, professors are limited to reading only books that criticize the thought of theologians such as Barth and Tillich. Obviously you gained approval and signed the waiver but then you failed to act in accordance with the waiver. You have not only lied to your denomination, you have committed the unpardonable sin of actually reading the works of heretical theologians such as Barth and Tillich with a view toward seeking an understanding of what these theologians were trying to say. Allowing their ideas to influence you to some degree has tainted you. You have illustrated why I personally believe that such works really should never be read. You must go Clearday. You must go now. I call for the vote immediately."

The Board met and without discussion voted unanimously to fire Clearday. He was charged with Barthism, Tillichianism, Hegelianism, a severe case of Schleiermacher's Syndrome, and with refusing to close the minds of intellectually curious students. As the fired president walked out of the meeting a throng of students who offered cheers of support greeted him. Clearday, who had been a Golden Gloves boxer in his younger days, fantasized about punching the dogmatism out of Pushey and Collie but he could not violate his commitment to pacifism and he certainly did not want to disappoint the students. So, Clearday walked among the students shaking their hands and hugging them and thanking them for their support. Ralph Pushey told the students that he had anticipated a riot and warned them that he had called the National Guard to be on the alert.

"If you don't disperse immediately, the Guard will enter this building and they just might open fire."

The frightened seminary students fled the scene feeling powerless and betrayed by the trustees. Many of the students left the seminary to study elsewhere. *Time's Up* magazine later did a story on the Clearday firing and when referring to the exiting students called it the beginning of the "brain drain" for Southwide Confederation. Seminary trustees called it good riddance believing that they now had the opportunity to revive a spiritually moribund seminary.

Immediately after Clearday's firing Megalo started meeting with Board members individually trying to convince the Board to place him as chair of the search committee to find a new president. The trustees met and did indeed vote to elect Megalo as the chair of the search committee. Megalo immediately thereafter called a special prayer meeting and asked all the trustees to kneel with him and pray that God would reveal to them His will for the seminary. Megalo prayed first.

"Lord, God, Jehovah Jireh, Son of God, Son of Man, Alpha and Omega, we come before you now to ask for your guidance. Please direct us as we seek to choose the next president for Southwest Seminary. May he be a well-known pastor in the denomination who humbly serves you and is a great man of prayer— someone who prays for your guidance, but who is of course a well-known pastor. Amen."

During the course of subsequent search committee meetings Megalo continued to pray that God would send a famous and beloved pastor to become president of Southwest Seminary.

Megalo told the trustees, "We need someone from the Confederation, someone like me, to lead the seminary; someone who is a visible and trusted pastor. Yet, I want to make it clear that I am not interested in the job so don't anyone think about asking me. Yes, we need someone who can reach out to the grass roots constituency and restore their faith in this seminary as a place that will simply train men and only men to become pastors of local churches instead of a place that turns them into thinkers. Besides, a pastor's real training occurs outside the classroom anyway. Let's not overestimate the importance of classroom preparation. But, please don't even consider asking me because God would really have to speak clearly to me in order for me to serve as president."

One of Megalo's friends and a fellow trustee, Curry Favor, stood up and shouted, "Megalo, stop being so stubborn. Just yesterday when you were praying God tugged at my heartstrings and then whispered in my ear, after straightening my tie and suggested to me that the committee ought to abandon the search and appoint Megalo as the president of Southwest Seminary. I failed to say anything because I was scared that God had come so close to me. I mean he literally had his hands on my tie! Then last night as I trembled and prayed earnestly in my room I saw a vision of you, Megalo, floating above me and you shone as bright as the sun."

Curry told the amazed trustees that this vision convinced him once and for all to put forward Megalo's name as the new president. Based on Curry's crystal clear vision the trustees voted unanimously to elect Megalo as the new president of Southwest Seminary.

In his first action, Megalo led the seminary board to change the name of the school to Credo Seminary. In his second action, Megalo demanded that all faculty and staff sign a statement that they affirmed **The Code**. Megalo brought the faculty one by one on the stage in the auditorium before a packed house of students and sat them down at a big desk and with a spotlight from above shining down upon the professors Megalo demanded that they sign the statement or be immediately fired. Every single professor except for one signed the statement. Many of the professors did not want to lose their income and retirement benefits so they simply signed the statement. The professor who refused to sign, Jim Grey, was a professor of church history. Jim had often warned his students about the dangers of credalism. Now, he felt he could not sign **The Code** and still maintain his dignity. Jim walked onto the stage and told Megalo and the students that he would sign a statement affirming his belief in the Bible but that he could not sign a creed.

Megalo muttered, "Jim, I've always known you were a troublemaking heretic and an impediment to true revival on this campus."

A group of students who had recently enrolled in the seminary after Ralph Pushey informed them that the seminary was now a "safe" place due to the firing of Clearday, hooted and hollered,

"Away with Grey, Away with Grey."

One student threw his *Oxford Dictionary of the Christian Church*, no small book, at Grey knocking the professor to the ground.

The students then shouted at Grey, "We don't need to study church history anyway; we just need to study the **Code** and the Bible."

Then the students began to chant simultaneously, "Sign the Code, Sign the Code." Grey lay on the ground wondering how students like these would have ever come into possession of the dictionary when suddenly both volumes of Justo Gonzalez's *The Story of Christianity* came whizzing by his head. He picked up the books and looked inside the front cover only to read his own name. The students had stolen the church history books from Grey's office. The students would never have spent good money on books that had nothing to do with the Bible and that would not help them be good ministers.

Megalo was surprised when he saw a young female professor come forward to sign **The Code**.

"Who is that? What is she doing here?" a confused Megalo asked Ralph Pushey. Pushey replied, "Well, her name is Festal Virgin. Dr. Clearday hired her to teach Church History a few years ago. She is very popular and the students have given her excellent evaluations and she claims to be under the authority of her husband at home so the trustees haven't tried to fire her."

Megalo replied hesitantly, "Church History is certainly not as important as Theology or Biblical Studies and so I suppose it is ok for a gal to teach in our seminary as long as she is not teaching courses in Bible or Theology. And she is popular. And she is willing to sign **The Code**. Ralph, let's give the little gal one more year and then fire her just before she is eligible to stand for tenure. On second thought, we just can't have gals teaching young men here at the seminary unless she is teaching Children's Ministry classes. She could teach those courses I suppose. But we must be true to what the Bible teaches. We don't want to be heartless either. Yes, the Christian thing to do is fire this gal now and give her one year of pay and benefits."

Pushey agreed. After Festal signed **The Code** she turned to Megalo and He smiled at her and her at him unaware that he had just sealed her fate.

When Megalo informed Festal that she had been fired Festal decided to sue the school for employment discrimination. Megalo became alarmed when he received a letter from Festal's lawyer. He went immediately to Pushey's office to talk about the issue. Pushey just laughed and remarked, Megalo, we have nothing to fear. Have you not heard of the ministerial exception? The Supreme Court recently ruled that an employee of a church or church related institution could not bring a suit against her employer."

An astounded Megalo suddenly remembered reading about the ministerial exception case before the Supreme Court in which a teacher of non-religious subjects at a Christian school was fired because she had missed some classes due to health problems. When the teacher sued the school the court declined to hear her case stating that she qualified as a minister and the court should not tell a church related school to fire or hire its ministers.

Megalo smiled at Pushey and stated, "This is great! Talk about the free exercise of religion! Since it appears that the courts are unlikely to hear such cases then we can fire whomever we like and not worry about getting sued by the enemies of God's kingdom."

Although some critics of ministerial exception argued that it failed to protect an employee from workplace bias or retaliation, for Megalo it enhanced his power and emboldened him to make even more dramatic changes at Credo Seminary.

Pushey, chuckling at Megalo's response to ministerial exception asked Megalo, "Brother, have you considered the irony here? We don't recognize Festal as a minister because we don't believe gals can be ministers but in ministerial exception cases the employees of churches or church related institutions are considered by the courts to be ministers even if the institutions don't recognize them as ministers and even if the employees don't even teach courses in religion. So, Megalo hire and fire all the liberals and gals you want. I believe the courts just gave us carte blanche."

Megalo spent a year firing only a few out of the closet liberals and hiring Confederation loyalist conservatives to replace them but eventually he became tired of spending so much time uncovering heretics. Megalo needed someone to assist him in his work. He needed a hatchet man. Megalo hired a childhood buddy Mediocre Norman as his Inquisitor to help him discover and dismiss all remaining heretics. Norman, who took the title Inquisitorial Provost and Vice-President of Doctrinal and Ethical Purity, had been an average student in seminary but became Inquisitorial Provost one month after graduating with his Ph.D. from Credo Seminary. Mediocre planned to rise through the ranks and eventually become president of the Southwide Baptist Confederation by demonstrating devotion to the denomination particularly by revealing heretics he encountered in seminaries and churches. A fellow student who went on to become an accomplished scholar once described Mediocre as "the perfect combination of ignorance and arrogance." In his second year as a graduate student at Southwest Seminary Mediocre had revealed to Megalo that professor Steadman Harmony believed that women could be pastors. Megalo, then a trustee, led the trustee board to demand that President Clearday fire Stephan. Clearday refused, but the trustee board went around Clearday and eventually forced Steadman out. Megalo arranged for Mediocre Norman to pick up Steadman's classes although Norman still had a year to go before finishing his advanced degree. Once Mediocre graduated Megalo, now the Credo president, hired him to be Inquisitorial Provost.

Megalo told Mediocre, "You and I know that the seminary is still filled with closet liberals who are going along with us only because they want a teaching job and a steady income. As Inquisitorial Provost your number one job is to keep this place pure. And it needs to be purified. You know that we are more spiritual than the old dead wood professors who have been here for years. We may not be able to fire the crumblies who are near retirement but I want you to go after the younger liberals. But, Mediocre, we must do all this in a winsome way so that we don't appear to be malevolent persons. But we must purify the seminary in order to save the school. And if we who are spiritual do not get rid of these unspiritual folks our seminary will continue to decline and we will never see revival come to our denomination. Before I became president I hated coming to trustee meetings on campus because I could literally feel the doctrinal impurity and spiritual deprivation in the air. My job is to cleanse this place. I have tried to cleanse this place but it is not completely clean. You are my cleaner. We must have a bumper crop of new conservative professors and get rid of the closet liberals or this seminary and our dear Southwide Baptist Confederation will continue its decline. I'm here to revive it and the way to do it is to get rid of impure professors. So, Mediocre Norman, go out there and find me some heretics, but remember to do everything in a winsome way! And please, don't worry about following the seminary handbook. We don't have to follow it if the ends justify the means. If a tenured professor needs to be fired we will do it without giving him a chance to defend himself even if the handbook states we must give him an opportunity to defend himself. We won't have to worry about fired professors bringing suit against us either. We are a private Christian institution and we can do whatever we want to do and hire or fire whomever we want to hire or fire. We are in power and we hold all the cards. Don't ever forget that Mediocre."

Mediocre conducted his investigations thoroughly and without notice. He conducted an exit interview with each student nearing graduation this being the usual practice. Yet, in past years the provost simply met with the students to see how they enjoyed their seminary experience and to find ways to improve the seminary education. Mediocre used the exit interviews to quiz the students about what their professors had taught them in class. The students shared freely what they had been learning from their professors unaware that the provost would use this information to try and fire their beloved professors. Mediocre also read the personal emails of the seminary professors hoping to find something incriminating. Mediocre loved looking underneath rocks to find something salacious but he never wanted anyone looking underneath his rock.

About six months into his presidency Mediocre brought Megalo his first sacrificial lamb. New Testament professor Milo Journey had recently gone through a divorce. Mediocre and Megalo never liked Journey because Clearday had hired him and they believed him to be a closet liberal. Mediocre had also discovered that Journey held "Creative Drink Night" once a year at his home where he invited select Southwest professors to bring their favorite alcoholic beverages to share and to talk theology. Megalo and Mediocre brought Journey into the presidential office and told him to resign or be fired.

"We cannot have a divorced professor teaching here. Your divorce has compromised your status as an ordained minister. You can no longer be effective in the classroom and I can't imagine that any church would invite you to preach," Megalo stated coldly.

Journey denied that his divorce compromised his ordination in any way but Megalo would not listen to anything Journey had to say. As Journey resigned he remembered how Megalo had offered to support and pray for him when news of the divorce first became public. Now, a dejected Journey realized how insincere and inauthentic Megalo had been. Journey left Southwest Seminary and the Southwide Baptist Confederation convinced that the denomination had fallen from grace.

About a year into his presidency Megalo learned through Mediocre's investigative work that one of his untenured professors had signed **The Code** but had been educating students and had also written some academic articles in a prestigious academic journal that questioned the value of credalism and suggested that it might not be constructive. When Megalo learned of the actions of Professor Alter he became livid. He brought Alter into his office and fired him on the spot for "failure to indoctrinate students and for opposing credalism."

Megalo also fired one of his theology professors, Salvatore Mundi. Salvatore had felt guilty for signing **The Code** and wanted to make it right. He wrote a book that he knew would get him fired and then started searching for a new job. Salvatore's book *Love Always Wins*, suggested that there is not a real hell and that God would ultimately forgive and save all persons from destruction. Megalo became livid when he became aware of Salvatore's work and fired him. When Salvatore left Megalo's office he put both hands in the air as a sort of Diet of Worms victory sign. According to Megalo's secretary, Salvatore also had both of his middle fingers extended in the air as he exited the building. Salvatore believed that Luther would have approved of his gesture.

To further counteract the damage done by Salvatore's book, which had become a best seller, Megalo wrote his own book. He entitled it, *Judgment Always Wins*. A few months later Megalo attended the annual meeting of the Southwide Baptist Confederation and brought the following motion before the delegates,

"Whereas some people in our culture have become victims of the leprosy of universal salvation and that even some persons in our denomination have been influenced by this terrible disease, Be it Resolved that the Southwide Confederation rejects the disease of universal salvation and affirms that hell is real, it is hot, it is eternal, and it is reserved for just about everybody in the world except authentic conservative evangelicals like us."

Megalo's motion passed unanimously. The headline in the *Southwide Searchlight* read,

"Southwide Confederation Votes to Approve Reality of Hell."

After the annual meeting of the Southwide Confederation Megalo had lunch at the Blazing Torch Grill where he remarked to his friends,

"If God had not created a hell the Southwide Confederation would have to because there are so many reprobates in the world."

After about a year on the job Mediocre decided to visit classes personally to ensure that all Credo professors were teaching orthodox

Southwide Baptist doctrine. One day he visited the homiletics course and discovered female students in the class. Mediocre ran to Megalo's office. Out of breath and clearly disturbed, Mediocre asked Megalo, "Did you know we had female students in our preaching courses?" Megalo screamed, "No! This is a liberal practice that we overlooked. Take care of this right away!" Mediocre went to the Registrar and withdrew all female students from the preaching classes and a few months later when the trustees met they passed the following motion:

"Since women cannot serve as Senior Pastors because the Bible clearly prohibits it, female students at Credo Seminary, although welcome to study here, are restricted from enrolling any in preaching classes."

A female student from Kenya, Beatrice Mwalimu, sent a letter to Megalo opposing the trustee action. She indicated that she had been ordained as a minister in Kenya and could not understand why she could not take a preaching course at the seminary. Megalo told Mediocre to withdraw Beatrice from the seminary.

Megalo explained to Mediocre, "Gals are welcome here Mediocre, but only if they are not ordained. We cannot allow ordained gals to attend the seminary. If we do allow it, we are supporting an unbiblical practice. This is also consistent with the policies of the Southwide Baptist Confederation mission agencies that will appoint gals as missionaries or chaplains as long as they are not ordained."

Mediocre met with Beatrice and told her she would no longer be able to attend Credo. Beatrice could not understand it. She tried to arrange a meeting with Megalo but he would not meet with her. She wrote Megalo a letter explaining that she was in the United States on a student visa and that if she were no longer a student she would have to return to Kenya and she could not afford to return. Megalo responded to Beatrice with a brief letter in which he simply wrote,

"The decision is final. You are no longer allowed to study here. We are not at fault here. You are solely to blame because you went against Scripture and were ordained. There is nothing I can do for you. I will pray to the Lord that you can raise enough money quickly to pay for your airfare to Kenya."

Beatrice had only been in the United States for six months and had few contacts. She did not know what to do. She made a quick call to the chair of the religion department at a nearby historically black college and told him her story and asked if she could enroll at the college to avoid having to return to Kenya. The chair could not believe how the woman had been treated but told her that his school offered only undergraduate courses. Beatrice already had a bachelor's degree. The chair helped Beatrice get in touch with Southern Methodist Seminary in Dallas, Texas, who gladly accepted her as a student in the Master of Divinity program. Her advisor enrolled her in theology courses and several homiletics courses as well.

Meanwhile, back at Credo Seminary Megalo and Mediocre founded the Southwide Baptist Preacher Boy Society. Each summer Credo Seminary would host young boys from junior high age to college who had "felt" the call to preach. The boys would go through an intensive two-week training program to help them learn the basics of preaching. The boys also attended doctrinal indoctrination classes and an apologetics course. Upon completion of the program all the boys received a special jacket resembling a high school letter jacket with a large patch on the sleeve that read, "Southwide Baptist Preacher Boy."

In order to hire orthodox preacher boys who would produce younger orthodox preacher boys Mediocre developed a series of questions for prospective candidates. He designed his questions to weed out any thoughtful professors and ensure that only SBC party line preacher boy professors would be hired. Mediocre asked potential candidates their views on abortion, women in ministry, homosexuality, and inter-faith marriage. If a candidate hesitated to reject unequivocally any of these practices Mediocre showed the candidate the door. Mediocre also asked the candidates to explain their view of God in five minutes, the concept of the Trinity in three minutes, and their eschatology in two minutes. His final question left all but the tried and true SBC evangelists baffled. Mediocre asked them what they would say to a "lost" person sitting beside them on a plane heading for a certain crash. If a candidate did not say quickly, "I will share a quick gospel message with the lost person as we descend to earth and certain death," then the candidate would not make the cut no matter how he or she had answered the other questions. Mediocre dismissed one professor from the room because the professor, with tears in his eyes, answered,

"I would call my family and tell them goodbye then pray like an apostle in a Roman prison about to be taken into the gladiator arena."

Megalo served for three more years as the president of Credo Seminary. After becoming convinced that Credo had established itself as the premier indoctrination station in the Southwest Megalo stepped aside and nominated Curry Favor to become the new president. When he made the announcement Megalo told the trustees,

"My work here has been completed. I have stemmed the rising tide of liberalism in the denomination and now I hand the mantle to Curry Favor who will continue the fight against Satan and his demons of liberalism."

As always, Megalo moved on to bigger and better things.

On another occasion Megalo served as a trustee of the Southwide International Mission Board. Southwide boasted over four thousand missionaries serving in over one hundred countries. With so many missionaries to oversee, the board of trustees felt compelled to insure that all missionaries were deeply devoted to the denomination. All missionaries had to sign a statement that they were in full agreement with **The Code**. And every missionary had to be baptized in an officially recognized Southwide Baptist Confederation Church. If a missionary candidate had been baptized in a church associated with another denomination then the candidate would have to be re-baptized even though he or she had already been baptized.

Fleroy Shygirl, who had once served as a Southwide missionary told her friends, "Imagine that, a veteran Christian undergoing an initiatory rite simply to satisfy a denominational requirement. Sounds petty and legalistic to me."

Missionary candidates also had to sign a statement in which they agreed not to engage in practices associated with the Charismatic movement. Fleroy was sensitive to Southwide's requirements because several years ago the Southwide Mission Board had fired her for speaking in unknown tongues and engaging in improper private prayer language. The Board brought Fleroy in to a special meeting and interrogated her with regard to her beliefs. Megalo, the chair of the board of trustees, led the inquisition session.

"Fleroy, you have been accused by a fellow missionary of engaging in heretical practices. How do you plead?" Megalo asked haughtily.

Fleroy responded, "Not guilty."

Fleroy went on to explain to Megalo and the board that as a young girl her parents had taken her to a Kenny Richman "God is a Cosmic Bellboy Convention" in which Kenny explained that God owed every person of faith present good health and lots of wealth. The keynote speaker of the convention, Crispo Greenbacks, preached his sermon in front of a mammoth sized $1000 bill. Crispo challenged his audience to give $100 to the Kenny Richman and Crispo Greenbacks ministries. He told them that if they gave $100 to God, then God would give them $1000. Greenbacks called this phenomenon, God's Irrefutable Law of Giving. After Crispo's sermon Kenny told the audience that everyone present who had faith in God stood to get lots of money from God so each person should demonstrate that he or she has faith by speaking in an unknown tongue. He said that anyone present who could not speak in tongues was not a Christian and would not get any money from God. Kenny told the audience that he wanted everyone to get some money from God. So, Kenny divided the audience into small groups and encouraged everyone in the groups to speak aloud in tongues.

"If anyone in your group does not exercise this gift, then circle the person putting them in the center of your group and pray for the person until the gift of tongues descends upon them." Kenny advised.

Fleroy explained to Megalo that her group placed her in the middle of the circle because she could not speak in tongues.

"The group kept praying and praying but nothing happened," explained Fleroy. "Then, group members began getting impatient with me and some of them started swearing at me in English, French, Spanish, Hindi, and other languages. So, I just started speaking in gibberish so they would shut up and leave me alone."

Fleroy went on to explain that she had told the story to one of her missionary friends who had turned her into the board for the crime of speaking in tongues.

Megalo banged his gavel. "Fleroy, you are guilty of publicly speaking in tongues. Yet this is not the only charge brought against you. You are also charged with using private prayer language when you pray alone."

Fleroy shot back, "How do you know how I pray in private?"

"We placed audio recorders in all the missionary houses so we could monitor the behavior of missionaries in their homes. We heard you praying in murmurs, whispers, and using unknown words."

A horrified Fleroy stood silent as Megalo, pronounced her guilty not only of publically speaking in tongues but of using private prayer language as well. The Board fired Fleroy and asked her to repent of her sins or leave the Southwide denomination. Fleroy not only exited the denomination but she left organized religion all together. She started a Blues band called the Exiteers and after doing well on the local scene for years the band had a top forty hit based on Fleroy's experiences with Southwide called, "Southwide In My Rear View Mirror."

Megalo also served his denomination as a trustee of the Home Missions Department of the Southwide Confederation. One day he dreamed up the idea that the denomination could win every person in the world to Jesus if people in the denomination tried really hard and gave lots of money.

"Why are we losing members? It's not because we are in a post-denominational era as some misguided historians have asserted. Our Confederation is losing members primarily because our pastors are not working hard enough and our laypersons are not giving enough. Let's challenge our people to work harder and give more." Megalo informed the Board of the Home Missions Department.

Megalo challenged the Home Missions Department to adopt his plan to win the world for Jesus. The Board of Trustees of the Home Missions Department adopted Megalo's plan. He called it Brazen Mission Thrust. When the executive director of the International Mission Board complained that the Home Missions Department should have consulted with the International Missions Department about such a plan and that such a mammoth undertaking should have been a cooperative effort between the International and Home Missions departments, Megalo told the executive director,

"You should have thought of it first. Since you didn't, then you don't get any credit for the idea. Of course, you may assist in the effort, but everyone will know that this was my idea."

Megalo had thought of Brazen Mission Thrust while he was on a missions trip to the western part of the United States. Southwide had blanketed the West with zealous evangelists and called the evangelism emphasis Pioneer Penetration. While on a Pioneer Penetration outing he conversed with some former Muslim men who had recently converted to Christianity and had joined Southwide. The men told Megalo that they had left Islam and converted after seeing a vision of Jesus telling them to leave their religion and come follow the true faith. Megalo surmised that if a heavenly Jesus actively engaged in converting persons that an earthly Megalo should join him. Of course, when Megalo talked to some former Christians who had become Muslim after Muhammad had appeared to them pleading with them to leave Christianity and come follow the true faith of Islam, he chalked it up to the work of Satan.

Nevertheless, a year after concocting the Brazen Mission Thrust idea Megalo stood before the annual meeting of the Southwide Confederation and challenged the people to give lots of money to the denomination, to encourage their children to become missionaries, and to go into the world themselves and evangelize the lost, especially Muslim men to whom Jesus had already appeared. In fact, on the spur of the moment Megalo proclaimed that the first year of Brazen Mission Thrust would be called the Year of the Muslim and all Muslims would be targeted for conversion. Megalo believed that the war on terror would be won by converting Muslims to the gospel since, according to Megalo, all Muslims were either terrorists or had the potential of becoming terrorists.

The next year Jews would be marked for conversion. Megalo had worked for many years with Messianic Jews in the Jews for Jesus movement to try and convert Jews to Christianity but had not been too successful. He wanted to make another run at the Jews.

Megalo once remarked to a Jewish rabbi, "It's a shame that Jesus was a Jew and yet so many Jews do not believe in Him as the Messiah. Of course, Jesus was not just a Jew but a Christian Jew. Jesus was his first name. Christ was his last name. So, his very name says that Jesus was a Christian Jew."

Megalo pleaded with the rabbi to become a Christian Jew and be like Jesus. Megalo was deeply saddened when the rabbi simply walked away shaking his head in disbelief.

"Won't you even consider watching *The Passion of Christ* movie with me? It will change your life." Megalo hollered at the rabbi as he continued his escape.

In the third year, Megalo explained to convention delegates, Southwide would aim its missionary strategy at the apostate Roman Catholics or as Megalo like to call them, "The Beasts." Megalo believed that although there were some secret Christians in the False Church of the Beasts, most Catholics were headed to a fiery end.

In order to facilitate the sharing of the "good news" that most everyone in the world faces eternally painful immolation Megalo invented the Evangicube. This was a small cube that presented Southwide's evangelistic message to the lost in four easy to learn phrases: 1. Whatever you are, if you are not a Southwide kind of Christian you are wrong. 2. Southwide Christians are right. 3. Faced with the choice of being wrong or right, you should choose to be right in order to avoid burning endlessly in a devil's hell. 4. If you choose to be right, then you can keep the Evangicube and share this message with others, but if you decide to be wrong you will be tied to a post and assaulted with Evangicubes until you do repent. The choice is yours.

Megalo reserved the right to cast the first Evangicube! Megalo also encouraged the Southwide convention attendees to engage in ejaculatory prayer for the Brazen Mission Thrust effort. He explained that ejaculatory prayer involved the one praying to ask God to go before the missionaries and plant the seed of the gospel in the hearts of those to whom the missionaries will evangelize. Megalo thundered from the podium at the convention,

"We want to challenge everyone here to engage in ejaculatory prayer so that Brazen Mission Thrust will be even more successful than Pioneer Penetration."

Megalo received a standing ovation from the crowd who seemed eager to follow his plan.

In one of his boldest moves Megalo presented a motion at the annual meeting that called for the Southwide Confederation to boycott Disney.

Megalo told delegates, "Disney is gay friendly, not family friendly as they used to be. I call upon our denomination not to go to any Disney theme park or buy any Disney products until they stop being gay friendly."

The motion passed unanimously and for several years the Confederation boycotted Disney. The Confederation eventually called the boycott off even though Disney continued its policy of hiring gays and providing health benefits for the partners of gay employees and holding an annual gay day at its theme parks. When a reporter asked Megalo why the Confederation put a stop to the boycott when Disney had not changed any of its policies he responded,

"Well, Disney still has some problems but the corporation has listened to conservative voices and has become more family friendly in recent years and we want to affirm them to continue in that direction. Disney is taking baby steps and eventually we hope to convince them to cease ungodly practices."

Megalo's faithful denominational service did not go unnoticed. He eventually received the coveted Southwide Baptist Confederation award for denominational service given only twice a century. Megalo received the *Confed*, as it was known, at a special celebration given in his honor. His old pal Grandeur Pompous made a fine speech detailing Megalo's accomplishments then Megalo gave a speech in which he also detailed all of his contributions to the denomination. Of course, Megalo's speech lasted much longer than Grandeur's address. In his speech, Megalo thanked the SBC for recognizing his God given gifts and providing him with opportunities to demonstrate those gifts in an abundant manner.

"I will always love and protect the SBC against all enemies, foreign, domestic, natural, and supernatural," Megalo concluded.

## Commercial Break

"Well, folks," an exhausted Natu the Narrator announced to the television audience, "our second show detailing Megalo's extraordinary life has come to an end. This has been exciting but really we're just getting started. Tune in next week as we examine the great schools that Megalo founded. I know you stand amazed in the presence of Megalo right now but after next week's show you will be awestruck by what I have to tell you about Megalo. But don't touch that remote control yet. Another one of our sponsors wants to tell you about some special products aimed solely at the evangelical world. Tonight's infomercial features Sue B. Maniac. Yes, folks, we get a special treat tonight."

Before Sue comes to share her products Daniel Shaddrach from Bible Fare Incorporated wanted me to thank you for your overwhelming response to his products. Daniel informed me just today that he has sold more products this past week than he has in the past year. If you loved Daniel's Bible foods you will certainly enjoy the products Sue B. Maniac has for you tonight.

Hi everyone. It's Sue B. Maniac. I know you are aware of my many beauty products designed especially for evangelical women but I want to share with you a few of my new products for women. Men, you stay tuned too, because I have something that will interest you as well. First, let me talk to the gals. Ladies, have you gotten tired of having to spend so much time putting and taking off your makeup? I know I have. If you are like me and think that spending two hours putting on makeup is way too long then I have a product for you. For the first time I would like to introduce you to my new spray on makeup I call Evangiglow. With Evangiglow you just point the can toward your face and spray and in an instant you have on beautiful makeup guaranteed to last throughout the day.

Let's say that you attend an evening revival or a Ladies Bible study and you get all emotional and start crying and your makeup begins to look terrible. Just take out a Kleenex, wipe your face and remove the old makeup, then spray a new coat of Evangiglow on your face and you will look as beautiful as ever. Imagine this scenario. You are on a plane and you encounter a rude flight attendant who makes you frown. I wish I had developed this product before I encountered a surly flight attendant on a recent trip to Phoenix. Anyway, just spray on Evangiglow and it will give you the appearance of having a smile even though you are really quite angry. In any tense situation, whether at church or at home or at work, or wherever, Evangiglow will allow you to mask your true feelings so that people will only see what's on the surface. You will be sporting a happy, beautiful countenance even in the midst of great heartache. That's the evangelical way! I tell you gals, this is a revolutionary product! It's so easy to use. Just point and spray and you're done. And the bottle comes in a small twelve-ounce container that you can easily slip into your faux Kate Spade handbag.

Now, men, I told you I have something for you. With the help of my husband Megalo I have developed the Submitter Transmitter. Your little gal will wear an electronic ankle device for which you have a remote. I know how you men love remote controls, but this one won't change the channels. No, this one changes your gal's attitude. Whenever she starts nagging you or tries to dominate you, all you do is push the remote button and it sends a signal to the ankle device which then delivers a shock to your little woman's ankle. The shock will remind your girl to be submissive to you. The device may take some time before it works without fail but eventually every time your gal receives an ankle shock she will associate it with submissiveness. Today I am offering a special deal. Gentlemen, if you buy the Submitter Transmitter I will throw in a free can of Evangiglow. You can't beat this deal. Something for you and something for the little lady. Simply call the number on your screen, 1-EVA-NGI-GLOW and we will send your order out right away. I am offering both products for $19.99 but after today you will have to pay $19.99 for each product. Don't delay. Call today. Good night all!

Chapter Three:

# Founder of World Class Schools

Megalo had attended public schools while growing up in rural Texas and he had enjoyed his time in school. After he entered the ministry however, Megalo had an experience that caused him to have a negative attitude toward public education. Megalo had been asked to preach a revival in Sour Grapes, Texas. He had been allowed at some schools to preach to the students during an assembly time and to invite them to the revival. Many times the superintendent of a Texas school served as a deacon at the local Baptist church and allowed Megalo to come to the school and evangelize or invite students to the revival to see the Frito Bandito. As he entered Sour Grapes High School the superintendent greeted him with kindness but would not allow him to preach to the students during the school wide assembly or invite them to the revival that Megalo was holding in a nearby Baptist church.

The superintendent explained, "If I let you evangelize the students then I have to open up my school to every religious group and I am not going to do that. I believe that allowing you to evangelize at my school flies in the face of the establishment clause of the First Amendment."

Megalo's face turned red with anger when the superintendent refused to allow him to talk with the students. He shouted at the superintendent, an elder in the local Presbyterian church,

"Our country is in ruins because we have taken God and prayer out of our schools. This is a Christian nation! Secular minded people like you are allowing our public schools to become godless. God will judge you!"

Megalo turned toward the door and hit it as hard as he could with open palms. He pointed his black Gucci's at the school and shook them as if he were shaking dust off of his shoes and mumbled something about God having abandoned the public schools. From that moment on Megalo became convinced that Christians should start their own schools and never attend the godless public schools because the public schools had kicked God out and refused to let Him back in. Megalo also became convinced that all state colleges had become bastions of heresy and most religious oriented universities had shaken off their Christian roots and had become corrupt at worst and spiritually anemic at best. So, Megalo founded Patriot Bible Academy, a K-12 Christian school that he marketed to fundamentalist and conservative evangelicals who agreed that the public schools were wicked dens of iniquity where secular humanism flourished. Patriot Bible Academy began flourishing almost immediately.

Megalo named his friend and fellow Southwide evangelist, I. Toot Myhorn, as president of Patriot Bible Academy. Known affectionately as "Toots" the new president touted the new school as a place where the political and religious leaders of the future would emerge.

"I would love for the world to be led by people who have a biblical worldview. And our aim at Patriot Bible Academy is to instill in our young people a certain, unmistaken, unashamed, unapologetic biblical worldview and to teach them how to advance in careers such as law and politics as well as theology," Toots declared at the first chapel meeting.

When A.C.A. Demic at Openmind University heard about the aims of Patriot Bible Academy he remarked,

"Which biblical worldview will they teach there? Will they promote polygamy, the cherem, theocratic government, and the stoning of disobedient children? If only there were one harmonious biblical worldview. Wouldn't that make the theological enterprise so much easier?"

Megalo also founded a Christian university he called Absolute Truth College in order to provide a place where Christian students could learn the absolute truth about life by embracing a biblical worldview which would of course give them ready answers for the most difficult questions about life. ATC did not grow as Megalo had hoped and after several years of meeting in a small store in a Houston strip mall the school folded. At the time only twenty students were enrolled. Megalo decided that the best course of action would be to plan a takeover of a prominent Baptist university and turn it in to Absolute Truth College. And he knew exactly how to get it done.

Megalo met with Grandeur Pompous and shared with him concerns he had about Mainstream Baptist University located in Waco, Texas.

"This school has abandoned its Christian and Baptist roots and is headed down the road of secularism. The light has almost gone out in Waco, Texas. We must do something drastic to get this school to return to its Christian roots. We turned Southwest around. Now, let's restore this school and turn the light back on in Waco," Megalo told Grandeur.

Grandeur agreed. Together the two men, who were having coffee and deep fried pancake puppies together at the Café Du Conspirateurs, hatched a plan of how to take over Mainstream Baptist University.

The two men had a simple plan and they executed it with precision, well almost. Megalo's Uncle Anthony had moved up through the ranks and had become the executive director of the state convention of Texas Baptists. Anthony despised many of the professors at MBU because they did not agree with his fundamentalist theology. More than anything he wanted to turn Mainstream Baptist University into Mainstream Bible College.

Uncle Anthony hated the liberal arts education offered at MBU but when he spoke a word of greeting at graduation services as the chief representative of the Texas convention he always stated,

"MBU has the best faculty members in the world."

Yet, all the faculty members knew that he did not care for many of them especially the teachers in the religion department.

Uncle Anthony once told Megalo, "MBU might be a place of academic excellence but the professors there do very little to make the students more Christlike."

Uncle Anthony enthusiastically gave Megalo the names of prominent pastors who were not happy with the teaching of a number of MBU professors. Megalo contacted these disgruntled Southwide pastors and encouraged them to question students from their churches who attended MBU about what they were being taught in their classes especially their religion courses. Megalo also suggested that pastors give scholarships to certain student spies and promise to reward them further if they could find dirt on some of their professors. Megalo also promised to reward the pastors with denominational appointments in the future if they cooperated. Although most students brought good reports to their pastors about what they had been learning, a few disaffected students and several of the appointed spies brought "heresy reports" to their pastors.

Uncle Anthony encouraged the pastors to bring the issue of alleged heresy at MBU before the Texas Baptist convention at its annual meeting and not the MBU trustees because Anthony had not been successful in taking over the trustee board even though he had tried diligently. Uncle Anthony had even used his authority as executive director to secure a permanent appointment as special consultant to the trustee board but he could not convince a clear majority of the trustees to investigate alleged heresy at the school. Uncle Anthony could not wait until he got the votes and decided to bypass the trustee board.

Upon Uncle Anthony's urging the pastor at Boondocks Riverby Landmark Baptist Church made a motion at the convention that a committee be organized to investigate the school. The pastor at Backwater Baptist Church seconded the motion barely edging out a second by the pastor from Rabbit Trap Baptist Church and without discussion the state convention delegates voted to organize "The Smelling Committee" to go to the school and determine the orthodoxy of MBU. Uncle Anthony was elated. As executive director he named Megalo chair of The Smelling Committee and thus Megalo became the new chief of the heresy hunters—the Southwide Grand Inquisitor.

President Jack Nips told an unhappy faculty that his hands were tied. I must work with The Smelling Committee no matter how I hate doing so.

"Just go about your work as usual and teach the way you normally do and I'm sure we will get a clean bill of health and this darkness will soon be behind us," Jack informed his faculty.

The Smelling Committee visited numerous classes at MBU and discovered evolutionary theory being discussed in science courses. Religion professors had their students studying process theology and reading the works of Alfred North Whitehead. New Testament students examined various types of biblical analysis such as Narrative Criticism. Students became familiar with liberation, feminist and womanist theology. One professor even had students reading the works of John Hick and Jurgen Moltmann. The World Religions professor even took his students to visit the local mosque and Hindu temple.

Megalo and the committee returned to the annual convention of Texas Baptists a year after the committee had been formed and gave its report to the convention. Texas Baptists attending the convention heard from the committee that MBU had serious theological problems that must be fixed immediately or the school would be lost. Texas Baptists voted to elect a brand new slate of trustees who would govern the affairs of the school. Once the new trustees began their duties they voted to remove Jack Nips as the president of MBU and upon the recommendation of Megalo's friend, Curry Favor, elected Megalo Maniac to be the new president of Mainstream Baptist University. In only one year Megalo had accomplished what he thought it might take him years to do.

"I love Baptist polity!" Megalo exclaimed after the convention meeting. "Get the ear of the people and you can change things in an instant."

Immediately, Megalo went to work changing the nature of MBU.

Megalo could not fire the old tenured professors unless he could prove they were heretics so he simply marginalized them until they took early retirement or found another job. Megalo immediately began firing untenured faculty members who were not fundamentalist but he often did it indirectly using lower level administrators to do his dirty work. Without going through a normal search process Megalo, working with Uncle Anthony, hired new faculty members who would be loyal to him and who he could count on to hold to the party line theologically and politically.

Together Megalo and Uncle Anthony brought the school into closer union not only with the Southwide Baptist Confederation but with the Southern Fried Baptist Convention of Inerrant Texans and the General Association of Infallible Baptists as well. Many of the professors in the religion department at MBU happened to be untenured, so Megalo essentially created a brand new religion department. First, Megalo hired a new dean for the religion department, Doc Trinare. Doc went to work immediately firing whomever he could. Then he named himself chair of all the search committees that were organized to find replacements for the fired religion professors. Doc, with the blessing of Megalo, hired his nephew, his best friend, his cousin's husband, his pastor's son, and the son of a prominent Texas pastor friend to teach in the religion department. A few critics called it nepotism. Doc called it, "putting God's people in places of service." After Doc assembled his new handpicked religion professors he and Megalo spoke at the annual meetings of the Southern Fried Baptist Convention of Inerrant Texans, the Southwide Baptist Confederation, and the General Association of Infallible Baptists. Megalo bragged to convention delegates about how he had kicked out the liberals and replaced them with Godly professors.

He roared, "Delegates, you can now have confidence again in our new religion department and in our school as a whole. You can count on our new professors never to teach anything that runs contrary to what you people in the churches believe as well. Please support us with your prayers and your pocketbooks."

Megalo had dreams of creating the flagship school for all conservative evangelicals but especially fundamentalist Baptists so he sought to network with as many right wing Baptist groups as possible in order to gain support. The GAIB only sponsored schools that would teach that the Bible is inerrant in every area of reality and is really the only book that one needs to read to learn about life. The Southwide Baptist Confederation voted to follow the policy of the GAIB.

Megalo and the trustees also changed the name of the university to Absolute Truth College and began recruiting students from conservative evangelical and fundamentalist churches. The school grew under Megalo's leadership and he viewed this as evidence of God's blessing for having turned the school back to the truth. The school also grew because Megalo offered many students an online educational experience using adjunct teachers from many different places who would agree to direct online courses. Even the students who came to the ATC campus could take online courses and many of them did. When ministerial student Jack Sloth graduated he bragged to his friends that he had not attended class a single day but had stayed in his dorm room for four years and had completed his degree in pastoral ministry.

Megalo crossed the country raising funds for his college. He preached in upper middle class churches across the upper Midwest and middle class churches down South. Megalo had a Big Donor Sermon for big givers and a Median Donor Sermon for middle class givers. Although Megalo did not know any poor persons firsthand he did have a Poor Donor Sermon for the impoverished. Megalo remembered how his daddy could sell Kirby Vacuum cleaners to poor elderly women. Megalo used the knowledge his daddy gave him to convince poor elderly folks to give everything they had to support his school so that God would be glorified and the giver would receive God's blessings.

The college received a huge boost when two of Megalo's followers, P.P. Trough and T.T. Stall, who made millions in the urinal and toilet business, donated millions of dollars to Megalo to provide scholarships and build new buildings. P.P. and T.T., who named their company Trough and Stall Incorporated, were politically and religiously conservative but also known for their unsavory business practices and crude speech. They made a deal with Megalo that they would "piss a butt load of money" Megalo's way only if strings were attached. Megalo agreed wholeheartedly. Megalo told P.P. and T.T. that if he had to he would require his faculty to teach that pickles have souls in order to receive their generous donations. P.P. and T.T. were pleased with Megalo's response.

The college had been accredited by a nationally respected accrediting agency but Megalo also sought accreditation from the Transglobal Union of Bible Colleges and Diploma Mills in order to demonstrate to his fundamentalist constituents that the school did not merely seek approval from the "secular world." The Transglobal motto was, "Show us the money and we'll accredit you."

Transglobal had over three hundred schools, most associated with the Baptist denomination, that it accredited and claimed to be the world's largest non-governmental accrediting agency. Transglobal had an embarrassing episode in its first few years of operation but overcame it due to the great number of Baptist ministers who sought substandard credentials. Evidently, a clever group of college students made up a bogus school and sent in the money to have the school accredited and the agency accredited it unconditionally. The school was called Donald Duck University. Faculty members listed were Daffy Duck, Mallard Season, Bugs Bunny, and Elmer J. Fudd. Fudd was listed as teaching creation science at Donald Duck University. The textbook for the class was entitled, *Where the Wild Things Are*, by Maurice Sendak. The school motto was listed as *Solum pro Anatidae Est Educatio whose meaning is rendered "Education is for Ducks."* Transglobal did not shut its doors after this prank became public but simply moved from Missouri to Arkansas.

When Transglobal representatives came to ATC after its first year of operation under Megalo he bragged that his school outstripped all secular schools in the country and many denominationally oriented schools because of the unique educational approach at ATC.

"Here at ATC we integrate faith and learning," boasted Megalo.

When a Transglobal representative asked Megalo to explain what he meant by integration of faith and learning, Megalo answered,

"Well, you have faith on the one hand and learning on the other hand and you simply bring faith and learning together and integrate the two."

In unision all the Transglobal representatives shouted,

"That's Brilliant. We've never heard anything like that in our lives. You are definitely on the cutting edge Megalo and we will gladly accredit your school for the coming year and all future years."

Megalo was not only proud of his integration of faith and learning approach to education he was also quite proud of the faculty that he and his Uncle Anthony and other pals had personally assembled at ATC.

Megalo had certain stars among the faculty that consisted of an inner circle and he referred to them in private as his "Dream Team." One of the most important members of the "Dream Team" was Megalo's professor of Homiletics Alvin D. Calvin Dort III. Alvin had made a name for himself in his youth as a member of the famous Southern Gospel singing group The Flaming Tulips. All of Alvin's sermons had five points and all had interesting titles. His students loved the sermons he preached in chapel aimed at all those folks he considered to be the non-elect or those Christ did not choose to receive salvation. One he entitled, "You're Going to Hell and It's Totally for God's Glory," and another he called, "You're Screwed and It's Not Even Your Fault." Among his beloved sermons for the elect or those whom Christ did choose to obtain salvation were, "If You Persevere, You're in the Clear," and "I May Be Depraved, but at Least I'm Saved."

Megalo and Alvin's father, Alvin D. Calvin Dort II had served together in their younger days as youth evangelists. Usually Alvin would preach one night while Megalo would lead the music portion of the service and then they would rotate duties throughout the week. Megalo remembered fondly Alvin's "sugar stick" sermon that often evoked a great response from the congregation. Alvin entitled his sermon, "God Does Not Call; He Chooses." Alvin would tell his listeners that he had no intention of inviting them to receive Christ because they did not have the ability to receive Christ. Instead, he informed the people that God had already chosen them to be saved and that if they had been given God's prevenient grace allowing them to realize that they were children of God then they should march down the aisle and publicly proclaim their election.

"If you do not come forward then it may be that God has not chosen you for salvation and you will be damned forever," shouted Alvin.

Inotta Sharpwun told those sitting beside her,

"Who wants to be damned forever? That's not for me. Cal has made it so very clear to me and now I know that God has chosen me for salvation. I recognize that I am one of His elect."

Inotta stood up from her pew and ran down the aisle to Alvin and shouted,

"I am chosen. I am chosen. I am chosen."

After one of their revival services Megalo and Alvin would go out to a local restaurant and eat and talk about their revival experiences. When Alvin preached and had a good response from the people he would often tell Megalo,

"Those who say that Alvin D. Calvin Dort II and men like him are not evangelistic simply don't know what they are talking about. I am as passionate about evangelism as Billy Graham. The only difference between us is that he is an inclusivist and calls people to salvation and I am an exclusivist who simply helps the elect ones see that God has already chosen them for salvation and they just need to recognize and admit it."

Megalo did not share Alvin D. Calvin Dort's view of election but he initially overlooked it because both of them shared a general fundamentalist outlook and believed in the absolute inerrancy of Scripture. Later, however, Megalo and Alvin II engaged in a serious dispute that led to Alvin's departure and to his being replaced by his son, Alvin III. The controversy started when Alvin II began publishing a journal called the Originator's Journal in which Alvin claimed that his theological orientation represented the original theological outlook of the founders of the Southwide Confederation and that the denomination as a whole must return to its original theology or slide down the slippery slope of doctrinal looseness. Alvin told his students frequently,

"If you don't accept predestination and limited atonement you are in direct rebellion against God!"

Megalo disagreed and rebuked Alvin II publicly.

The feud expanded and became a big mess for the entire Southwide Confederation. Alvin II formed a group called the Archetypes who used the Originator's Journal to advance their cause. His son, Alvin III, formed a competing group called the Garden Variety Calvinists. This group held to the same theological ideas as the Archetypes but did not believe their views represented the standard theology of the denomination and refused to impose it upon others. Then there were the Semi-Arminians such as Megalo who only believed in the idea of perseverance of the saints but not the other aspects of Calvinist theology. Some of the Semi-Armianians preferred that others call them the Modified Dorts because they feared some uninformed persons might confuse them with Semi-Arians and they certainly did not want to be associated with Arius, the heretic who taught that Jesus was a created being and not co-eternal with the Father.

Megalo believed the only way to bring the controversy to an end was to fire Alvin II. Megalo brought Alvin II into his office and scolded him,

"All these years I thought you were a Garden Variety Calvinist not an Archetypical Calvinist but either I was wrong or you have changed and now you must go."

Alvin II left the room and the denomination and founded a competing denomination he called the Original Southwide Confederation. Alvin D. Calvin Dort III promised Megalo that he would always stay a Garden Variety Calvinist. So, Megalo hired Alvin D. Calvin Dort III to replace his father and the controversy subsided at Megalo's school but continued for many years in the Southwide Confederation.

Another of Megalo's inner circle faculty members was an evangelist turned Bible professor named Billy Hyperbole. Billy held the prestigious Chair of Embellishment at ATC. According to Billy over the course of his career he had preached to millions of people, had baptized thousands, and constantly had to turn down speaking engagements because the demand for his services was so great. Billy claimed to have three doctorates, two masters' degrees, and two bachelor's degrees. Billy loved telling people how he had completed all three of his doctoral degrees in a span of three years. Billy had received a PhD in Applied Ministry from Easy Credit Seminary, a PhD in religious studies from Simpleton Online Seminary for Lazy Asses, and his third PhD in ministerial ethics he earned at Dimwit Seminary. According to Megalo, Billy was the most brilliant professor in America who held degrees from the most prestigious institutions in the land.

With Megalo's assistance Billy had created a website entitled askGodanything.com. Megalo and Billy advertised the site through newspapers and television and invited anyone to ask them questions about God, the Bible, or any religious matter. The questions began coming in so quickly that Billy and Megalo became overwhelmed and did not have the time to answer all the questions that came to them so Megalo hired two of the brightest students at ATC to answer questions.

Megalo and Billy eventually agreed to shut down the web site when an anonymous young female student at ATC asked if God would send her to hell if she admitted that she was a lesbian. The ATC students had no idea how to answer the questions so they brought it to Billy who told them,

"Tell the young woman that Satan is tormenting her and that she just needs to tell him to go away. Then she needs to tell the ATC administration her name so we can kick her out of school. We won't just kick her to the curb. We will send her to Jimmy Joe Dobson's Fix

Everyone's Family headquarters in Colorado where she can undergo Reparative Therapy. She can overcome this disorder. After therapy she will have to start going on weekly dates with boys and eventually God will remove those unhealthy desires from her midst."

Although the young woman did not reveal her name to the ATC administration her roommate did and Megalo removed the girl from ATC and informed her parents,

"Your daughter is unwholesome and may not study with the pure young men and women at ATC. Bad company corrupts good morals."

Immediately the story of the student's ouster became big news. A group of activists called the Equality Riders visited ATC and protested the treatment of the student. Whenever some of the protestors walked on campus to attend chapel services they were arrested for trespassing and had to spend the night in jail. Another group of students went to the library to donate some books that dealt with homosexuality but the librarian threw the books in the trash and called the campus police who came and arrested the students and sent them to jail as well.

Megalo told students in chapel that he hated to see young people sent to jail but "sinners must pay a high price for their sin or they will continue in it and lead others astray."

Megalo explained to the students that their parents had sent them to ATC to protect them from the evil influences of the world and that their parents depended upon him to be "Lord Protector" of all ATC students.

"The enemy is on all sides attacking us because we stand for God's truth. An attack upon us is an attack on God. We must defend God against His enemies because He has appointed us to be His ambassadors in this fallen world," Megalo explained to ATC students while they nodded approvingly.

Megalo did not like the Equality Riders and feared that gays in America had an agenda to turn all heterosexuals gay. Because he felt harassed by the Equality Riders Megalo hired a bus called Prayer Force One to follow the Equality Riders' bus around the country. Prayer Force One, America's Flagship of Prayer, had as its primary objective to "unite America's praying majority." The bus, painted with the exact same paint as Air Force One, regularly toured the U.S. promoting prayer for a national revival. Megalo filled the bus with devout conservative evangelicals who prayed constantly for the Equality Riders to give their lives to Jesus. The Prayer Force One riders believed Jesus would then turn the Equality Riders into heterosexuals. On one occasion the Equality Riders stopped to eat at Two Dudes Bakery in Lynchburg, Virginia and so the Prayer Force One praying saints also stopped at the bakery to eat.

When the Prayer Force One saints exited the bus, Dick Encephalon exclaimed, "We're in Jerry Falwell country now. These gays don't have a chance. The spirit of Falwell rests so heavy here. Can't you feel it? I can expect we will soon see a mass conversion of Equality Riders. Wow! I just had a vision of all the Equality Riders switching busses! That's right. I believe that in the next few moments those Riders will repudiate their homosexuality, exit their bus, and get on our bus."

None of the riders exited the bus and boarded the Prayer Force One Bus. They simply entered the Two Dudes Bakery. The Prayer Force One Saints marveled at the tastiness of the soup and sandwiches. The saints also could not resist the delicious cupcakes. None of the Prayer Force One saints realized that they were eating at a bakery owned by two gay guys until one of the Equality Riders shouted,

"You guys just ate soup, sandwiches and cupcakes made by gays."

Several of the Prayer Force One women fainted. Danny Praysalot took it all in stride and commented to his friends,

"Well, I have to hand it to them. Despite their agenda to take over the world, these gay people can make some damn good cupcakes."

Another member of Megalo's Dream Team, Flapjack Schlaapy, loved pancakes, women, and studying erotic passages in the Bible. Flapjack referred to these passages as the "hard" sayings of Scripture. In class he would turn to passages, especially from the Psalms, to show students how to develop an intimate relationship with God that is as intimate as marriage partners who are engaging in sexual intercourse. Flapjack read to the class Psalm 119:30.

"It says here class, 'I have chosen the way of truth: thy judgments have I laid before me.' That word laid is a sexual term and it literally means the same thing as a husband having sex with his wife. David gets even more graphic when he writes, 'I have stuck unto thy testimonies: O LORD, put me not to shame.' The word stuck refers to the act of a husband entering his wife. The Word of God is saying that the Bible should be our intimate lover. Nothing should be closer to us than the Bible."

Flapjack also explained to his students that when a person eats the bread during the Lord's Supper he or she is not actually eating Christ's body as the Catholics teach.

Flapjack stated, "Transubstantiation is a weird dogma that is frankly unbelievable. When a worshiper partakes of the bread that person becomes female in the spiritual realm and the person is receiving the body of Christ as a lover. Eating the sacred bread is spiritual intercourse. Now, that makes perfect sense doesn't it students?"

Megalo's favorite professor in the inner circle was his old pal Angus Huxter who later became Megalo's brother-in-law. Angus and Megalo had served together on youth evangelism teams when they were in college together and that is where Angus met Megalo's younger sister Meg Maniac. In fact, Megalo employed many of his relatives and friends to work at ATC. His cousin served as the head of the grounds crew, and several of his female cousins served as secretaries at the school. Megalo only wanted employees at ATC whom he could trust to be loyal to him. So, only Megalo's friends and family members could ever get an interview much less be hired.

"Nepotism is necessary in today's chaotic world. You can't trust anyone you don't know and even some people you do know," Megalo was fond of saying.

Yet, Megalo loved his brother-in-law Angus and was very proud of his many accomplishments although they did pale in comparison to Megalo's many undertakings. In most recent years Angus had a robust television ministry and his religious broadcasts reached all 50 states and Mexico and Canada. Angus had very few special guests on his programs because he enjoyed the spotlight. He preached sermons, sang solos, hawked for funding to keep his TV ministry afloat, and for a while served as emcee of a game show he created called, "Are You Smarter than a Southwide Baptist Confederation Preacher." The show pitted 5th grade students against Southwide pastors in a contest to see who could answer the most questions about basic math, science, geography, social studies, and other subjects. Although initially popular the game show lost its place with viewers because the 5th graders won every time. Angus pulled the show but displayed no embarrassment about the performance of the pastors.

"These guys don't need to know nothing but the Bible and how to preach the gospel," Angus told his viewers at the end of the final show.

Megalo brought Angus on board at ATC to teach courses in New Testament. Angus held the Roxanna Don Chair of New Testament. Roxanna Don had taught history courses at one of Southwide's Colleges and upon retirement gave money to establish the chair in New Testament at ATC. Roxanna told Megalo that she would like to see a woman fill the Roxanna Don chair. Megalo agreed, took Roxanna's money, and walked out her door with no intention of hiring a woman to teach in the religion department. Soon thereafter Roxanna died. Immediately upon her death Megalo called up his old pal and brother-in-law Angus and said,

"Angus, I want you to hold the Roxanna Don Chair of New Testament. Roxanna did prefer that a woman fill the chair and she did stipulate that we had to interview a woman for the position, but she did not demand that a woman be hired. She told me that the best person should be hired. We are going to bring Maryanna Duped in for an interview but I want you to know right now that you are the best candidate."

Maryanna did well in her interview and impressed the entire faculty at ATC but they were under strict orders from Megalo not to choose her for the position and so the faculty followed his will. When Megalo introduced Angus to the faculty as the new Roxanna Don Professor of New Testament, he exclaimed,

"After considering two very fine candidates we have decided to go with the most qualified candidate, Angus Huxter."

A few months later Maryanna secured a job teaching in the religion department at Princeton University and immediately upon her hire praised God for guiding her steps away from ATC.

Angus made quite a name for himself while at ATC. He wrote a number of books about Jesus that won evangelical book publishing awards. His most famous book he entitled, *The Quest for the Historical Jesus: Over and Done*, in which Angus claimed that he had ended the quest by proving conclusively that the theological Christ of the church and the historical Jesus are one and the same. He also wrote a bestseller about the Apostle Paul entitled, *The Real Apostle Paul: Lost but Now Found.* Here Angus used the book of Acts and the thirteen canonical letters ascribed to Paul to build the argument that Paul was a conservative Christian who condoned slavery, subordinated women, and condemned homosexual behavior.

Angus also won favor with Megalo and gained many fans in the larger evangelical world when he invented Fundapedia. Fundapedia was an online encyclopedia that offered a fundamentalist slant to every topic. Only Angus, Megalo, and a number of their colleagues and friends had control of the content. Angus did not want just anybody putting material on his web site. One of the most talked about topics in Fundapedia had to do with evolutionary theory.

Sham Fraudster, a scientist at ATC wrote the entry. Sham had received his degree from Cornell University. In his dissertation he admitted that the earth was millions of years old but according to his entry in Fundapedia his literal interpretation of the Bible compelled him to believe that the earth could not be more than 10,000 years old. In an interview with FBN (Fundamentalist Broadcasting Network) Fraudster explained that in his classes at Cornell and in his dissertation as well he had to follow the "rules" of secular science if he wanted to graduate and be viewed as a legitimate scholar in his field. Yet, he said that since his days as a youth he had embraced young earth creationism and that thankfully his experience at Cornell had merely reaffirmed his commitment to young earth creationism. Fraudster also told FBN that in the museum at ATC one could find a fossil he had unearthed of a 3,000-year-old dinosaur.

Megalo wanted his school to put on Broadway style productions that reflected Christian themes so he hired the celebrated evangelical actor Richard Denise. Confused about his sexuality early in life Richard lived the gay life for years before being "cleansed" from his homosexuality. He married and had fifteen children. After the fifteenth child was born Richard told his former gay friends,

"So, now will you believe I'm not gay?"

Evangelicals embraced Richard Denise because he was living proof that the homosexual disorder could be overcome by prayer and by the power of the Holy Spirit. Megalo brought Richard to ATC to do Christian theatre. In the initial interview Richard told Megalo,

"Friend, you will see the drama department put on productions such as The Passion of Christ or The Chronicles of Narnia and Fireproof. You will never have to worry about me putting together a production such as Hairspray. After all, Hairspray is replete with sexual innuendo, has a man dressed as a woman, and flouts an interracial relationship. All these things I abhor although the interracial relationship is not as bad I suppose."

The final member of Megalo's Dream Team was Megalo's longtime friend Dakta Rotunda. Rotunda loved fried chicken and eschatology. He founded the Pretribulation Research Center locating it across the street from Wanda's Chicken Ranch. Rotunda crossed the street every day at lunchtime to get his chicken and to visit with Wanda. Wanda had a crush on Rotunda and usually gave him extra chicken and biscuits. At the Pretribulation Research Center Rotunda developed some impressive charts and graphs based on his study of apocalyptic material in the Bible and had them enlarged so he could use them when he preached in churches. Rotunda always informed his listeners,

"I am a premillennial, pretribulation rapturist because that's what the Bible teaches."

Megalo invited Rotunda to teach at ATC after hearing a presentation Rotunda made at Maranatha Baptist Church in Perouse, Arkansas. Rotunda agreed to teach at ATC as long as he could continue operating his research center and his preaching engagements. Megalo agreed.

Rotunda, surrounded by his giant charts, informed students and congregants that humans were definitely living in the last days and that he had a pretty good idea when Jesus would come back to earth to get His children but he did not want to reveal this information out of fear it might cause widespread panic.

Rotunda often proclaimed, "I don't want to set a date, but it's getting very late, so you better not wait, don't leave it to fate, take Jesus as your mate, and enter the heavenly gate."

Megalo's school flourished under his leadership so that he opened an off-campus center in a converted strip mall in Dallas, Texas. Due to the generosity of Trough and Stall Megalo later built a nice educational facility on the site where the old Dallas Cowboys stadium once stood. The original stadium was partially enclosed but had no roof and rabid Cowboys fans said that the Cowboys organization had it constructed that way so God could watch His team play on Sunday. Megalo, a huge Cowboys fan, decided that to honor the Cowboys he would build himself a huge office at the Dallas campus and put a rectangular skylight in the office so God could look down upon him while he studied. In front of the main building on the Waco campus, now called Trough and Stall Hall, Megalo placed a giant bronze statue whose body resembled the Greek god Apollo but the head was undoubtedly that of Megalo. Behind Megalo's statue stood a small cross barely visible to campus visitors. When visitors went into the ATC Bookstore in Waco and Dallas they not only could purchase "We Love Megalo" T-shirts and Hoodies but numerous Megalo Bobble Head figures adorned the shelves as well selling for $20 apiece. If one purchased the Charles Spurgeon Bobble Head as well the Campus Bookstore offered a $5 discount.

On Grand Opening Day at the Dallas campus Megalo and his administrative staff rented horses and rode them onto the campus as students cheered. Megalo preached to the students while atop the horse.

"Students, the West was won by determined Cowboys who would not be denied by their opposition. And near this spot another group of Cowboys won a bunch of Super Bowls because God was on their side. We too will win the West for Jesus and will ride herd on all the lost people west of the Mississippi. We will round them up and move them on out to the Savior in that great Super Bowl in the sky."

During the first chapel service at the main ATC campus President Megalo led in a dedication for the Trough and Stall Chapel. Megalo had wanted the chapel to be named the Megalo Maniac Chapel but Trough and Stall provided the money to build it giving them naming rights. A deflated Megalo offered a dedicatory address and thanked Trough and Stall publicly for their generosity but privately Megalo wished the chapel could have been named in his honor. During the second chapel service at the main ATC campus Megalo introduced his faculty to the student body who had gathered in the massive rectangular shaped Trough and Stall Hall Chapel and bragged that he had assembled the finest faculty in the world. He told the students that he trusted his faculty completely then he called upon each faculty member to come up on the stage in front of the student body and sign the Chicago Statement on Inerrancy, the Danvers Statement, the Manhattan Declaration, Francis Schaeffer's A Christian Manifesto, the Apostle's Creed, and of course, **The Code**.

The drafters of the Chicago Statement had made the incisive observation that the Bible is inerrant when properly interpreted. The Danvers Statement, issued by the Biblical Council of Studhood and Ladyhood, called for women to follow the clear counsel of the Bible and accept their inequality, be quiet about it, stay home and away from the workplace, and not to try to interpret the Bible any other way than how the Council interprets the Bible. The Manhattan Declaration, issued by a host of Protestant, Catholic, and Orthodox Christian leaders, called upon Christians to reaffirm traditional marriage, discriminate against homosexuals, and complain that their religious liberty was being violated when they weren't allowed by the government to discriminate against homosexuals. Schaeffer's A Christian Manifesto, called upon Christians to fight against the secular humanists who had rooted out from the public square the biblical principles on which the United States was founded. Megalo had the professors sign the Apostle's Creed because of its historic value and he had them sign **The Code** because he wrote it and it so he knew that it definitely contained absolute truth.

To underscore how much Megalo trusted his professors to teach what he wanted them to teach, Megalo also determined what textbooks they would use in their courses. Megalo chaired the Textbook Committee that approved all textbooks used by ATC professors. The Textbook Committee did its job of repressing any controversial or doctrinally aberrant textbooks. Yet, on one occasion a popular Christian radio personality and Messianic Jew, Zollo Lotto, whose son attended ATC, began reading the text used in the New Testament Survey course and accused the textbook author of teaching Replacement Theology— the idea that the Christian Church has now replaced Israel as the people of God and that God's promises are now for the church alone. The author denied that he advocated Replacement Theology and ATC faculty denied that they advocated the concept as well. Nevertheless, Zollo, who had garnered quite a following especially after forming the Freedom from Thought Foundation several years earlier, used his radio program to lead a successful crusade to get the textbook removed from ATC classes. Megalo publicly reaffirmed his support of the Textbook Committee and privately excoriated Zollo calling him "that little bastard Messianic Jewboy."

Megalo's most severe controversy at ATC however occurred when one of his philosophy professors, Zeno Spirituel, began attending academic conferences with philosophers from schools throughout the world. Zeno even presented philosophy papers at some of the conferences. He published one of his papers in a prestigious journal and won the admiration of his philosophy colleagues. The article asserted in one place that Zeno's argument did not hinge upon either a literal or non-literal understanding of Genesis 1-11. No one at ATC ever knew about Zeno's article because it had appeared in a prestigious academic journal. Nevertheless, Zeno had his philosophy students read the article. Two of his students, C. Ben Spies and Uri Spineless, were troubled by the article and took it to Megalo who read it and wept. Megalo then prayed with the students,

"God, help us to stand strong in the midst of this terrible tragedy as we have allowed Satan to creep back into our school after we had cleansed it. He has found a way to infiltrate our ranks with base heresy despite our efforts. We kicked him out once before so Lord please help us as we excise this disease from our midst once again."

Megalo told C. Ben and Uri to attend their classes as usual and he would take care of Zeno. Megalo brought Zeno into his office and rebuked Zeno harshly.

"I knew I should have never allowed philosophy courses to stay in the curriculum. We should have just replaced philosophy with apologetics so that we could provide students with all the answers they need instead of bringing questions before them. Our students need to be prepared to refute all worldviews besides the superior conservative Christian worldview. Zeno, I am sorry but you need to pack up your things and leave immediately. Satan has his hold on you and you must go."

Zeno tried to explain to Megalo that he had not taught anything heretical but had only made an innocuous statement in his article that his argument did not depend on a literal or non-literal reading of Genesis 1-11. Megalo would not listen to Zeno's protests.

Megalo chided Zeno, "Zeno, your pastor came and met with me several months ago and told me you had expressed some doubts about Genesis 1-11 being actual history. Is that true?"

"What I said to my pastor was in confidence and he told me that anything I discussed with him in his office was confidential," Zeno protested.

"That doesn't matter Zeno. What matters is that your pastor is a trustee of ATC and he told me he would be prepared to make big waves if I did not dismiss you from the faculty. I was contemplating what I should do with you when two of your students approached me with the article you wrote. That event led me to my decision. Now, this does not mean we are not brothers in Christ. Don't be angry or say anything you might regret Zeno, because you are still my brother in Christ."

Immediately Megalo dismissed a confused and dazed Zeno from his office and the school. The day after Zeno's dismissal the ATC school newspaper, *The Absolute Advocate*, ran a story on Zeno's firing and the headline of the story read,

"ATC Deals a Sharp and Decisive Blow to Heresy in its Midst."

Many of the professors at ATC were upset that Zeno had been fired and although they grumbled among themselves no one really spoke up and said anything for fear that one of them might be the next to go.

"I have a mortgage and young children. I feel sorry for Zeno, but I can't get involved," said the Faculty Senate Chair, B. E. Safe.

So, Zeno packed up his things and his family and moved in with his parents while he tried to find another teaching position in a very competitive market.

After the Zeno affair Megalo decided that he had to approve any articles or books that his professors wanted to publish in order to do a heresy check on the professors.

"Education is a dangerous game. It's a necessary evil. The educated must beware of falling into the trap of intellectual elitism that leads to a decreasing emphasis upon the spiritual aspects of life. Yes sir, the more educated you are the more you have to guard against being unspiritual. There is definitely an advantage to being ignorant. You never have to worry about being unspiritual," Megalo often said.

When Megalo's science professor Willy Recant wrote a book entitled *The Beginning of the End of Christianity*, Megalo thought he would enjoy it immensely because Billy and he had talked many times about the dangers of evolutionary theory. Megalo had even allowed Willy to send his book to the publisher without Megalo performing the standard heresy check because Megalo believed he would find nothing unorthodox in Willy's book. After all, Willy's title reflected his view that evolutionary theory threatened to bring an end to Christianity if the public found it to be credible. However, as Megalo read the book he discovered that Willy had bought into the idea of an old earth.

Willy stated in the book, "I would really like to be a young earth creationist but the evidence for an old earth is so strong."

Recant also wrote that that Noah must have survived a regional rather than a universal one. After reading the book Megalo immediately called a meeting with Willy and other high ranking officials at ATC and demanded that Willy repudiate what he had written or be fired. Megalo called the publisher and told them to stop the presses immediately before distributing any books. Meanwhile, Megalo told Willy that if the book had been published he would have had to fire Willy for denying the full trustworthiness of the Bible. Since the book had not yet been published Megalo informed Willy that he needed only to make a public statement affirming the inerrancy of Scripture and denouncing the unorthodox ideas in the book.

Willy gladly complied stating simply, "I really do believe the earth is young. I don't know what got into me. I would definitely have stated things differently if I had it to do over again. I also believe the Genesis flood was universal. I should have stated my view more clearly. What I meant to say is that the flood covered a large region of the earth, well, all of it. I also want everyone to know that I believe Adam and Eve were real people and that Moses wrote the Pentateuch. In the end, I believe what Megalo believes."

Whenever a colleague from another school told Willy privately that he had been the victim of academic persecution, Willy denied it saying,

"I never should have taught anything that brought into question the full verbal inspiration of the Bible and that challenged the views that ATC deems orthodox."

Whenever a local Houston news station reported on the incident and a reporter asked if ATC had engaged in academic persecution Megalo told the reporter,

"There is absolutely no truth in the accusation that ATC doesn't allow academic freedom. What occurred here could best be described as intellectual interchange, not academic persecution. Only secular schools engage in academic persecution. These secular schools and even many religious schools have for years been successfully marginalizing or excising the Christian perspective from their midst and you reporters never say anything about it. The minute you think that a biblically based school is engaging in academic persecution you can't wait to jump all over it. Well, I've got news for you. There is no story here. Willy is a fine scientist who will remain on the faculty and his academic freedom will not be threatened in any way."

Willy kept his teaching job at ATC and never wrote another book. The rest of his days he never taught his students anything that challenged their views or ran counter to Megalo's views in order to keep the peace and his job. He cultivated a friendship with Megalo and on Willy's tenth anniversary of service at ATC he wrote a note to Megalo thanking him for saving him from the perils of scientism and liberalism. In the course of Willy's career he won the distinguished teaching award on three separate occasions, something no other professor at the school had accomplished.

After the Recant incident, one of the older New Testament professors at ATC, who had been at the school for over 30 years, published an introductory book in New Testament studies that Megalo read and tentatively approved. Yet, when the book was published the cover of the book had on it a picture of Jesus upon the cross. Megalo brought the professor, N.T Writes, into his office and forbade him to sell the book or use it in his classes.

"With Jesus on the cross, this looks like a Roman Catholic book. Evangelicals will think we are promoting Catholicism here at ATC. Don't get me wrong. I like a few of those conservative Catholics who are against abortion and homosexuality, but generally speaking Catholics aren't Christians so it is best to stay a country mile away from them. I'm sorry N.T., you can give copies to family members and a few colleagues but then we are going to have to tell the publisher to destroy the remainder of your books," Megalo said stoically.

N.T. ran out of Megalo's office deflated and in tears because he had worked on the book for over ten years and had poured his life into the book. N.T. would not be alone in being censored by Megalo.

One of the longtime Old Testament professors, H.E. Brewer, had written a book about the Pentateuch. Megalo read the book and refused to approve it for distribution because H.E. did not state clearly that Moses wrote the Pentateuch. Megalo also did not like the cover of the book that showed a partially nude Adam and Eve walking in the Garden of Eden holding hands. He believed the picture to be immodest and thought that the school would receive many complaints about the book.

As the tenth year of Megalo's tenure at ATC approached, Megalo asked one of the ATC history professors, Frank N. Direct, to write a ten-year history of the institution. When Frank finished the project after working on it for over a year Megalo read it and did not like some of Frank's interpretations of events that had occurred on the campus.

Megalo called Frank in to his office and said, "We're not going to publish this Frank. Now, we paid you. You got your money. That fulfills our contractual obligations to you, but I don't like this history you wrote. Your interpretations of events reflect your own biases and you refuse to follow my example and simply say whatever our Southwide Baptist constituents want to hear. We don't want any book going out of ATC to our constituency that might challenge their cherished beliefs about any area of reality. Since you refused to adopt the party line I am forced to get someone else to write something with which I am in complete agreement and that will reflect the thinking of the average Southwide Baptist member."

Frank protested but Megalo had his mind made up. Megalo brought the dean of the Business School, Darvy Witlus Pricker, into his office after Frank left and asked Darvy, known around campus as "Prick," to write the ten-year history of ATC.

Prick had written one other book, *Solomon the Wise Business Man*, a collection of devotional stories about how to succeed in business as an evangelical Christian. Prick, one of Megalo's golfing buddies, agreed and after consulting continually with Megalo wrote a history of the institution that made Megalo proud. Prick entitled his work, *Ten Years of Miracles: Megalo and the Founding of a Flagship Christian School*. Megalo was the hero of the book and when it was published he and Prick held a book signing in the ATC student center during homecoming festivities. At the book signing Megalo leaned over to Prick and commented,

"Prick my good friend, you have written such an outstanding book. You are a shoe in to win the Meritorious Service Award this year. In fact, I think I will give you the Outstanding Teacher Award and the Professor of the Decade award so that you can be the first Triple Crown award winner the university has ever had."

Prick beamed with pride. He had finally reached his ultimate goal in life. Meanwhile, a disheartened Frank left ATC and moved on to Ban Banning University.

Megalo also personally vetted every speaker who came to ATC, especially weekly chapel speakers who spoke to the entire student body. A perennial chapel speaker at ATC, Hamas Faker, claimed to be a former Muslim and a member of Hamas but had left the organization after finding Jesus at a revival led by Megalo. He held students spellbound as he recounted his amazing story in chapel. According to the charismatic Faker he grew up in the West Bank where he learned Arabic from his devout Muslim parents. His mother taught him how to make bombs and his father taught him the Qur'an. He told the students that he gained such a reputation for his successful terrorist activities against Israelis that Hamas recruited him as a teenager to come to the United States to form an underground group who would hatch and carry out terrorist plots on U.S. soil. Faker claimed that he carried out several terrorist attacks on American soil but did not specify which attacks he was behind.

Faker claimed that while in the U.S. he befriended a white Christian woman whom he called Kali. Kali provided a cover for his activities and he attended a Southwide Baptist church with her frequently. According to Faker he went with Kali to a revival led my Megalo and while Megalo preached Jesus hovered above him in the form of a hummingbird, looked him straight in the eye, spoke to him in an audible voice and said,

"Faker, Faker, why are you persecuting me?"

According to Faker he fell down on his knees immediately and gave his life to Jesus and left Hamas and turned his back on his terrorist past. Faker told the students that he began telling his story to churches and that before long he had so many speaking engagements all he did was travel the country "telling my amazing story." Faker, who claimed that he often received death threats from angry Hamas members and had to hire round the clock bodyguards to protect him, had gained wealth and fame from his many speaking engagements. He became a household name in the evangelical world, however, when his book *Unveiling Islam* sold a half million copies. In his book Faker referred to Muhammad as a "demon possessed pedophile" claiming that Muhammad had been possessed by an evil spirit who disguised himself as the angel Gabriel and that Muhammad had married a six year old girl and a nine year old girl. Although American Muslims who read the book criticized it for its numerous inaccuracies and its strident tone the book won the Evangelical Book of the Year Award sponsored by *Christianity Today, Tomorrow & Every Day After Magazine*.

Faker's reputation received a slight blow among evangelicals when some Muslims investigated and discovered that Faker had never been a member of Hamas and that he had grown up in a Southwide Baptist church in Iowa since the age of four. His mother, a Christian, never made a bomb but instead made wedding cakes at a local bakery. Faker had never been to the West Bank but he had visited his non-observant Muslim father who worked as a teller at the local Bank of the West. Muslim critics also pointed out that when Faker did use Arabic words and phrases in his speeches that he did not use correct pronunciation. They doubted that he knew how to speak or read Arabic. Faker also claimed to have debated publicly a number of high profile Muslim leaders in America. Yet, although they had heard of Faker none of them had ever had any contact with him.

Megalo encouraged a cursory investigation into Faker's past and concluded that the criticisms of Faker were not legitimate and were part of a Muslim extremist plot to discredit a fine, honest, Christian leader. Evangelicals continued to buy Faker's book and invite him to their churches to speak. Only a few churches and individuals in the evangelical world denounced Faker. Megalo loved Faker so much that after Faker published his second book, *Debriefing Islam*, Megalo appointed Faker as a member of the faculty and placed him in an endowed chair. Students in chapel gave Hamas Faker a standing ovation on the day he was officially installed as the Faker Professor of Islamic Studies. During the installation ceremony Megalo proclaimed to the students,

"Hamas Faker is the foremost authority on Islam in the world and we are so fortunate to have him here as a professor at ATC. His opponents simply castigate him because he is edgy and controversial but he stands up for the truth so we here at ATC our proud to stand up for Hamas Faker."

Another of Megalo's favorite chapel speakers, who came once a year to ATC, was Paulie Gist. Paulie referred to himself as an "evangelist to the intellectuals." According to Paulie he had grown up a skeptic so he understood the thinking of thoughtful secularists. One thoughtful scientist who read Paulie's book, *The Art of Apologetics*, wrote that Paulie's arguments were sophomoric. The scientist critiqued the modern evangelical apologist in general stating,

"Today an evangelical apologist is merely someone who offers simplistic answers to complex questions and who normally addresses issues that are of no concern to intellectuals."

Megalo believed Paulie to be one of the most intelligent persons he had ever known. Paulie and his wife home schooled their four children but since Paulie had a seminary degree and his wife did not even have a college degree he didn't teach his children advanced science, math, history, and English. Paulie taught his children how to use the Bible to argue against anyone who might try to use rational persuasion to argue against the Christian faith. When Paulie came to ATC to lecture he proudly told students that he had not come to make them ask questions but to give them answers.

One of Paulie's favorite lectures was "Hula Hoopin' with Jesus." Paulie placed a hula-hoop on the stage and then jumped inside and told students that as long as they were in God's will they would prosper and do well. Then Paulie jumped outside of the hula-hoop and told students that if they were outside God's will they would have a lot of problems and would not prosper. Paulie would jump in and out of the hula-hoop quickly while preaching,

"In His will, all is good. Outside his will, all is bad. Get it students. Get it."

Paulie gave students at ATC a nice, tidy set of answers to life's ultimate questions while dismantling all other worldviews but the Christian one. After Paulie's lectures students at ATC would walk proudly across campus with head held high because their questions had all been answered and all they had to do now was to go out into the world and share those answers with all the poor ignorant people of the world who had many problems because they didn't have the answers. Students at ATC had the White Christian's Burden.

Of course, Megalo loved speaking in chapel and he did so often. One of his addresses entitled, "The Curse of Liberalism," upbraided liberal Christians.

Megalo pronounced, "Today liberals call themselves moderates. A skunk by any other name still stinks!"

Students whooped, hollered, and cheered wildly. On another occasion Megalo painted himself red, dressed in tattered clothing, and presented a monologue entitled "Pilate in Hell." Megalo as Pilate screamed that he had been burning in hell for about two thousand years because he sent Christ to be crucified.

"Don't believe the Catholics when they celebrate Pilate's Day in honor of me. They believe I repented and received Christ as Savior. I did not. I'm in hell and you will be here too unless you repent because even though I delivered Christ to be crucified your sin actually sent Christ to the cross," Pilate moaned.

Frequently when Megalo preached in chapel he would end his sermon in tears. He used this tactic when he preached at summer youth camp as well. All the campers loved Megalo because he cried when he talked about Jesus. One Southwide pastor at the camp upon watching one of Megalo's tearful sermons commented,

"What a spiritual giant. When a man is big enough to cry about Jesus in public, he is a spiritual titan"

Megalo brought the campers to an emotional high when he delivered his favorite line with his voice quivering and tears running down his face.

"Jesus took the hit for me and for you. Won't you take the hit for him?"

Campers would rush down the aisle to be saved after Megalo continued a tearful plea for them to turn their backs on sin and receive salvation. Megalo would counsel the young people to accept Jesus and sign an ATC enrollment card. Megalo would tell the young men that if they enrolled at ATC he could guarantee that they would meet some beautiful girls there.

One of Megalo's favorite moments to address students occurred during graduation exercises at ATC. Megalo would stand before graduates and announce,

"Today, graduates, you are now a part of the ATC family unless you turn liberal or gay. In any event, we will support you with our prayers and we expect you to support us with your money. And if you send us gay or liberal money we will accept it after purifying it for the kingdom of course."

The female students at ATC had the biggest burden to carry. They had to take numerous Bible courses not so much that they might learn the Bible but so they could have the opportunity to meet a nice, clean cut, ATC boy and marry him. Female students were especially encouraged by the administration to snag a future pastor and become a pastor's wife. All the female students at ATC, but especially the women who had their sights set on becoming a pastor's wife, had to take extra courses in homemaking. A special building, resembling a two-story country style home, stood on the northeast end of the campus, and served as the Center for Homemaking Studies.

The initial class the women took consisted of instructions on how to make tea and knit at the same time. Next came the course on entertaining guests in the proper fashion. When the students mastered Serving Cold Beverages 101 then they would take a course in Serving Hot Beverages 102. Newspaper, Slippers, and Coffee for Your Husband 103 proved to be one of the most challenging courses in the program. The most difficult course for most women, however, was the clothes construction lab in which they had to learn to make suits and casual wear for their future husbands. A course entitled, How to Please Your Husband in All Things that He Demands 104, also proved to be a challenge for many of the women although most of them were up for the challenge.

The women got all giggly in the final course of the curriculum called Mastering the Missionary Position 105. The women held mock demonstrations in which they would lay flat on their backs on a bed and scream out a name of a prospective husband while pretending to engage in missionary sex. The students were not allowed to make any movements at all that might simulate sex and they most definitely could not make any groaning noises. The other young women would stand around the bed and cheer on the screamer,

"That's it, honey. Great job. Way to lay still and scream. You are gonna make a wonderful wife."

Faculty member, Lottie Girth, told the students that these exercises would help them for when it came time to implement them in a real life situation it would make their husbands feel powerful and that would lead the men to do better in their careers.

"You will benefit in the end because your husband will be happier and make more money so that you can have a comfortable lifestyle. In marriage you have to be on the bottom in order to make it to the top," Lottie told the smiling students.

Although all the girls enjoyed the mock demonstrations some of the girls thought that Debbie Dutiful screamed a bit too loudly during the demonstrations and that Martha Meek needed to increase her volume considerably and decrease her thrashing about on the bed.

The only women who taught courses at ATC were faculty members at the Center for Homemaking Studies. Lottie, a self-proclaimed former beauty queen, had lost every pageant she had entered until finally she won the Miss Calico County beauty pageant at the age of 28. She beat the only other contestant in the pageant, a 16 year old whose talent was reciting the Pledge of Allegiance in Latvian and who refused to enter the swimsuit portion of the pageant because she had a giant mole on her left thigh. Over the years Lottie's rugged beauty had faded as she packed on the pounds due to her love for eating out often at Applebees and the Texas Roadhouse Cafe. Lottie tried every diet that came along but her semi-fast food addiction kept her from being successful. Her library consisted of various translations of the Bible, an etiquette book, a host of diet books and of course books by Beth Moore. Serving along with Lottie as a faculty member at the Center was Fanny Bumpus. Fanny excelled in the area of beverage service and had become a legend at serving both iced and hot tea. She could also knit sweaters so quickly that others commented that Fanny seemed possessed by a wild yarn spirit when she went to work. Fanny never married but had always wanted to have children of her own. She viewed the female students at the Center as her children and she tried to live out her dreams through them. She often told the women,

"Snag a man quickly, and I mean quickly girls. If you are not married by the time you graduate from college then you are unlikely to find a good man because all the good men will be gone."

Ironically, Fanny taught a one-hour course on how to catch a good husband. Snagging 106 became one of the most popular courses at the Center.

Fanny often told the students, "If you don't snag, you'll soon be a hag!"

Although the Center for Homemaking Studies brought many female students to ATC Megalo thought initially that it might be controversial and perhaps dangerous to have too many women gathered together in one building because he believed that when women met too frequently in large groups they tended to get egalitarian ideas. So, Megalo placed a former policeman Edward Autocrat in charge of the Center and Edward kept a close watch on the women to ensure that they maintained submissive attitudes. Although Edward was not allowed to be at the Center during the mock missionary position demonstrations, he would often be invited by the women to do some role playing as a pretend pastor husband and the women students would make him tea and biscuits, cakes and pies, engage him in polite conversation, and make shirts and pants for him. Edward was especially fond of a tweed jacket that Carley Compliant had made for him. When it came to making clothes, Carley had all the women beat. Only Darlene Docile could come close to competing with Carley although Darlene was a better at making tea and coffee.

The best conversationalist among the women was Sherry Subservient. Edward loved talking baseball with Sherry who had memorized many baseball statistics because she had her eye set on marrying Sabbatarian Domingo, who had left a career in baseball to attend ATC so that he could become a mega-church pastor. Sherry told the other girls that Sabbatarian was the only guy she ever let get to first base with her. Sabbatarian, however, had gained the nickname "Hammerin' Hank" because everyone on campus had heard rumors that he had covered all the bases with Sherry as often as Hank Aaron had crossed home plate. Megalo investigated the matter and even brought Sherry into his office to interrogate her. Sherry tearfully denied the rumors and became so upset she began coughing uncontrollably. Megalo apologized for questioning Sherry's integrity, handed her a cherry cough drop and sent her back to the Center.

Edward loved talking with Sherry and watching after the other female students. He felt at home at the Center. He told his former policeman buddies that God had shown him a glimpse of what heaven will be like.

"Young ladies waiting on you and making cookies and pies and stuff for you and smiling at you and greeting you as Sir Edward, yes sir, I have seen a foretaste of heaven and I like it."

Of course, Edward's wife didn't care too much for his job. Since he played house all day he didn't want to talk to her or pay any attention to her when he came home. She constantly pleaded for Edward to give her some attention and affection but Edward just sat on the couch and drank Blue Moon beer and watched ESPN all night. Although ATC had a no alcohol policy for its faculty and staff, Edward rationalized his six-pack of Blue Moon a night habit telling his wife that the alcohol helped relieve the stress that came with his very difficult job at ATC. After his wife went to bed and fell asleep Edward would then crawl into bed and dream that he was sleeping next to one of the young ladies at the Center for Homemaking Studies. Yet, in the morning he would wake up disappointed to be lying next to a seemingly lifeless woman who he believed desperately could have used a course in homemaking when she was younger.

Megalo, of course, loved visiting the Center for Homemaking Studies and would often drop by for a piece of chocolate meringue pie and a cup of hot tea and to make sure the women weren't planning to engage in any subversive activities. After Megalo left the Center Fanny Bumpus would tell the students,

"Now girls, that's the kind of man you want to get. He is successful and godly and wealthy."

Then Fanny would turn and walk slowly to her room, shut the door, and lie on her bed and cry. She had dated Megalo once during her college days but Megalo broke up with her after their first formal date. After dinner Megalo had asked Fanny if she was a virgin. Taken aback, Fanny blurted out,

"Megalo, I have to be honest with you because a relationship cannot be built upon lies. No, I am not a virgin. I tried to follow the True Love Waits program in high school but I found a true love who wouldn't wait. He seduced me and I gave in again and again and again and again. After numerous encounters I felt so sick inside that I went to church and repented of my sin and I haven't had sex since. Even though I got kicked out of the True Love Waits program and was placed in the Easy but Forgiven program I have lived a celibate life since my transgression."

When Megalo heard Fanny's confession his countenance fell and with sadness in his voice he remarked,

"I appreciate your honesty Fanny and you are a really nice girl but God has told me that He only wants me to marry a virgin so I enjoyed the dinner and all but I'm going to have to call this our first and last date."

Megalo dropped Fanny off at her dorm room and never spoke to her again and when he visited the Center for the first time he didn't recognize her. Till the day of his death Megalo had no recollection of Fanny Bumpus.

## Commercial Break

"Another show is in the books," announced Natu the Narrator to Megalo's vast audience.

"This next show is probably my favorite one as we explore all the books that Megalo has written throughout his career. I know you all have gone from amazed to awestruck as we have revealed the great accomplishments of Megalo Maniac. But after next week's show you will be absolutely mesmerized. Now, stay tuned for another evangelical infomercial from one of our sponsors. Tonight we are going to hear from Tommy Torquemada from Torquemada Industries in Madrid, Ohio. And, before I turn it over to Tommy Sue B. told me to give all of you a big thank you for buying her Submitter Transmitter and Evangiglow. Sue had so many orders that she could not process them all. She wanted me to inform you that most everyone will receive their order in two weeks but backorders won't go out until another month."

Hey folks, I'm Tommy from Torquemada Industries and I have developed something that no evangelical should be without. Years ago I became concerned about religious schools allowing heretics to teach in their schools and I also became aware that there were heretics attending our evangelical churches. In the old days we had to weed out these heretics with old fashioned methods such as sending spies into classes or tape recording lectures of certain professors, or reading some of their publications for the purpose of discovering heretical ideas. At Torquemada Industries we have brought heresy hunting out of the dark ages and into the modern era with a new electronic device I call the Heresy Detector. The Heresy Detector is a small device that looks much like a Turnpike Pass. Inside the Detector we have placed a small computer that holds the orthodox answers to thousands of theological questions. All you do is simply place the Heresy Detector near the back of the head of the suspected heretic and the Detector, using amazing technology developed at Torquemada Industries, will conduct a brain scan of the suspected heretic. The scan will reveal the true theological ideas of the person scanned checking them against the preloaded answers in the Heresy Detector. If the individual does hold to heterodox theological views a red light on the Detector will begin blinking. If the person is orthodox, a green light will blink. If you do encounter the red light then you have all the evidence you need to bring formal charges against the person. If the heretic is a professor then you should take the Heresy Detector to the school administration and show them the results so that they can begin the process of firing the professor. If you use the Heresy Detector on a church member then take the Detector to the pastor and staff so they can begin counseling with the person to turn him or her back to the orthodox fold. If counseling doesn't work then the pastor and staff should remove the individual from the fellowship of the church before the heretic infects the entire congregation with liberal notions. I know some of you are probably asking,

"How could I use this device without being detected?"

It's easy. In church, sit behind the suspected heretic and hold the device to the back of the person's head while holding the church bulletin between you and the Heresy Detector. Everyone in church will believe you are simply reading your bulletin. Using the Heresy Detector on professors is more difficult because professors in religious schools are experts at concealing their heresies. At times seasoned professors are able to unconsciously block the scanning mechanism of the Heresy Detector and cause the device to misread the professor's thoughts. With professors I suggest you invite them to lunch. Their guard will be down in a relaxed atmosphere of a local deli. When they are standing at the counter to order, simply stand behind them and scan them. Others in line may wonder what you are doing but they won't really have a clue what you are doing. The Heresy Detector does not come cheap. This baby will cost you $3,000. It's really ideal for institutions rather than individuals but I will sell it to individuals. Encourage your church and school to buy the Heresy Detector today and let's keep our churches and schools doctrinally pure and theologically safe. Call us at TOR-QUE-MADA and order your Heresy Detector today! Good night all. Good night all and God bless!"

Chapter Four:

# Prolific Author

Over the course of his career Megalo had written and edited numerous books. He thought surely this could be considered his primary contribution to the evangelical Christian world. As a young pastor in Ding Dong, Texas he published his first book with a local publisher, Longhorn Church Publishers. His *Simple Sermons for Sunday Simpletons* sold well locally as did his second book, *Pounding the Pulpit and Pelting the Parishioner: A How to Manual*. Deacon Troll loved both books and sent copies to family and friends as gifts. After Megalo published his second book Deacon Troll told his fellow deacons,

"That A.C.A. Demic thought he was so smart and the whole time he was here he never published a book and Megalo has published two books while he has been here and all the while he has pounded the pulpit, stepped on our toes, and preached about a hell so hot it would incinerate Satan himself. Megalo is remarkable and is just what we needed."

Megalo titled his third book *Whores of the Bible*. Initially, Megalo had titled his book *Jesus and the Whores* but the publishers thought that the book might not sell with such a title. He then changed the title to *Really Awful, Horrible, Easy Girls of the Bible* but the publisher would not approve it so the two parties eventually agreed upon *Whores of the Bible*. In his book Megalo went from Genesis to Revelation telling the stories of easy women of the Bible. Megalo's list of loose women included— Tamar in the book of Genesis; the anonymous immoral woman who wiped Jesus feet with her tears; Mary Magdalene; and the woman caught in adultery that Jesus saved from being stoned to death. Megalo's purpose in writing the book was to demonstrate that "God loves all people, but that God has a special affinity for loose women." When one reader wrote Megalo explaining that he did not think that Mary Magdalene was a prostitute Megalo responded in a letter,

"Dear Reader, anyone who had seven demons cast from her had to have been a prostitute. At least one of those demons had to have been a prostitution demon."

Megalo did not receive much attention for this first book making him all the more determined to take another crack at publishing. His next book he wrote in a matter of days and had it published a month later. *How to Give a Circus Style Invitation* gave instructions to pastors on how to manipulate people into getting out of their pews and walk the aisle and be saved. Megalo's advice included earnest pleading, a pianist playing sad but sentimental hymns, shouting followed by whispering, cracking one's voice and getting weepy when talking about Jesus, and perseverance.

Megalo wrote, "Sing and plead until someone comes. Tell your congregation that you will stay all day until someone comes. Eventually, someone will break and come down the aisle crying and this could influence others leading to an emotional outpouring and a true revival experience."

Megalo's fifth book came within a year of his fourth one and it turned out to be the book that made him famous in the evangelical publishing world. He entitled this book, *The Jesus Shaped Cheeto*. The idea for the book came to Megalo after he had an amazing experience while eating lunch. One ordinary afternoon Megalo had gone down to the Ding Dong Diner to eat a sandwich and chips and he picked up a Cheeto that looked like Jesus. He wrapped it carefully in a napkin and on Sunday displayed it to an amazed congregation. Megalo then did research on the internet and discovered that people all over the world had discovered Jesus, Jesus' mother Mary, Peter, and even the Apostle Paul in such objects as wood, stone, a fish stick, pancakes, potatoes, carrots and other vegetables. One gentleman in Ohio thought that his Rib Eye Steak looked like Joseph, Jesus' father. He had the steak preserved and mounted on his wall at home. People from miles around came to gaze at the Father Joseph Rib Eye.

When Megalo discovered that so many people had an experience similar to his own he decided that he must write about all the events so he could prove to the secular world that God is actively working in the world.

Megalo told his wife Sue, "This cannot be a coincidence that all of these people have had these amazing sightings. I must write about it so that the world can see that God is everywhere at work revealing Himself to humans. He is even in a Cheeto!"

Megalo pitched the idea to Imprudent Publishers, who jumped at the idea. Imprudent needed a boost since the last book they published, *Building Pergolas with the New Hampshire Mennonites*, turned out to be a complete flop. Once Megalo's book appeared in print he held a well-publicized book signing at the local Christian bookstore in the Quail Creek Mall in Austin, Texas. People stood in line for hours in order to get Megalo to sign his book but Megalo made it worth their while by giving them a coupon for a free pretzel. One lady even brought a Frito that she claimed looked just like Mary Magdalene.

An amazed Megalo commented to her, "My extensive research has proven that the apostles and other New Testament characters, even minor ones such as Rhoda in the book of Acts, tend to show up more often in potato chips than in any other item. Why? I have no idea. Just chalk it up to the providential hand of God."

After gaining a great deal of attention for *The Jesus Shaped Cheeto* Megalo churned out *A Dummies Guide to the Bible.* In less than two hundred pages Megalo explained to readers the story of the Bible from Genesis to Revelation. For Megalo, the only true way to understand the entire Bible was to see that from beginning to end it is a story about Jesus.

He told his readers, "Always look for Jesus in the text and you will find Him there. In fact, the Old Testament makes no sense whatsoever unless you can discover all the references to Jesus sometimes hidden but other times clearly presented. Some scholars think only a few references in the Old Testament have to do with Jesus but Jesus is in every page of the Old Testament. Oh, there are a few parts of the Old Testament that don't have to do with Jesus and these passages are not unimportant but just not as important as the parts that reference Jesus. Jesus was one of the angels that appeared to Abraham and Sarah informing them they would have a son named Isaac. Moses is a prototype of Jesus. Jesus is the Suffering Servant in Isaiah. He is the one in the furnace with Daniel's three friends. He is the one that Jeremiah predicts will come and establish a new covenant that will replace the old covenant. He is found in various places in the Old Testament but especially in the prophetic books. Jewish readers don't see Jesus in their so-called Hebrew Bible because they have been temporarily blinded. One day their eyes will be opened and they will start referring to the Scripture as the Old Testament and they will see Jesus in the Old Testament text. Of course, Jesus is all over the New Testament. And when Jews come around to seeing things from the Christian perspective they will also embrace the New Testament and toss aside that silly Talmud which, unlike our New Testament, is not a harmonious document but contains numerous competing ideas. Someday Jews will no longer want to debate theology as they do now, but when the time is right they will be in complete agreement with the perfect text of the New Testament."

Megalo had wondered for many years why the Jews did not accept Jesus as the Messiah when God had made them His chosen people long ago. For Megalo Jews had a history of being obstinate and disobedient to God and that is why they had suffered so much over the years. He believed that the suffering they had endured and would encounter in the future would cause them to see the error of their ways and accept Jesus as the Messiah someday in the future. But for now, Megalo considered the Jews to be just like everyone else who didn't believe in Jesus—they were lost and needed to be saved so they could go to heaven. When Megalo attended an interfaith prayer breakfast on one occasion he purposefully sat by the Jewish rabbi so he could share the gospel with him. When Megalo asked the rabbi if he would be saved so he could go to heaven the rabbi looked at him and said,

"What in the world are you talking about? Every day of my life I seek to follow God and be obedient to Him."

Megalo shrugged and replied, "You Jews just never seem to get it right. Why does God continue to put up with you? You were His chosen people but there will probably be more Jews in hell than any other group of people. God's heart must surely be broken that He invested all that time with you people and most of you have refused His free gift of salvation while still claiming that you love God and follow Him. You don't know God at all."

Megalo never attended another interfaith prayer breakfast mainly because the president of the interfaith alliance told him that he could not use the occasion to proselytize.

Megalo responded, "I am being persecuted because I'm a Christian. I'm sure you wouldn't censor the rabbi because he is so open-minded and tolerant. You say the interfaith alliance is tolerant but you actually refuse to tolerate my intolerance so you are not really tolerant after all. I won't be a part of such a hypocritical organization."

After enjoying brisk sales of his "Dummies" book Megalo followed with *Highway to Heaven* in which he explained that there is only one way to get to heaven.

Megalo wrote, "Some say it is old fashioned to believe that belief in Jesus is the only way to heaven but this is none other than biblical Christianity. Secular America says that Sikhs, Buddhists, Muslims, Jains, Hindus and others can find ways to God through their religious beliefs and practices. Roman Catholics and Protestant liberals have embraced all forms of inclusivism including the idea that all religions have highways that lead to God. In fact, the ClearMount School of Theology, a school with historical ties to Methodism, recently became a multi-faith center for the training of clergy. Now the school will train Buddhist, Hindu, Muslim as well as Christian leaders. This is what happens when churches and denominations fail to prevent their educational institutions from embracing theological liberalism. A multi-faith seminary, and there will likely be more to come, is a repudiation of classical Christianity. A true Christian is an exclusivist. A biblical Christian only believes in the exclusivity of the gospel of Christ. There is only one highway to heaven and that is through belief in Christ, not Krishna or Mithra or anyone else. If evangelical Christians become inclusivists then biblical Christianity will be dead."

*Highway to Heaven* sold well to evangelicals over the age of 65 but evangelicals under the age of 35 didn't buy it. For the first time Megalo realized that a generation of younger evangelicals not represented by any of the students at ATC had different ideas about the Christian faith than the older generation. Megalo became determined to reach these young, rebellious, evangelicals. After meager sales of *Highway to Heaven* Megalo implored his publisher to let him turn his attention toward eschatology because evangelical Christians of all ages "seem obsessed with the end times."

"Eschatology is the vehicle that will allow me to speak to the new generation of evangelicals." Megalo surmised.

Long fascinated with the book of Revelation, Megalo went to work and wrote several books that dealt with the last book of the New Testament. He entitled his first book on Revelation, *Premillennial Party Poopers*. In the book Megalo expressed his longing for the end of days when billions of people on earth would be destroyed through war, famine, and other atrocities while he and his few righteous friends and relatives would be taken to a heavenly paradise by Jesus.

"I get so excited when I imagine the rapture and I'm flying up toward heaven while I gaze below at the molten lava engulfing this sad old earth and its wicked inhabitants," Megalo wrote.

Another popular book that also dealt with end time matters Megalo entitled *God's Animal House: A Red Heifer, an Unblemished Lamb, a White Horse, and a Herd of Goats*. Here Megalo shared with precision the events that would occur as the world ended. First, a red heifer would be born in Israel signaling to the Messiah, sinless Lamb of God, to mount his white horse and prepare to leave heaven and come to earth to gather faithful Christians and bring them to heaven.

Megalo wrote, "Jesus will rapture His church in an instant. Jesus' appearance on a white horse will certainly be confusing to Hindus who will think that the Messiah is Kalki an avatar of Vishnu who has come to set up an era of Hindu ascendance. All Hindus will be surprised however whenever they realize that Cowboy Jesus did not come for the Indians and He will leave them behind. The Indians always lose to the Cowboys."

Megalo continued, "When Jesus comes for His people they will be driving cars down the highway one minute and in a second the cars will be without drivers. Crashes will be abundant. The bumper sticker that reads, 'In case of rapture this car will be unmanned,' is no joke. Stay away from those cars unless you enjoy placing yourself in dangerous situations. Only atheists, Hindus, Buddhists, Daoists, Sikhs, Jains, Muslims and other sinners will be driving around after the rapture. This will lead to numerous instances of road rage because all the considerate Christian drivers will be gone. The most fortunate Christians will not be driving cars but will be visiting their deceased loved ones in the cemetery when the rapture occurs. Since the Apostle Paul stated in I Thessalonians that when the rapture occurs the dead in Christ will rise first followed by the living, it will be rather easy for a living Christian to grab an arm or a leg of the deceased loved one and hitch a ride as he or she bursts from the ground and soars heavenward. Wouldn't it be great if Jesus came on Memorial Day? Christians who are working on roofs of houses will also get a head start when Jesus comes again. Perhaps Jesus will come on a Sunday morning so that many Christians will already be dressed and ready to meet the Savior. What a bummer if Jesus came really early during a weekday and raptured many Christians while they were taking their morning showers. That could be embarrassing. It would be much better for Jesus to see his people in their Sunday suits, not their birthday suits."

Since the Messiah could not possibly come to earth until the birth of a completely red heifer as stipulated in the Old Testament book of Numbers, Megalo had spent thousands of dollars shipping red heifers to Israel from the United States in hopes that a red heifer would be born. Megalo even received some financial help from some orthodox Jews who also wanted a red heifer to be born in Israel. Rabbi Wacko Screwbalstein gave Megalo land for his imported heifers and also paid workers to feed and care for the animals. The workers formed The Red Heifer Society in order to ensure that everyone who worked with the animals believed fully that they were working to help bring the Messiah back to earth.

For Wacko and members of the Red Heifer Society, the birth of the heifer would signal the Jewish Messiah to appear. For Megalo, the birth of the heifer would compel Jesus the Messiah to come to earth again. Even though Megalo and Wacko were working together at cross-purposes neither of them cared for each one knew the other one was dead wrong. Megalo and Wacko both became elated last year when a red heifer was born in Israel, yet their excitement turned to disappointment when white hair began to appear on the animal's face.

Wacko told his orthodox friends afterward "Do not be dismayed friends God must be waiting for His perfect timing."

Megalo shrugged off the disappointment as well commenting, "God is giving us more time so we can save more people from the dark side."

According to Megalo, after the red heifer is born and the Messiah does come to earth and rapture His followers, everyone else, the goats, will be left behind in a completely corrupt world filled with violence and utter chaos and of course, mean and inconsiderate drivers. Some of the goats will repent of their sins and become sheep but because they decided too late in the game to become sheep they will have to suffer through seven years of tribulation. The seven years of chaos and disorder is God's judgment against all the bad people who refused to follow Him. He could have wiped them out in a flood as in earlier times but He said He would not do that again and besides drowning is too quick and painless. Bad people deserve at least seven years of incessant pandemonium and who knows whether the suffering may encourage them to turn from their evil ways.

At the end of seven years of horrific living on the earth Jesus will call time and come again to the earth and set up a Messianic kingdom here on earth. It is unclear whether He will come to earth riding on a white horse on this occasion or whether He might choose another riding animal such as a beautiful peacock or a huge elephant to demonstrate his support for the Republican party. He definitely won't be riding a donkey. Last time he did that by the end of the week he found himself on a cross. Whatever the case, Jesus will come to earth for the third time. Unlike the first two brief visits, this time He will stay awhile. The Messianic kingdom on earth will last one thousand years, which makes perfect sense because five hundred years is too short and two thousand years far too long. During this time Satan will be cast into a deep dark dungeon so he can think about all the bad things he has done to everyone.

At the end of a thousand years, after Satan has been in time out long enough, Jesus will release him from the dungeon to see if he has decided to become a good guy after all. Unfortunately, Satan will be mad as hell when he comes out of the dungeon and will try to wreak havoc upon the earth once again and destroy Jesus and His people. Satan will gather a huge Muslim dominated army and try to fight against Jesus' people here on earth. The Christian Messiah will defeat Muslims in a final battle at Armageddon and then he will convert all the Jews to the Christian religion. The Jews will finally be on Jesus' side having seen the error of their outdated, legalistic, short-sighted religion.

(Earlier in his life Megalo taught that a Russian led army would fight against Jesus but he changed his mind after the Cold War ended and the era of "Muslim" terroristic activity began). Jesus, having had enough of Satan's bad boy ways, will do what he realizes He should have done a long time ago, and knock Satan off for good and destroy his army and bring all the sheep together into one heavenly pen so they can enjoy eternal life where there is no more suffering and the old will sing Southern Gospel hymns while the young belt out Contemporary Christian Pop music all day every day for eternity.

All the goats will be cast into a fiery pen where they will be tormented by fire throughout all eternity. Of course, all lost people are goats, but the lead pack of goats is the Muslims out of whose midst will arise the chief goat beast, the Anti-Christ. Megalo stumbled across a sort of secret Bible Code that allowed him to understand that Muslims are the main pack of goats among the lost. A numerological analysis of the numbers 666 in the book of Revelation reveals the cryptic meaning of the numbers: **Islam = Goats**. Each letter of the alphabet has a numerical value. A = 1; B = 2; C = 3; and so on. Using this method assign all the letters in the world GOATS a number. G = 7; O = 15; A = 1; T = 20; S = 19. Subtract 7 from 15 and you get 8. Subtract 1 from 8 and you get 7. Subtract 19 from 20 and you get 1. Subtract 1 from 7 and you get 6. So, one can clearly see that goats are the beasts represented by the first number 6. How could Megalo be certain that the goats are the adherents of Islam? This is where it gets really interesting. I = 9; S = 19; L = 12; A = 1; M = 13. Subtract 9 from 19 and you get 10. Add 12 and 1 and 13 and you get 26. Add 10 and 26 and you get 36. 6 x 6 just happens to be 36. So the final two 6's of the number of the beast is Islam. For Megalo, clearly anyone who has the ability to do simple math can see that 666 means **Islam = Goats**. Further, the reason there are three 6's is because Islam the goat beast is the anti-Trinity. And everyone knows that Muslims reject the Trinity. The Muslim Anti-Christ will emerge to challenge Jesus' divinity as well as engage Him in battle. The Muslim beast will certainly be surprised when the Father, Son, and the Holy Spirit team up to put on a goat barbecue. Nobody will want to order the Cabrito, however, because it will be way past well done.

At least all the goats will have Satan in their company so they will have someone to blame for their situation while they burn. The sheep won't be sad that the goats are burning because God will somehow give them a case of heavenly amnesia and they won't have any recollection of anyone burning for eternity. Of course the sheep will recognize one another in the heavenly pen. If any sheep had relatives or friends that they can't find in the heavenly pen they won't even have the ability to consider that they were sent to the burning pen. They will simply not remember those relatives or friends at all. And in all this God will be glorified."

One unsympathetic online reviewer of Megalo's book asked, "Hey Megalo, what if a Jewish Messiah comes soon and He is pissed about how Christians have treated Jews over the years? What will you do then? And what if a Muslim Mahdi appears and he wants to kick both Jewish and Christian butt for past offenses against Muslims? What then?"

Megalo actually read the review and responded briefly, "The only Messiah who will come again to earth is Jesus and when he comes to rescue His people He will also blow his enemies away. And, if truth be told I would love to blow you away in the name of the Lord."

A year after Megalo's book appeared the Evangelical Theological Society for Amateur Theologians (ETSAT) gave Megalo their prestigious Islamaphobe of the Year Award. The president of ETSAT, when presenting the award to Megalo introduced him as the noblest Islamaphobe he had ever met. He stated that Megalo had now received three awards in the last ten years from ETSAT. Earlier Megalo had received the

Complementarian of the Century Award and the Anti-Semite of the Decade Award.

Megalo wrote often about heaven and hell. Two of his bestsellers he wrote after having two separate visionary experiences. *30 Minutes in Hell* tells the story of Jesus' visit to Megalo on one occasion in which Jesus transported Megalo to hell so he could see the horror of it and warn people on earth to stay away from it. Megalo describes in his book that he witnessed the devil, many demons, and millions of people crying out in anguish as they were tormented by the fires of hell. Not only did the devil scream out loudly he also went around punching people in the face and calling them stupid and idiot and other names. When they tried to punch back the devil would move quickly enough never to receive a blow. The demons would swoop down on people and pull their hair and shout expletives at them. Not only did people in hell endure all this pain, they also had to stand in long lines for no apparent reason. When the line didn't move quickly enough, which always happened, people would get into fights with each other and throw fire balls at one another.

Megalo wrote in his book how Jesus pointed out to him such figures as Voltaire, Catherine de Medici, Charles Darwin, and Michael Servetus. Megalo also saw some people he knew in hell. Megalo said he was not surprised to see the Catholic priest he had known for years who had just recently died.

"I knew Father Wilcox was a real SOB although he tried to hide behind all his social work such as feeding the poor and building houses for low income families," Megalo thought to himself.

Megalo did quite a surprise when he saw one of his former Ding Dong deacons, Eddie Getty in hell. Megalo remembered how as a young man Eddy loved to study eschatology especially the books of Hal Lindsey and John Walvoord. Eddy used to tell Megalo often,

"I can't wait until Jesus comes again to take me home."

While in his twenties Eddy had even joined the Southern Gospel group The Left Behind Singers. Although late to every gig once they arrived they did not disappoint their fans as they sang old favorites such as *This World is Not My Home, I'm Just a Passin' Through* and *I Wish We'd All Been Ready.*

Megalo called out to Eddie from afar, "Why are you in hell Eddie? I don't understand."

Eddie shrieked, "Megalo, I don't understand it either. I thought I was saved, but apparently I was wrong."

A baffled Megalo then remembered that in his late thirties Eddy had left the Ding Dong church and had joined a moderate Baptist church in a nearby city and had abandoned premillennialism and other basic doctrines.

Megalo mused, "So, Eddy never really was saved because he did not persevere in the true faith. People can wrongly believe they are saved when all the time they are headed straight for hell. That's incredible. Of course, no one should live in continual fear that they are not saved. That is a form of doubting God. I'm so glad that I know I am saved because I can clearly see the signs in my life of an authentic faith. What a bummer to think you are headed for heaven and then you wind up in the fiery pit where flames do rage and glow. Well that's what happens when a person doesn't really believe in Christ or embraces some confused ideas about the gospel of Christ."

Megalo also saw his Uncle Billy, who had been baptized and attended church all his life, and he lit up hell like a Roman Candle. Jesus allowed Megalo to talk a few moments with Billy since they were related.

Billy shouted, "I bet you wonder what in the hell I'm doing here, Megalo?"

"Of course I am more than curious," Megalo answered.

Billy explained, "Well, Megalo even though I claimed to be a Christian over the years I harbored these secret doubts about my faith and about Jesus being the Messiah and those doubts landed me here. Megalo, go back to earth and tell people never to have any doubts or they will end up like me."

Suddenly a big ball of fire enveloped Billy and the devil grabbed him and whisked him away while punching him repeatedly in the face while a group of demons pulled out his hair and shouted at him,

"You're a stupid dumb ass hick."

A horrified Megalo pleaded with Jesus to lead him out of hell. He had seen enough.

Megalo warned his readers at the end of the book, "I saw so-called Christians in hell. Are you sure that you are saved? You better make certain. I spent 30 minutes in hell so that you won't have to spend an eternity there."

Megalo's other book he entitled *60 Minutes in Heaven*. After Jesus had taken Megalo to hell He felt obligated to show Megalo the wonders of heaven and to allow him to visit twice as long as he had been in hell. During Megalo's one hour in heaven with Jesus acting as his tour guide he saw amazing things that he felt compelled to write down. Megalo explained to his readers that there are no gates in heaven just a big castle that looks a lot like the one at Disneyworld.

"I walked through the entrance to the castle past two beautiful women who both wore one piece swimsuits with sashes across the front one that read, 'Miss Heavensent' and the other 'Miss Immaculate' I could tell right away they were heavenly virgins. As I entered the castle before me I saw the Lord sitting on a huge throne. Jesus left my side and took his place at the right hand of God. God told me that the chair to the left was reserved for the Holy Spirit who was present but that I could not see him because the Spirit cannot be seen with human eyes. I could not see God clearly because a bright light shone around him. Numerous winged creatures flew all about Him as well obscuring my view. All I could see of his face were big bushy eyebrows, a mustache, and a long white beard. My belief that God was indeed male had been confirmed.

Jesus took me away from the throne room and into a huge mansion next door to the castle.

'This is your heavenly home, Megalo.'

I hooted, 'I'm living in a mansion next door to Jesus just like I had always hoped.' Jesus continued, 'We have rewarded you for all the work you have done for us on earth. We have equipped this home with all the comforts you could ever want. Ipads, Ipods, Macs, a state of the art theater room, an Olympic size swimming pool are all yours. Your home will be filled with male and female servants who are here to do your bidding. They are happy to be of service to you and do not mind being servants at all because these are folks who barely made it into heaven. They had just enough faith to get by so they are happy to be servants here rather to be frying in hell.'

I could not believe that God had provided such as beautiful and expansive mansion for me in heaven and that it looked so much like my earthly home. God is good to His faithful servants."

Megalo had a wave of sadness come over him suddenly as he remembered his Uncle Billy being tormented in hell.

Megalo thought to himself, "If only Billy had not doubted he could have been one of my servants in heaven instead of roasting in hell. I'm so glad when I make this my final home I won't have any remembrance of Billy roasting in hell."

Megalo wanted to see more of heaven and he had so many questions.

"Will I still be married in heaven?"

"Do I get to have sex with my female servants?"

Who else lives in my neighborhood?"

But Jesus told him that this glimpse of glory would have to do for now. Jesus took Megalo back to earth where he had a difficult time adjusting to living in an imperfect environment again. Then, one of his servants brought him a Mocha Malt Frappuccino and this brought Megalo great comfort.

One of Megalo's personal favorites among the books he had written had to do with hermeneutics. Megalo considered it to be his most scholarly work. Bible colleges across the country used his hermeneutics book that he entitled *The Power of Proof Texting*. Megalo set forth his tried and tested principles for interpreting the Bible that would give Bible students the ability to get at the exact meaning of the text. Megalo placed his five major hermeneutical principles in order. 1. Always read the Bible literally, never figuratively. The Bible is a plain book that speaks plainly. 2. The first question to ask when reading a passage is what is this text saying to me? 3. Ignore context. 4. Avoid using those destructive higher critical methodologies, especially the ones invented by the German liberal infidels. 4. Skip over seemingly difficult passages and focus only on clear ones realizing that only theological experts should handle difficult passages. 5. If a Catholic or Episcopalian or anyone from one of the so-called orthodox traditions disagrees with your interpretation of the Bible simply say to them,

"I'll pray for you that God will give light to your eyes and that He will illuminate your heart."

Megalo provided examples of proof texting for his readers so that they could see his principles at work. One of his primary proof texts came from the Pastoral Epistles. Megalo saw in 1 Timothy 2:11-12, 3:2 and Titus 2:5 clear teaching that only a man can serve as senior pastor of a church, a woman can never teach a man, and that a woman must be silent in the church and learn quietly, and she must be a homemaker. Megalo challenged anyone to refute "the clear teaching of Scripture."

Megalo wrote, "God said it. That settles it."

Megalo pleaded with his readers, "Don't listen to those liberal Bible teachers who say that Paul didn't write the Pastorals and that he actually encouraged women to use their gifts in ministry. Phoebe was not a deacon, just a servant. It is not Junia a woman, but Junio, a man, who Paul calls an apostle. Priscilla stood under the authority of her husband Aquila as the two of them taught Apollos. In fact, she probably just sat there and offered encouragement to Aquila while he instructed Apollos. Those who try to argue that Paul taught equality of men and women by appealing to Galatians where Paul states that there is neither Jew nor Greek or male and female in Christ Jesus do not understand that Paul is merely talking about salvation, not ministry. Paul is simply stating that anyone can be saved, not that all are equal in Christ. Remember, Jesus chose twelve men as disciples, not any women. Those who want to appeal to Luke 8:1-3 to assert that Jesus had female disciples do not realize that these women were just plain old vanilla followers of Jesus who had no authority. They did not stand in a special place with Jesus as the chosen twelve did. Even Mary the mother of Jesus, great as she is, could not stand in the shadow of any of the male disciples with the exception of the traitor Judas Iscariot of course."

Megalo also appealed to the Pastorals to argue that a pastor must be a married man because if he were single he would be susceptible to sexual advances or he might be gay. According to Megalo, the most normative New Testament texts describing the office of pastor come from

I Timothy 3:1-7 and Titus 1:5-9.

Megalo wrote, "These passages clearly state that the minister must be a husband of one wife. Marriage is the default state for the minister. And the pastor must have believing children as well. So, a pastor must not only be married but he and his wife must have children. If they cannot have children naturally they should adopt children. Evidently (and this is God saying this not me) in order for a pastor to lead a church effectively he must also have the ability to lead a family. Now, some Bible students will want to appeal to I Corinthians 7:6-9 where Paul exalts the gift of celibacy and Matthew 19:12 where Jesus says that some have 'made themselves eunuchs for the sake of the kingdom of heaven.' These passages are not addressed to pastors but to all Christians who might want to remain single so they can devote full attention to the Lord's work. So, Paul is in no way contradicting himself here because these latter passages are not addressed specifically to ministers. In the end, marriage is a basic requirement for pastoral ministry. My advice to young single ministers is to go get married if they want to be a pastor because churches want married men with children to serve as their pastors."

Megalo's interpretations of several Old Testament passages left his hearers in awe as he brought to light otherwise ambiguous passages.

Deuteronomy 23:18 states, "You shall not bring the hire of a whore, or the price of a dog into the sanctuary."

Megalo told his followers that God does not allow dogs in church. Megalo told his followers that he had to appeal to this passage only on one occasion. Back in Broomville the church held a Wednesday night talent show and a woman in the church wanted to bring her dogs to church and have them show off their tricks for the church members. Megalo told her that God would not allow dogs in the church and so the woman held a reception after church at her house and invited the church members to see her dogs do their tricks. On another occasion at the Little Bigger Church a blind man with his canine companion tried to enter the church and Megalo refused to allow the man to enter the church with his dog. The man went down the street to the Methodist church. Megalo told one of his deacons, "A blind man headed for a blind church. We don't need him here. If he had enough faith he wouldn't be blind anyway. We don't have anyone who can sign for him anyway."

The deacon turned and walked away stunned and confused.

A number of passages in the Old Testament have the phrase, "he that pisseth against the wall."

For example, I Kings 14:10 states, "I will cut off from Jereboam him that pisseth against the wall."

One Sunday at ArenaChurch Megalo announced that he would be preaching a controversial message and that might not be suitable for everyone. He offered the opportunity for anyone to leave who did not want to hear the message. No one left. Megalo read I Kings 14:10 and then began his sermon.

"Hundreds of years ago pastors stood up behind a pulpit to preach that a man needs to be a man. A man pisses standing up, not sitting down. Only females and males pee sitting down. This text tells us that true men of God piss while standing but the problem in our churches is that we have too many males who refuse to be men and stand up for what is right. We have too many males who pee sitting down. I'm gonna tell you one thing. I'm not going to pee sitting down. I'm going to pee standing up because I am a man. I am a man of God."

At the conclusion of the sermon an astonished yet exhilarated crowd exited the building and not one person stopped to use the restroom on the way out.

Megalo loved preaching the parables of Jesus and demonstrating how His parables promoted a free market system.

He proclaimed, "Jesus said more about money than any other subject. You might think he said more about the Kingdom of God but not in my Bible. The parable of the laborers in the vineyard in Mt. 20 clearly demonstrates that God rewards those who work hard. Some people think you can't have money and be a Christian. They quote verses such as Mt. 6:24 and try to say that you can't be slaves to both God and money. Now, what Jesus meant here is that you can't be a slave to God and money unless God gives you the money. If God gives it to you then you should enslave the money to use it in service to you. You can be slaves of both God and money if God gives you the money."

Megalo also preached that Christians could judge others.

He told his parishioners, "Some people think that in Mt. 7:1 Jesus told us not to judge others. This is generally true unless God gives you a special insight into the minds and hearts of others then you can judge others. And you will not be judged for judging others because Christ has given you His mind and heart in order that the judgments you make and the standards you use are absolute. I must say, this happens to me all the time. It is quite a burden to bear, looking into the hearts and minds of others, but I bear it as a humble servant of Christ."

Megalo's interpretations of Scripture had the ring of infallibility. His hermeneutical circle consisted of himself, God, and the text. The relationship between the three was seamless. God gave Megalo the correct interpretation of the text and Megalo delivered it to his followers.

Megalo's most popular book had to do with one of his favorite activities— evangelism. *How To Convert Muslims, Jews, and Just About Anybody* made Megalo more money than all his other books combined. His instruction on how to convert Muslims included the following advice.

"First, if you are a woman stop reading. This advice only applies to evangelical Christian men. Christian women should never try to evangelize Muslims. The Muslim man will try to make you his wife and Muslim men are very convincing. Muslim women will try to persuade you to become a Muslim and they are very convincing as well. So, mature Christian men, find a Muslim friend by going to the local mosque. Be careful when you go to the mosque because it is well known that extremists run over 80% of the mosques in America. Several members of Congress have said this and I believe them. Don't really befriend the Muslim because he can't be trusted. Just pretend you like him so you can get him to become a Christian and always watch your back. He may have easy access to hidden weapons of destruction such as a personal pocket launcher which releases a tiny fast moving missile designed to hit your face and explode upon impact. Further, only go to the mosque once so you will not risk the danger of converting to Islam. Muslims are aggressive evangelists inside their mosques but not outside. When you are inside the mosque watch the Muslim men pray but do not join in. After the prayers are complete, invite your Muslim friend to go to church, go to lunch, and do other fun things but keep an eye on his shirt pockets. I'm telling you those pocket launchers are deadly.

After you have had several encounters then take the Qur'an and show him all the passages that demonstrate that Islam is a violent religion. Tell him that Muhammad was a violent man and prove it from the Qur'an. Do everything you can think of to insult his religion so that he will be ashamed of being Muslim and want to become a Christian. If you have to use the 'Muhammad was demon possessed pedophile' line then use it but only as a last resort and only after you have checked all his pockets. Of course, you will have to have a working knowledge of the Qur'an. You should become familiar with the book but do not spend too much time reading it so as not to be convinced to become a Muslim. Memorize the 'Sword Passages' so you can prove to the Muslim that the Qur'an promotes violence. Remember, you are only reading and memorizing the Qur'an to refute its message. After you have convinced your Muslim friend that his religion is worthless then pull out your Bible and tell him that Jesus loves him and wants to save his soul. Then pray with him and help him pray the saving prayer of faith in Jesus. Please note that if your Muslim friend gets angry with you at any point and leaves that he is not rejecting you but only Jesus. Remember too that you are only responsible for sharing the good news. You are not responsible for the results. And if you lose a friend, remember that he wasn't really your friend in the first place. Then go to the local mosque and find another friend and repeat the process."

Megalo provided sage advice on how to win Jews to Jesus as well.

"Converting Jews is especially tricky because we share part of the Bible with them. Nevertheless, you should first pretend befriend a Jew. You should try to meet a Jew from the Conservative tradition because the Orthodox are too strict in their practice and won't likely listen to you and the Reform Jews are so liberal and screwed up that they are beyond redemption. Both women and men can evangelize Jews because they are not as persuasive and cunning as Muslims and Christian women ordinarily do not find Jewish men attractive. If possible invite your Jewish friend to my theme park that I opened in Tampa, Florida called AppleWorld.

I opened the AppleWorld park in order to get Jews to visit so that they would hear the gospel message and repent and believe in Jesus. My theme park was initially called Three Flags Over Jesus (A Christian Flag, a Jewish Flag, and the U.S. Flag) and the flags flew proudly. Yet, some of my Messianic Jewish friends told me that having the Christian flag flying next to the other two flags might offend Jews and prevent them from coming to the park. So, I renamed my theme park AppleWorld. AppleWorld is an ancient working interactive Jewish village in which first century Jewish customs are acted out and explained. At one time we actually practiced animal sacrifice in order to amaze Jews and make them long for the good old days of blood and guts rituals but the state of Florida shut that down.

Even without the animal sacrifices, we do have a working Temple that resembles Herod's Temple. Visitors can hear choirs sing antiphonally and even enter the Holy Place. We do not allow visitors to enter the Holy of Holies however, but you should see the crowds we have on Yom Kippur. We offer half price admission for Jews on the Day of Atonement. AppleWorld also has a synagogue where one can attend services and even read from a scroll. At noon every day we reenact the episode in which Jesus read from the book of Isaiah in his hometown synagogue of Nazareth and offended the home crowd by claiming to be the Messiah. Visitors can also have their picture taken with Pharisees and Sadducees who walk the grounds in abundance. We have authentic first century Jewish homes where visitors can see common Jews cooking, farming, and herding sheep. After Jewish visitors spend the day viewing the life their ancestors lived then we hit them with the finale. We put on a drama called The Really Bloody Passion of Christ in which we demonstrate how the Jews killed Christ. We want these Jews to see what their ancestors did to Jesus so that they will repudiate the religion of their bloodthirsty ancestors and they will accept Christ. Those who repent are given directions to a nearby Messianic Jewish congregation and encouraged to join. We tell the repentant Jews that believing in Jesus does not mean that they must give up everything Jewish in their lives. They simply have to adjust all their Jewish practices to a Christian context.

If a trip to AppleWorld is too difficult for you and your Jewish friend, then let me suggest an alternative strategy. Simply ask your Jewish friend if you can join him/her for the Seder meal. When you arrive bring a nice bottle of red wine. In fact, you should probably bring two bottles because Jews like to drink a lot during the Seder meal. They say they only drink four cups of wine during the meal but their cups are as big as Mason Jars. And they won't stop guzzling just because the meal is over. Jews will drink until whatever it is they are drinking is all gone. Don't get near Jews during Simchat Torah unless you enjoy being around people who are drunk on their asses. One Jewish rabbi, who was especially fond of drinking Crown Royal Whiskey during Simchat once told me,

'On this day I drink until I can't tell my kippah from my tallit.'

After you enter the home, ask your host which chair is reserved for Elijah. Go and sit in Elijah's chair and then quickly explain to your surprised Jewish host that you are sitting in the chair reserved for Elijah because he is not coming, he has already come. Explain to your Jewish host that Jesus is the Elijah who has already come. Share a gospel message but tailor it to your Jewish host. Keep reminding him that Jesus was Jewish just like him. After the meal is over invite your Jewish friend and his family to church and be sure to invite them to your house the next week for ham and pepperoni pizza night."

Megalo also had a number of books that he had written as a part of his "Steps" series. *Twelve Simple Steps to Beat Depression, Ten Proven Steps to Affair Proof Your Marriage, Eight Easy Steps to Happiness, Six Effortless Steps to Build a Mega-Church,* and *Three Painless Steps to Superior Sermons,* all sold well in the evangelical world.

In what he called his *Twelve Step* book Megalo explained to depressed persons that among other things they should read the Bible, pray, go to church, be happy, and stop feeling so sad all the time because it depresses everyone around them. In his *Ten Steps* book Megalo indicated to his readers that the key to a happy marriage includes going to church together and holding hands while listening to sermons. He told husbands that they should love their wives by allowing the wives to wait on them and take care of all their needs, especially their physical needs. Megalo told the wives that the key to a happy marriage was doing everything they possibly could to serve up good food and good sex.

Megalo wrote, "If your husband wants oral sex but you think it's gross then close your eyes, hold your nose, and go down on him quickly. He won't mind a fast and furious approach. And for God's sake don't make him Hamburger Helper every night."

Megalo's *Eight Steps* book outlined the essential keys to happiness.

"Remember that God loves you and wants the best for you. Think often of how you can get happiness for yourself. Be good to yourself first then think of others next if you think it necessary. Think positively and happiness will definitely come your way. Avoid depressed people who will try to ruin your positive outlook on life. Seek a career in which you will make a lot of money. Find an attractive spouse and remember that single people are generally not happy people. Finally, after you have become happy, protect your happiness by beating down anyone who would try to steal it away from you."

Megalo's *Six Steps* book gave sage advice on how a pastor could move from Second Street to Superdome. Originally titled, *The Little Church That Could,* Megalo changed the title to satisfy his publisher. Although he claimed to give six easy steps on how to build a mega-church in the end it came down to one simple step— Be like Megalo.

Megalo's final book that rounded out the series provided sermon help for busy pastors. Megalo preached superior sermons because he followed three painless steps:

1. Pay attention to delivery. Delivery is everything. Walk around. Don't stand behind a pulpit. Sit on a stool at times. Bring objects onto the stage such as tanks and animals. Be animated and bombastic in the pulpit. Raise your voice at appropriate moments in the sermon and at other times use a softer tone. Whatever you do, do not scream. Screaming is out. I used to be a screamer as a young preacher but I changed my ways. If you scream like a fat kid on an out of control rollercoaster you will lose your audience. Your members equate screaming preachers with hellfire and damnation sermons. You should still preach about hell but when you preach about hell today you have to do it without screaming or nobody will listen to you. And you have to convince the elite Christians in your congregation that the hell sermons are not for them but for those who are not present such as people they work with or Democrats. You have to preach about hell to be faithful to the biblical record and to God, the author of the Bible, but just make sure you look like it really hurts you to preach such bad news even though you might secretly enjoy it especially when you look out in the audience and see people who have opposed you and wish that they would indeed go to hell.

2. Pay attention to your looks. Dress casual. Suits and ties are out. I used to wear suits but no more. Wear dark jeans and a Daniel Cremieux collarless shirt and a pair of Sanuks without socks. You have to look hip to appeal to the younger crowd. If any older people object to your look then they should just find another place to worship if they are going to be so fussy. If your hair is thinning go ahead and shave it and grow a long chin beard. That look is really in for cool pastors and praise band leaders. For the younger pastors a small fish tattoo on the forearm or perhaps a Greek or Hebrew word from the Bible is appropriate. Nowadays you have to get the punk ass look or none of the younger folks will respect you.

3. On most occasions preach sermons that could be termed "pop psychology." Tell your members how wonderful they are, how gifted they

are, how God wants to bless them with an obscene amount of material possessions. Tell them not to ever get down on themselves but to be happy and keep reaching for their dreams. I used to be strictly a "guilt" preacher and it still works for older evangelicals. But use guilt sparingly. In recent years I realized that guilt doesn't work as well with younger evangelicals. They want affirmation. Only on rare occasions should you preach sermons that confront your members but then only tackle certain issues. Tell them to tithe or God won't bless them. The church won't run without money. Tell them to be revived or God won't bless them. You need to keep the people excited and emotional. Tell them to obey you or God won't bless them. They have to obey you if the mega-church is to survive. In general, do not make your members feel guilty or uncomfortable very often because you will lose them.

4. When you preach about social and political issues you should be certain only to reflect the political and social views of the vast majority of your members. This should be easy to do since conservative Republicans and liberal Democrats are not attending church together these days. In fact, if you ever find a liberal Democrat in church on Sunday you have discovered something rare or you simply made a mistake. In the unlikely event that you do have an even a moderate democrat in your evangelical mega-church then just wink at him while you are preaching your conservative political and social views and that will likely appease him. Whatever you do, don't ever preach prophetically and challenge your members intellectually, socially, or politically. You don't want your members to leave your worship service with questions or with a feeling of confusion. You should preach in order to give people answers so that they will come back again next Sunday. Remember, the most important thing about preaching is to keep the members you have and add new members to the flock. You have to keep your members happy in today's competitive environment. If you want to be a mega-church pastor it's all about the numbers and the money of course.

Although Megalo had never taken a science class beyond high school he had become acquainted with some Christian scientists who criticized evolutionary theory, especially the scientist at ATC, Willy Recant. Recant and his Christian scientist friends were members of a scientific think tank called the Suppression Institute. The Suppression Institute had founded the Biblical Creation Museum and the Noah's Ark Park in Saint Petersburg, Kentucky. At the Creation Museum visitors can see a video detailing how God most likely created the universe in six days completing His work about 10,000 years ago. One display has humans interacting with animatronic dinosaurs. At Noah's Ark Park visitors can see a life size replica of the Ark and many types of animals. There are animal shows, a petting zoo, and a movie showing how Noah could have gotten numerous animals, including dinosaurs, onto the Ark. A replica of the Tower of Babel can also be found at the park. For only a few dollars visitors can hear an audio presentation, available in many different languages, about what happened at the ancient Tower of Babel. Visitors can also take a fast moving water ride in a miniature replica of the Ark. The park also includes restaurants where one can purchase unique food items such as Noah's Noodles, Canaan's Corned Beef, and the Ham and Japheth egg omelet. Visitors to the park can stay at the new state of the art Forty Days and Forty Nights Inn.

Officials at Noah's Ark Park put together a special two-hour dramatic presentation of the Noah story but decided early on to edit the part of the story where a drunk and naked Noah places a curse of servitude on his grandson Canaan because Canaan's father Ham saw Noah naked. Too many visitors complained about Noah being "nekked." Park officials also became a bit uneasy when a good number of visitors asked them why the U.S. no longer sanctions slavery when it is clearly a biblical concept.

Both the Creation Museum and Noah's Ark Park received millions of dollars in tax rebates from the Kentucky state government. The governor of Kentucky supported the tax rebates because the Creation Museum and Noah's Ark Park had created hundreds of jobs and brought millions of tourism dollars into the state.

The governor commented, "In Kentucky we are known for Breeding, Betting, Basketball, Bourbon, and the Bible, but not the Big Bang. We don't consider it to be a violation of church and state separation to subsidize these biblically based enterprises and even if we could be convinced otherwise it wouldn't matter. We love the Bible and we love money."

According to Ken Sockdolager, the park and the museum had two million visitors in their first year of operation. Sockdolager founded Slam Dunk Answers in Genesis Ministries and also created a web site called simplisticanswersingenesis.org. The web site refutes any scientific discovery contradicting the biblical record. Slam Dunk Answers in Genesis serves as one of the major sponsors of the museum and park along with God Is On Our Side Ministries.

Another controversial aspect of Noah's Ark Park has to do with a movie that features Megalo explaining how he discovered the original Ark on an archaeological expedition years ago. In the video Megalo informs listeners that the ark is not on the modern Mount Ararat as some have suggested. Rather, it is on another mountain that in ancient times was known as Ararat. Visitors to the museum can see pictures of the ark that Megalo took during the expedition.

Several scientists not associated with the Suppression Institute who went to see Megalo's ark first hand indicated that what Megalo had found was not a boat but simply a rock formation. Megalo and the SI scientists would not buy the rock formation conclusion for a minute. After all, scientists at SI believed in examining evidence that only supported their biases and either ignoring or suppressing evidence that ran counter to their preconceived notions. Nevertheless, SI scientists had coined the popular phrase "Intelligent Design."

After reading several of their books and watching a couple of their videos Megalo felt that he must use his fame in the evangelical world to debunk the theory of evolution. Megalo believed the theory of evolution had to be discredited because Darwin's theory made it possible for persons to be "intellectually fulfilled atheists." Megalo believed that without the "Dogma of Darwinism" that atheists would be without a coherent worldview. Megalo had to destroy Darwinism so he could annihilate atheism because in Megalo's opinion the United States was in danger of being overtaken by secular atheism on the one hand and religious extremists (Muslims) on the other hand. According to Megalo, the Darwinian atheists had a clear agenda. They wanted to use evolutionary theory to marginalize Christians and bring into disrepute the study of Christian theology. For Megalo, one could not believe in evolution and have any integrity as a Christian.

He often said, "Evolution represents one the greatest challenges to the Christian faith in our times. It is incompatible with true Christian theology."

Megalo's *The Intelligent Designer* hit the stores and immediately began flying off the shelves. Whenever the SI scientists who advocated Intelligent Design read Megalo's book much of the material looked familiar. Megalo had borrowed profusely from their works, even from Willy Recant's book that Megalo had censored earlier, without giving them credit. The SI scientists did not want to get a fellow brother in trouble so they suggested that the publisher issue a statement from Megalo and the SI scientists that they gave him permission to use their material even when Megalo used their exact wording, which he often did. Megalo's readers greeted the statement issued by the publisher with a giant yawn. They did not care where or how he got the material for the book, they were just happy that he had spoken boldly against the theory of evolution.

One of Megalo's primary arguments in favor of creationism, and one he had borrowed from an evangelist pal Louis Gigolo who claimed a molecular biologist had provided him with this decisive conlusion, had to do with glycoproteins known as Laminin. Gigolo's video, in which he discusses how God made Laminin, had received over 3 million hits. Megalo knew that including a discussion of Laminin in his book would be well received. Megalo explained in his book that Laminin molecules are cell adhesion molecules that "literally hold us together. Without them we would fall apart."

Megalo wrote, "Do you realize that the glue that holds us together physically is in the shape of a cross? The one who holds us together spiritually made that which holds us together physically in the shape of a cross. Do you know what this means? This is proof that our wonderful Lord designed this universe and everything in it with perfect meaning and purpose. Read Colossians 1:15-17 and you will discover that all things were made by the Lord Jesus and 'in him all things hold together.' The presence of Laminin in our bodies supports this passage unequivocally."

Megalo provided a molecular diagram that he had borrowed from a textbook demonstrating that Laminin is indeed in the shape of a cross.

A molecular biologist wrote to Megalo and explained that Laminin is not the only essential bonding agent and that the shape at any given time is transitory.

"Proteins change conformations. They don't hold to a given shape. Your theory is based on a molecular diagram found in a textbook and these representations are merely approximations not exact reproductions. The structure of Laminin antedates Jesus by thousands of years. Was the cross event predetermined so that Jesus had no choice in the matter? Isn't a cross a simple structure that can be found in other natural elements? Some would say that Laminin resembles a sword or a caduceus more than a cross. Also, consider that the molecule ribose that makes up the backbone of DNA (which contains the information that determines who you are) is in the shape of a pentagram, a Satanic symbol. Perhaps, we are tools of Satan on this earth. Further, potassium channels are in every nerve cell of your body and they look like swastikas. So, are we to assume that because the swastika is an emblem of the Hindu god Vishnu and since Vishnu is known as the Sustainer, that it is Vishnu who literally sustains us? In the end, to say there is some hidden message in these shapes is pure nonsense! And by the way, I don't really believe that Louis Gigolo received his information about Laminin from an actual molecular biologist."

Megalo responded to the molecular biologist, a faithful Catholic, by telling his parishioners in a Sunday morning sermon,

"I'm being persecuted for my faith by one of the Beasts. Pray for his soul that he may turn his back on his atheistic scientific knowledge and embrace the Savior who holds him together whether he wants to admit it or not."

Megalo's congregation cheered in approval.

Of course, Megalo did add some material to the book that he had not borrowed. He contributed none of the scientific material but he did provide some interesting illustrations. For example, Megalo told the story of how eating breakfast one morning had given rise to his belief in an Intelligent Designer of the Universe.

Megalo wrote, "I poured my Honey Nut Cheerios and peeled my

banana to put in my cereal when it suddenly hit me. Look at the design of the banana I said to myself. It is easy to peel and then it is bent so that it goes straight into my mouth. A simple fruit helped me to see that God designed the world perfectly. And I think it is so ironic that bananas are the favorite food of monkeys. God does have a sense of humor."

Megalo became livid whenever a science professor from the UK called him up one day and said he had read Megalo's book and that he had only one question for Megalo—

"What about the coconut? And what about the pineapple? God really screwed up those didn't He?"

Another scientist wrote to Megalo accusing him of leading the church into intellectual catastrophe by causing scientists to look upon Christianity with incredulity. Megalo wrote back informing the scientist that the church will in no way capitulate to scientism.

Megalo continued, "Certainly the world looks old. If I were only armed with naturalistic assumptions I would agree with you and your Darwinian evolutionist friends. But I do not share your worldview. The Christian faith is based upon supernaturalistic assumptions and a plain reading of Scripture will lead the common sense reader to reject evolutionary theory along with its naturalistic assumptions. When Christians look at the cosmos they understand that while it appears to be old it really isn't. The cosmos has been ravaged by sin and God's judgment to such an enormous degree that it just looks worn out. The cosmos is simply a 30 year old man who looks 80 due to years of hard living."

Despite a few negative reviews from those outside evangelicalism, Megalo's book received rave reviews and was nominated for a *Fundy* Award. Imprudent Publishers along with other evangelical publishers created the *Fundys* to celebrate the achievements of those who used the printed word to combat liberalism effectively. Megalo prayed that he could win a *Fundy* so he could add it to his trophy case. When the night came for the awards show Megalo had a speech prepared because he thought he might win. The other three books up for a Fundy had not sold as many copies as his and the authors were not nearly as famous as he. Megalo could not believe his ears when the presenter called out his name. He had won his first *Fundy* and had beaten out three fine books: *The Chiliastic Calvinists Outwit the Unorthodox Unitarians; How to Beat a Liberal at Almost Anything;* and *A History of Heresy Hunting.*

When Megalo returned home after the awards show he placed his *Fundy* next to his *Narci.* The year before Megalo's show had won a *Narcissus* (*Narci* for short) because viewers had voted his show the best religious television program of the year. The *Narci* looked like an Oscar except it was designed to bear the likeness of the winner of the award. Megalo would often stare at his trophy cabinet for hours admiring his *Narci* but now he could also stand in awe of his *Fundy* as well.

"A *Narci* and a *Fundy*," he would repeat again and again to himself as he gazed at his awards.

## Commercial Break

"Did I tell you that you would be mesmerized after this week's show? Yes, I did and I did not disappoint," Natu the Narrator exclaimed to the viewers. "Join us next week for our final show in which we will discuss Megalo's significant political contributions. At the conclusion of the show we will take an audience vote to determine which of Megalo's contribution is most significant. Next week's show promises to captivate and fascinate. You will want to tune in for sure. Sit back and enjoy a special five minute presentation from one of our major sponsors, Premillennial Motors."

Hello folks, I'm Mary Natha, spokesperson for Premillennial Motors. I am here today to introduce you to our newest vehicle. Yes, Premillennial Motors is proud to present to you the Rapture 1000. The Rapture 1000 should be the vehicle of choice for evangelicals living in the last days. Besides getting excellent gas mileage, the Rapture 1000 comes equipped with all sorts of Second Coming Sensitive equipment. You will drive with confidence knowing that your car has Sonroof and Ejector seats for passengers in the front and back seats. When the rapture occurs the Sonroof will automatically open and the Ejector seats will toss you up in the air giving you that little extra boost that will make for an easy exit. The Rapture 1000 also comes equipped with a steering wheel lock so that when you do exit through the roof of your vehicle your vehicle will not swerve out of control and crash into the vehicles of lost persons killing them before they have an opportunity to receive the gospel. After you exit through the roof the Rapture 1000 will shout the following Second Coming Warning to nearby motorists, 'Stay back, this vehicle has no driver. Driver has been raptured. Driver has been raptured.' Your through the roof exit will also automatically set off a mechanism that releases gospel tracts into the atmosphere so that nearby left behind motorists can pick them up and read them. The tracts will explain clearly to those left behind what they just witnessed and what they should do now since they were not taken to heaven. And of course, your Rapture 1000 comes equipped with a special iridescent bumper sticker warning other drivers that in case of rapture your car will be without a driver. When the rapture occurs the bumper sticker automatically begins flashing the phrase, 'Rapture has occurred. No driver in vehicle. I told you so.' I could tell you so much more about this special vehicle but my time is up. Please, folks, come on down to Premillennial Motors and test drive a Rapture 1000 today. Do not delay. You don't want

Jesus to come while you're driving a Yaris, a Prius, a Chevy Aveo, or a Honda. Come right away because you don't know how much time we have left here. Hurry on down to Premillennial Motors and purchase the car that Evangelical Car and Driver Magazine has named evangelical car of the millennium."

# Chapter 5:

# Political Guru

Megalo claimed that he was the most politically active preacher in America and that God had called him to this work. Megalo began his political activism when he founded the Reclaiming America for Christ organization in the early 1980s when the government made a decision to block Megalo's college from receiving federal funds due to the school's discriminatory enrollment procedures. Absolute Truth College allowed minorities to enroll in the school as long as they signed a letter that they would only date "their kind." Any minority student caught dating one of the Caucasian students would be dismissed from the school. Megalo believed that the government had overstepped its authority by intruding into God's business on this issue and a host of others.

The RAC organization was also determined to get evolutionary theory thrown out of public schools and lobbied Congress to pass a law that required every public school student to start the morning by pledging allegiance to the Christian flag and the flag of the United States of America. RAC actually merged with two other groups that shared similar aims; the Patriotic Creationists and the Intelligent Design Club. The Patriotic Creationists originally called themselves the Wooden Literalists due to their belief that Genesis 1-11 not only contained a religious message, it also provided a detailed scientific explanation for how the world came into existence. A key leader of the Wooden Literalists who later become one of Megalo's chief advisors and the vice-president of Absolute Truth College, Davy Pseudepigrapher, had made a name for himself by writing bestselling books such as *Earth, Young and Fabulous*, and *The Six Day Universe*. The Wooden Literalists had developed close ties with the Intelligent Design Club. The latter group spent a lot of time and money lobbying to influence the appointment of new Supreme Court Justices who would support mandatory daily prayers as well as the teaching of creation science in public schools. The Suppression Institute encouraged them not to use the phrase "creation science" but "Intelligent Design." The Suppression Institute thought the group might be able to convince scientists that Intelligent Design was actually science and not creation science dressed up in different garb. On the recommendation of the Suppression Institute the group took the name the Intelligent Design Club. While most scientists dismiss the Intelligent Design movement as unscientific and are convinced that it is merely a repacking of creation science, the Designers simply call these scientists "secularists who were out to discredit God and His people."

Ironically, most Designers did not send their children to public schools but taught them at home or sent them to Megalo's prep school, Patriot Bible Academy. Many Literalists also sent their children to PBA as well and so the two groups began to mingle. When the Literalists hosted their weekly meeting at the Patriot Bible Academy someone suggested changing the name from the Wooden Literalists to the Patriotic Creationists and everyone agreed. Not long after the name change the two groups began to discuss a merger. Under Megalo's leadership the two came together and formed the Patriotic Intelligent Literalists (PIL). Eventually PIL joined with the Reclaiming America for Christ organization in order to carry out a unified approach in fighting against the liberal forces that sought to marginalize the Christian influence in America.

The first major action of RAC was to authorize the publication of a new Bible that the organization hoped would be embraced by the typical conservative evangelical in America. While Megalo's *Ultimate* Bible had been marketed for a global audience, RAC hoped that the *New American Patriot Bible* would serve the needs of American evangelicals who were tired of the liberal agenda in Washington. The group employed Megalo's childhood buddy Rodney Revisionist to translate the NAPB. The *Patriot Bible* prided itself on what its translator called "gender exclusive" language. All references to persons in the Bible were in masculine form.

Revisionist explained his rationale, "The secular liberals in America have been pushing the feminist agenda for years in this country and this is simply an effort to push back against that agenda."

Nevertheless, in the *Patriot Bible* Deborah in the book of Judges was now called Delbert and Jael who slew Sisera now went by the name Jake. Mary Magdalene was now called Marvin Magdalene. When one reader pointed out that even the mother of Jesus is called Mack, Rodney simply responded,

"Hey, it was a virgin birth, she wasn't really necessary anyway, so I really don't see the problem. Besides, those damn Catholics elevate her too highly so this will bring Mary down a notch. She's just a woman after all. If the Eastern Orthodox Church and the Eastern Catholics want to refer to Mary as a Theotokos fine by me but she's still just a mother even if she is the mother of God."

The *Patriot Bible* also featured Jesus delivering his Sermon on the Mount against the backdrop of a giant Roman flag while each of his twelve disciples stood around him holding twelve giant flags representing each of the tribes of Israel.

Jesus taught them, "Blessed are those who seek governmental support for their religious agenda for they shall inherit the earth."

The *Patriot Bible* also contained select quotes from America's Founding Fathers placed right alongside the biblical text in a parallel format. Next to Jesus' words about denying yourself, taking up your cross daily and following him one could read a quote from George Washington that he delivered to Delaware chieftans who wanted their young people to be educated in American schools.

"You do well to wish to learn our arts and our ways of life and above all, the religion of Jesus Christ. These will make you a greater and happier people than you are. Congress will do everything they can to assist you in this wise intention."

For Rodney, this quote proved that George Washington, America's first president, was a devout Christian, not a Deist, an inactive Christian, or a theistic rationalist. For Rodney this quote from Washington proved that our first president wanted Christianity to have such a pervasive influence in society that even the youth in our public schools should receive a Christian education.

The *Patriot Bible* also contained copious commentary notes throughout all written by Revisionist. About Israel's monarchy, Rodney wrote in the commentary notes on Exodus 18: "What was Israel's form of government before it degenerated into a monarchy? It was what may be termed a "republic." In Exodus 18:21, the people were told to choose out from among themselves leaders of tens, fifties, hundreds, and thousands – that is, to select officials at what we could call the local, county, state, and federal levels. Understanding this original form of governance, the early colonists who arrived in America therefore established representative governments."

Rodney definitely believed that the American form of government had explicit biblical foundations. He thanked God every day for the colonists who discovered that truth so long ago.

Revisionist had originally wanted to call his Bible the *New American Patriot Polyglot* in order to demonstrate his ability to use scholarly language but the publishers nixed the idea stating,

"Evangelicals wouldn't know a polyglot from a pollywog."

One independent scholar who reviewed the *Patriot Bible* indicated that the only persons who would utilize the Bible would be conservative evangelicals so it would be "highly unlikely that readers will complain that the quotes from the Founding Fathers had been cherry-picked, lifted out of context, that that some of the statements attributed to the Founding Fathers were fabrications, that there were no quotations from the Founding Mothers, and that none of the Deists among the Founding Fathers were quoted."

One of the primary aims of Revisionist's *Patriot Bible* that undergirded the entire work was to demonstrate that the nation had been built upon the foundation of the Christian religion and that Christianity today should receive special favor from the government.

"America is a Christian nation no matter what you might hear from pseudo-historians on the left," Revisionist wrote on the dust jacket of the *Patriot Bible*.

One of the biggest fans of the *Patriot Bible*, Key Proselytizer, an Air Force Major, ordered numerous copies to be distributed to cadets at the Air Force Academy. Major Proselytizer, a friend of Megalo's, worked with other evangelicals to make the U.S. Air Force Academy a place to recruit evangelical Christians as well as a place to train future officers. Major Proselytizer worked with the Superintendent of the Academy to change its stated mission. The Academy's stated mission was "to educate, train, and inspire men and women to become officers of character, motivated to lead the United States Air Force in service to our nation." The revised mission read that the Academy's mission was "to educate, train, and inspire men and women to become Christian officers, motivated to lead the United States Air Force in service to God and our nation."

Major Proselytizer also worked with the Superintendent to arrange an annual leave time program for cadets called Aim High. Cadets would receive two days leave time if they attended a special evangelistic service at the nearby Aim High Baptist Church. At the service each cadet would be given a copy of the *Patriot Bible* and listen to an evangelical sermon. Major Proselytizer would share his personal testimony and tell cadets that if they converted to evangelical Christianity then their chances for advancement would be enhanced greatly. The Major would then encourage all evangelical cadets to use the *Patriot Bible* to witness to fellow cadets who were not Christian.

"You especially need to witness to Jewish and Muslim cadets. We need to have a united evangelical Air Force if we are going to fight effectively against our godless enemies abroad. The Jews are God's people who are no longer acting like God's people so we need to bring them into the light. The Muslims are infidels who advocate Holy War against Christians. We must help them step into the light or kick them out of our ranks. Besides, in battle how could you trust a fellow Muslim soldier if you happen to be fighting against a Muslim enemy? You couldn't. So, all of our cadets must be Christian if we are going to have a unified Air Force. Not just the Air Force, but the entire U.S. military is in service to God and our nation to fight against all godless enemies," Major Proselytizer pronounced.

When Adir Akiba, a Jewish cadet, refused to attend the Aim High service, some evangelical cadets ridiculed his faith.

Cadet Brash Swagger told Adir, "What's the harm in going to a church service so you can get a little leave time?"

Adir responded, "I believe in the separation of church and state and this leave time program is clearly a violation of church-state separation."

Brash laughed and stated, "Adir, come on. You're a Jew. There's no separation of state in Israel so what's your big problem? Don't you want to fit in and be one of the guys? Who cares anymore about separating church and state anyway? That's an outdated secular concept."

Brash then offered Adir a copy of the *Patriot Bible* but Adir refused it.

A stunned Brash declared, "Who would refuse a Bible? Are you a secular Jew or something? I mean this Bible has the Old Testament in it. Don't you Jews believe in the Old Testament?"

Brash walked away from Adir shaking his head. Adir would continue to be the target of evangelistic actions throughout the remainder of his time at the Air Force Academy despite his complaints to officers who told him to "man up" and "stop whining" and "stop stirring up trouble" and to "focus on more important matters."

When Rodney Revisionist discovered that Air Force officers at the Academy distributed the *Patriot Bible* to cadets he was elated. Rodney believed that the affirmation his Bible received from the Air Force demonstrated that God had ordained his work. Rodney also loved the publicity. Even prior to the publication of the *Patriot Bible*, Rodney Revisionist had won the hearts and minds of many evangelicals through a slick marketing program involving, cheap videos, books, and pamphlets. His first book he entitled *The Godly Constitution*. Revisionist argued that although God's name is not mentioned in the Constitution He had a hand in its formulation because He guided the Founding Fathers to write it. According to Revisionist, the Constitution advocated preferential treatment for Christianity while at the same time granting religious liberty to other religions.

"Everyone in this country has the freedom to worship as they feel led, but that doesn't mean the government should show them favoritism. We Christians were here first and so we should get special treatment," Revisionist wrote.

Revisionist followed *The Godly Constitution* with another book that sold well in the evangelical world, *Declaration of Dependence Upon God*. Here, Revisionist argued that the Declaration of Independence may have

141

advocated liberty from British tyranny but it also spelled out clearly that "our nation should use its freedom to depend upon God and serve Him freely." Revisionist's video, *America's Godly Legacy*, sold even better than his books because conservative evangelicals would much rather watch a video than read a book. The video featured Revisionist interviewing actors who played the parts of the key Founding Fathers all of whom kept repeating during the video,

"I am not a Deist. I am an orthodox Christian. Take that you arrogant secularists!"

Revisionist also made numerous appearances on emotion laden religious television shows led by evangelicals who hawked for money so they could afford their private jets and beach homes. He always wore a denim shirt with the American flag emblazoned across the front. No one could accuse Revisionist of being neither unpatriotic nor unchristian. In fact, Revisionist had a difficult time separating the two. Revisionist, who had no formal training as a historian or a Church-State scholar, also went to Washington D.C. at the behest of a Republican Senator from his home state of Texas who asked Revisionist to share his view on church and state with U.S. legislators. Revisionist described to the lawmakers that separation of church and state is a liberal myth. He quoted a letter that Thomas Jefferson wrote to the Baptists in Danbury Connecticut and concluded that Jefferson believed the state should support religion in general but not one particular denomination.

He stated confidently, "Of course at the time the Christian religion was the only one here in America so Jefferson must have believed that the state should support the Christian religion in general but not one particular denomination."

Revisionist also explained to the legislators the American people had been duped by secular historians who had taught them falsehoods. Revisionist described his God given task.

"It's what I call historical reclamation. I am just trying to get history back to where it's accurate. If you're going to use history, get it right."

Although Church-State scholars to the person debunked Revisionists arguments he continued to win over many ordinary evangelicals who felt threatened by the pluralistic environment in America and believed that the government had become hostile to Christianity in recent years. After his big visit to Washington, *Time's Up* magazine voted Revisionist the second most influential evangelical of the year. Unhappy with this result Revisionist conducted his own poll that named him America's most influential evangelical of the year.

Another popular figure in the RAC movement was one of Megalo's closest friends, Mani Pulate. Mani had started out as an evangelist but had gotten a hot stock tip from a friend and gave up being an evangelist when he became wealthy almost overnight. Mani invested in Windpower Inc. a company that placed huge windmills on their so-called windmill farms and then sold the harnessed energy to nearby communities. Mani's friends immediately began to refer to him as Mani Money. Mani had a dream of using his millions to take down the big liberal machine in the U.S. but he had not worked out the details until one day he had a flash of insight.

Mani invited Megalo out for dinner one evening at Constantine's Imperial Steak Pit to share his thoughts. Mani loved to talk business at Constantine's because he loved the Creeds of Christendom Crab Bisque and he knew Megalo loved the Imperial State Church Chicken Fried Chicken that Constantine's served. Nonetheless, Mani informed Megalo that he had bought out a major news network that would now be known as Cougar News Network. Mani explained how all the other major news networks reflected liberal bias in their news stories so the aim of Cougar News would be to present a conservative slant to the news but claim objectivity.

Mani explained his approach further, "Megalo, I am going to get some 30ish very attractive feisty females, and a few who are downright nasty, and some handsome and pompous males in their 40s to serve as news anchors and hosts of politically oriented shows. These men and women will be on the front lines every day denouncing the liberal agenda in America and presenting a wholesome conservative viewpoint. While we will tell our viewers that Cougar News is a no-spin zone network we are going to spin the hell out of everything we cover that it would make a Whirling Dervish dizzy. We will present the news in the briefest yet most provocative way in order to catch people's attention and gain a large viewing audience."

Megalo liked the idea but had no idea what a Whirling Dervish was. Megalo also expressed concern that women would play such a pivotal role at Cougar News instead of serving in their God given roles as homemakers.

"Aren't you giving a great deal of power and authority to the gals? And these little gals you have described don't seem like submissive types," Megalo added.

Mani comforted Megalo by telling him that "this is not an ideal situation but in order to fight against liberalism it is necessary to use an end justifies the means mentality."

"Besides, I will make sure that female employees sign a statement that while on the air they are to be tough as tigers at home they are to be as submissive as sheep." Mani added.

Mani appeased Megalo and when Megalo watched the initial broadcast of Cougar News and saw the beautiful yet forceful Sherry Spite deliver the news that reflected his point of view he was hooked. When he watched Willy O'Leary's show, "No Spin Zone," and witnessed Willy overpowering his liberal guests by continually talking over them and not allowing them to finish their sentences Megalo thought O'Leary had put on a brilliant display.

Mani also spoke to Megalo at Constantine's Steak Pit about engaging in a new style of evangelical politics.

"Megalo, we need to reinvent the Reclaiming America for Christ organization and become more aggressive politically. We have worked hard but have only won a few victories and we need to win what the liberals call the "culture war" and not just win small battles. We have been able to get a lot of our evangelical churches that the government refers to as faith-based organizations to participate in government-funded social service programs. We have some good programs in place such as job training and drug treatment services and the government is basically providing funding to help us propagate the evangelical faith and that is a good thing.

You and I both know that this is no culture war. This is a war between right and wrong. We are on God's side of the argument, as you well know. Make no mistake this is a war between the children of light and the children of darkness. Now, down in the South there is a grassroots organization that has recently developed called the Kool-Aid Brigade. The name arose when a soccer mom while serving her son's team some Grape Kool-Aid just before a game heard that the local school would not allow school sponsored prayer at any more athletic events. She gathered a group of folks from the local churches in town and they marched into the superintendent's office and told him to 'put the prayers back in or we will see that you are booted out on your ass.' They intimidated the superintendent and he caved in to their demands. When they won this small victory they became emboldened and thought that if they could get organized on a national scale that they could win bigger more important victories. They started calling themselves the Kool-Aid Brigade and I'll tell you Megalo I'll drink what they are serving. I like these people. They are my kind of folks. I detest that elitist liberal news reporter who called them the 'Kook-Aid Brigade' and described them as 'typically uneducated, racist, overweight Caucasian men and women who prefer to gorge on the Lou Ann Platter at Luby's, love to go to church on Sunday and Wednesday, enjoy sitting in the recliner and watching Cougar News every night during the week, and who hold religious and political views that are simplistic and completely self-serving.'"

Mani continued, "Megalo, these folks may not be highbrow but they are good, common folks who know are country is on the wrong track and they are serious about making some changes in our country politically. They are a bit disorganized right now so I think RAC should join up with the Brigade and support their efforts and you should lead them into battle."

Megalo loved the idea and soon RAC and the Brigade had their first joint meeting. Mani nominated Megalo to become the official head of the RAC and the Brigade and the members elected Megalo unanimously. Megalo and other leaders developed a strategy to further the political aims of RAC and the Kool-Aid Brigade that now went by the name The Alliance. First, The Alliance sponsored *Taking Back Our Country* from the Infidels rallies in big cities across the U.S. in order to galvanize the grass roots support. The rallies were held in the parking lots of Big Crappie Pro Shops. Megalo and Mani spoke to large crowds everywhere they went encouraging the people to vote the infidels out of office and to vote for faith based politicians.

Megalo cried out to the audience vast audience in the Big Crappie parking lot,

"We have been called the Silent Majority but we will be silent no more. We will win the victory over the immoral minority in our country who have been controlling Washington, the mainstream media, and our public schools and universities. We will win because we are God's faithful people and He won't let us down and we won't let Him down."

The Big Crappie rallies worked as Megalo reached a sizeable number of disaffected persons most of whom had a penchant for camouflage wear and also enjoyed looking at Bass boats.

Megalo and Mani and other members of The Alliance used the rallies and personal phone calls to recruit a huge number of "faith based politicians" to enter Senate and Congressional races. When a reporter defined a faith based politician as "one who is committed to imposing the Christian religion upon the American people via the political process," Megalo responded angrily, "A faith based politician is one who is committed to reestablishing the Christian foundations of our country."

Jimmy Jack Lanky in Oklahoma had been a Baptist youth minister with no prior political experience but with the support of The Alliance he won a seat in Congress handily. A reporter from California commented on Lanky's win.

"In Oklahoma, where you can't throw a stick without hitting a conservative Baptist, apparently the only qualification necessary for being an elected official evidently is to be a conservative Baptist."

Lanky shot back, "Having served as a leader at summer youth camps will serve me well in Congress."

In Nevada, Shelly Angel, a self-described faith based politician who claimed that praying daily to God qualified her to hold office, told reporters that God had called her to enter the Nevada Senate race to defeat her liberal opponent. She told a Christian Nationalist Network (CNN) reporter,

"When God calls you must answer even if He asks you to do something at which you are completely unqualified."

Although Angel lost her bid to become a Senator because The

Alliance could not find an effective way to discredit her popular opponent, she vowed to run again in the future.

"I have a feeling God will call on me again in a few years," Shelly told CNN.

In Texas a pastor's wife who taught elementary school for many years decided God had called her to run for Congress as well. Of course, a phone call from Megalo urging her pastor husband to recruit evangelical politicians influenced her as well. As Cally tells it, she could not sleep one night because God had put it on her heart to run for a seat in Congress.

"I argued with God. I said to God, 'I can't do this God. I'm a first grade teacher.' But God spoke to me in a still small voice, not an audible voice, but He spoke to my heart and said, 'Cally, you are here on earth for such a time as this.' Well, I just thought of Queen Esther and how she saved her people because she stepped up and spoke to the king in their behalf. So, right then and there I told God, I said 'God, I'm your girl. I will save my people from the evil Haman's of this world who want to destroy your Christian people.'"

Cally Simpletonius entered and barely won her race against a flamboyant drag queen who had recently lost his job at The Queen's Palace Ballroom and decided to give politics a try. Cally headed off to D.C. ready to serve God and country. While there Cally became alarmed when she saw what she described as numerous gay protestors pleading for certain rights. Cally came back to Texas and made a public statement condemning the aggressive gay agenda in the U.S. that sought to force Americans to accept homosexuality as a legitimate lifestyle and to "turn our children gay." Cally stated, "homosexuality is more dangerous than terrorism." Unhappy gays criticized Cally's remarks calling her statements hateful and mean-spirited. Cally's supporters held a huge Rally for Cally at the state capitol building in Austin where they cheered for her, made inflammatory remarks against gays, and ate cookies and drank grape Kool-Aid. Cally claimed later that at the rally God reached down and touched His child and whispered in her ear,

"I'm on your side. Stay strong. Keep the world straight, not gay. It's all up to you."

Cally asked Megalo to speak and he gladly complied with her request. Megalo stood behind the podium and thundered,

"I have just received word from one of my pastor friends from Minneapolis, Johnny Pipedown, that members of the Evangelical Lutheran Church of America meeting in Minneapolis for their annual meeting had a serious debate on whether to liberalize its policies towards gays. During the debate powerful tornado force winds ripped through the city and caused damage at the convention center where they were meeting. Also, the Lutheran church across the street, which had been used as a meeting venue, lost its steeple and many of its stained glass windows were damaged. Friends, Johnny Pipedown told me, and I agree with him, that Jesus brought those winds as a gentle but firm warning to the Lutherans that they better not condone sin and dishonor God by being gay friendly. If God had really wanted to make a statement the storm would have killed a few of the Lutheran leaders. God is more patient with people than I am. But I digress. Johnny Pipedown also told me that the Minneapolis storm is a warning to America that if we continue to give homosexuals rights and start treating them as human beings God will probably send devastating tornados across our entire nation that will kill many gays and gay friendly citizens but of course will spare innocent citizens. It only storms on the unjust, not the just."

Cally then took the podium and agreed with Megalo that American citizens must stand firm against the gay agenda or suffer the consequences. Cally informed her listeners that she would soon publish a book that would detail how radical, subversive forces had attacked her because of her Christian faith.

She told her audience, "The conservative Christian minority is under attack from a group of unsavory folks who want us to accept their unholy lifestyle. In my new book, *The Stoning of Cally Simpletonius*, I will share the many instances in which my opponents in the gay community have spread rumors about me and have written and said hateful things about me. I know that I must be right because so many of these people have been mean to me. Yes, their meanness proves that they are wrong and I am right."

After the rally a local reporter interviewed one of Cally's longtime friends and asked her if Cally's rhetoric could be considered as "hate speech."

Cally's friend responded, "Cally is the nicest person you will ever meet. There is not a hateful bone in her body. She is simply standing up for the truth and not being mean at all. These gay people are the ones who are being mean. They are a bunch of sick deviants and they are trying to ruin our country. But, of course, I am saying this all in the love of Christ just like Cally did and I pray for them every day because the Bible tells me to do so."

Cally further pleased her constituents whenever she refused to accept as a gift a copy of the Qur'an given to her by the President's Ethnic American Advisory Council. The president organized the Council to promote healthy religious dialogue but Cally and fifteen other lawmakers refused to accept the Qur'an. The year before the Southwide Baptist Confederation handed out Bibles to members of Congress and Cally gladly received that gift but she would not accept the Muslim Scriptures saying,

"I cannot accept a book that endorses the killing of innocent women and children. I know that not all Muslims are terrorists, but I don't know of another religion or ideology that employs terrorism and the threat of terrorism,"

With Megalo by her side Cally also stated publicly that she refused to accept the Qur'an because internationally known evangelist Frankie Cracker had been disinvited by Pentagon officials to speak at the National Day of Prayer event last year.

She told reporters, "My friend Megalo Maniac informed me that Pentagon officials had disinvited Frankie because they said he made inflammatory remarks about Muslims. According to Megalo all he said was that Islam was a violent and wicked religion and that the God of Christians is not the same God of Muslims and that Christianity and Islam is locked in an "earth-shattering struggle that will end only with the Second Coming of Christ when He comes to kick Muslim ass. Megalo helped me to see that Frankie's "dis-invitation" represents intolerance toward biblical Christianity and is actually a violation of Frankie's religious liberty. Megalo rightly stated that what Frankie said is simply that Christianity is an exclusive religion and he should not have to apologize for that. His remarks reflect nothing other than classic Christianity. The Pentagon pulled Frankie from the program for making statements that are required if one is to be faithful to Christ."

A reporter asked Cally and Megalo, "But wouldn't you two agree that making the statement that Islam is a wicked religion is different than stating that Christianity is an exclusivist religion?"

Megalo shot back, "No! Islam is wicked because it doesn't lead to salvation. That's not inflammatory. That's pure gospel. Any teaching that leads to damnation is not only false but evil."

When the reporter asked Cally and Megalo what resources they had studied to learn about Islam Cally replied,

"I conducted extensive study on the internet at many Christian web sites that provide helpful information about this cult."

Megalo agreed with Cally that Christian web sites had also helped him understand this "wicked" religion but he quickly added,

"I don't hate Muslims as individuals. I just hate their religion that blinds them from seeing the truth."

The chair of the President's Council, Marjan Salaam, told reporters that the Council never intended to force anything on anyone they simply wanted to introduce Islam to leaders in the nation through a peaceful and kind gesture. She wept when she saw the news reports about the derogatory statements that Cally and Megalo had made about her religion.

Cally pleased her constituents on another occasion when making a speech before the legislature she suggested that minorities earn less than white people because they don't work as hard and have less initiative.

Cally declared, "As a school teacher I saw a lot of people of color who didn't study hard because they said the government would take care of them. There's a high percentage of blacks in prison and that is tragic, but are they in prison because they are black or because they don't want to work hard in school?"

Cally also acknowledged that women generally don't work as hard as men and enjoy more leisure time than men therefore most women should stay at home and not pursue a career.

A reporter from the *Daily World* asked Cally, "Didn't you teach first grade? Your first graders said the government would take care of them? Really? And why have you, a woman, pursued a teaching and a political career if women should stay at home to enjoy leisure time or fix sandwiches for their husbands?"

Cally declined to answer.

Another major undertaking of Megalo's Alliance involved fighting to get or keep crosses and Ten Commandments displays on government land. In Alabama Judge Roy Hokey had to remove a 2 and ½ ton granite Ten Commandments display from the court house when the Supreme Court ruled that the display stood as an "in your face" structure that communicated to the populace that the government favors the Christian religion. When workers came to remove the granite behemoth a member of the Kool-Aid Brigade shouted,

"Get your hands off my God."

Roy Hokey would not be denied. He simply loaded his granite Ten Commandments shrine on a flatbed truck and sent it on a well-publicized tour around the country. Hokey showed up with his megalith in the parking lots of Big Crappie Pro Shops and large crowds came to see it. He handed out "Honk for Hokey" bumper stickers for free and hawked miniatures of the display for $10 each, Ten Commandments key rings for $5 each, and a signed poster of him standing beside his granite monument for $3 each.

Clarence and Juanita Muckrake of Trifling, Oklahoma waited with great anticipation until finally Hokey showed up at the Broken Arrow Big Crappie Pro Shop near their home. The cold breezy winds of March compelled Clarence to wear his jacket to see Hokey and the Ten Commandments. He could not decide whether to wear his green colored camo jacket or his Iraqi desert brown camo jacket. Finally, he decided on the green camo jacket because Spring had almost arrived and he could zip it up over his "too many pork ribs and potato salad" gut. Juanita donned her bright yellow polyester pantsuit that she had worn to all special occasions since 1961 no matter what the season. Although the threads of her pantsuit were clearly under great stress due to Juanita's giant paunch and whopping booty, she thought she looked stunning. Clarence and Juanita were delighted to meet Judge Hokey and touch his huge display. They even bought a miniature display to hang on the rear view mirror so they could admire it while they drove down the highway.

When Clarence and Juanita got in the car to leave, Clarence, with tears in his eyes, said to Juanita,

"Our country is headed for hell Juanita and I feel powerless to do anything about it. Let's do something. Let's travel around the country visiting courthouses where Ten Commandments displays are still found. We will take pictures of the displays and stand in front of them handing out flyers that read, 'Keep Your Hands off My Commandments.' We will also meet with elected officials encouraging them to keep these displays. We will meet with elected officials responsible for removing displays and we will give them a good chewing out. We will see if others from The Alliance will join us and if so we will create an unstoppable conservative convoy."

With the blessing and encouragement of Megalo, Clarence and Juanita embarked on their journey. They planned to make their final stop in Washington D.C. to view the tableau at the Supreme Court building and to invite the Supreme Court Justices out for a Whopper at Burger King and to explain to them how important the Ten Commandments are to our country's legal system. Their first stop, however, was at the courthouse in Stifler, Oklahoma. Although a church sat across the street from the courthouse and a Ten Commandments display could have easily been placed there, the local judge wanted the display to be put on the lawn in front of the courthouse. Clarence and Juanita took pictures beside the display, met with the local judge who told them that the display would be removed over his dead body. The judge took them to lunch and told them about the town.

"One of the ironies of Stifler is that our mascot here is a Black Panther yet not a single black person lives in this town. And that's the way we want it too. We want our Ten Commandments to be displayed proudly at the court house and we don't want no black people," the judge said proudly.

Clarence and Juanita smiled and nodded approvingly. Before leaving Stifler Clarence and Juanita visited the display one more time when Juanita noticed that one of the commandments read,

"Thou shall not commit adultry."

"Clarence, I believe the word adultery is misspelled on the display," Juanita said unconfidently.

"No, honey, the word is spelled just how it sounds, adultry. Anyway, who cares about spelling? Now, let's go to the capitol building in Austin, Texas to see that big ole 6 foot tall Ten Commandments display," said Clarence as he climbed into his lime green Ford F-150.

Megalo also led The Alliance to sponsor the Save Christmas Campaign. Megalo had been shopping at the mall a few days before Christmas when the clerk in Dillards handed him his packages and said,

"Happy Holidays."

Megalo became angry.

"You mean Merry Christmas don't you?"

The clerk gave Megalo a puzzled look and went on her way. Megalo began visiting other stores and noticed the same trend. So, he became determined to save Christmas for the United States of America. Megalo preached to Alliance members across the nation telling them to go into stores and say "Merry Christmas" to everyone they met.

"And if a clerk gives you any of that Happy Holidays crap, politely but firmly tell the clerk, 'You say Merry Christmas to me right now or I'm putting back all this stuff I just bought.' And folks, you need to be prepared to put your stuff back because a clerk working during Christmas may be a secularist or a Jew celebrating Hanukkah or one of those crazies who celebrates that weird new Kwanza thing."

In the meantime Megalo met with some faith based politicians in Washington encouraging them to sponsor a Merry Christmas bill that would require everyone in the U.S. to greet one another by saying "Merry Christmas" from December 10-25. Those who refused to comply would receive a $1,000 fine and would have to stand beside the Salvation Army ringers and say "Merry Christmas to 1,000 persons. The politicians thought it to be a splendid idea but doubted it would pass until more faith based politicians made it into Congress.

"This is definitely something we can anticipate doing ten or twenty years down the road," said the senior Senator from Oklahoma.

The Alliance also lobbied Congress encouraging them to support Israel against her enemies no matter what. In fact, The Alliance formed a special committee called Christians United for Israel whose aim was to convince the politicians in Washington never to denounce Israel and to be prepared always to offer military assistance to Israel.

Megalo told his congressman, "God is going to be on the side of His people, no matter what, so if the U.S. refuses to side with Israel at any time the U.S. will find itself fighting against God himself."

An aide to the congressman who had studied theology at Princeton asked Megalo, "How can you equate the modern nation of Israel with the Israel of the Hebrew Bible?"

Megalo answered, "Son, Israel is Israel no matter what the time period."

The next Sunday Megalo preached a sermon about the need for Christians to rally to support Israel by denouncing the Palestinian thugs who were trying to destroy God's people. A local reporter heard Megalo's sermon and asked him afterward,

"Rev. Megalo, I thought you did not care for Jews too much? You have made disparaging remarks against them in the past haven't you? Remember when Congressman Tony Bonner sexted his package to young girls and at first said he just wanted to show off his circumcision to Gentiles but then resigned amidst the scandal and then later entered a rehab program for sexual addiction? Remember what you said? You told him that Jesus, not rehab, would solve his sexual addiction problems."

Megalo cut in, "Well, I do believe that if the Congressman were a Christian instead of Jew then he wouldn't be sending pictures of his package to young girls on the internet. People that are high on Jesus simply don't do that sort of thing. But people who are high on Moses do that sort of thing."

The reporter added, "And didn't you once write in one of your books that you believed Henry Kissinger to be the anti-Christ?"

Megalo responded quickly, "I love Israel. The nation of Israel is what I love. I don't care so much for Jews as individuals and I never liked Kissinger but I love the people of Israel." The reporter walked away scratching his head and sporting a rather confused look.

Megalo claimed that all the recent Republican presidents sought his advice on foreign policy matters and that he constantly encouraged both Republican and Democratic presidents to embrace a pro-Israeli foreign policy. Megalo even set up a special web site in which visitors could offer virtual prayers in a virtual White House. Visitors could click on the door of the White House and enter and then click on the door of any room and go in and offer prayers for the president and his advisors. When visitors to the web site entered the oval office the president and Megalo greeted them. The virtual president would tell visitors how he and Megalo had been discussing political and spiritual matters but did not mind being interrupted in order to engage in a time of prayer.

Megalo even hosted a debate between the Republican and Democratic presidential candidates in his church but things didn't go so well. Megalo's clear Republican bias surfaced regularly during the debate. Four years later during the next election Megalo invited the presidential candidates to attend another debate at his church but both candidates refused his offer. A spurned Megalo, who had already put tickets on sale for the event, told his followers he cancelled the debate because the campaigns carried on by both candidates had become so uncivil he wanted nothing to do with either of them.

Megalo not only claimed to have a special relationship with presidents, he also claimed to have a special relationship with several governors. Megalo did in fact meet with the governors of South Carolina, Oklahoma, Texas, and Arizona one at a time and encouraged them to legalize the use of "I Believe" license plates for cars.

Megalo told the governors, "Specialty license plates can have all sorts of messages on them, so why shouldn't a Christian be allowed to put an "I Believe" license plate on his or her car? The message of the plate is clear but still vague enough that it should please secularists."

All the governors loved the idea and soon evangelical drivers from those states sported new "I Believe" plates. The Supreme Court, however, ruled the plates to be constitutionally invalid and soon "I Believe" license plates adorned the garage walls of many angry evangelicals.

"You see what our country has become. We Christians are being persecuted for our faith when our government should offer us special treatment," Megalo told Sherry Spite of Cougar News during a special report.

Megalo basically took over Sherry's News Report by going on a lengthy rant. Megalo complained about the government not allowing crèches and crosses on public property in many instances.

Megalo fumed, "Sherry, along with the bald eagle and the American flag the cross is one of the greatest patriotic symbols of our country. Yet, our government is taking down crosses from public lands and taking crosses off of city and county seals just to appease the secularists who refuse to believe that we are indeed a Christian nation. God will judge us. In fact, God is already judging us with a bad economy and then we have had terrorist attacks and threats of future attacks. And it's all because we are taking down crosses while at the same time giving rights to homosexuals. Sherry, God is judging our country and that is why the American people must support The Alliance. We must take our country back and put it safely in Christian hands once again. And, by the way, my I say that you are looking rather stunning this evening Sherry. I watch your show all the time and think you are great. I was so excited when I learned that you had invited me to be on your show."

After the show Megalo invited Sherry to have coffee with him but she declined until Megalo told her that he had an American Express Black Card that he needed to use and he would be willing to use it to by her some nice things.

"Isn't that the card that in order to apply you have to receive a special invitation and you have to agree to spend at least $250,000 annually? Sherry asked with excitement in her voice.

"That's the card Sherry and I have only spent $150,000 so far this year and I really need to use the card and I would love to use it to buy you some nice things." Megalo said as he grabbed his jacket ready to head out the door.

Sherry grabbed her coat as well and the two headed out to do some serious shopping. Sherry did ask Megalo to avoid walking down Subsistence Street on the way to the exclusive shops because too many homeless people littered the sidewalks there and she did not like having to step around and over them.

Megalo agreed saying, "Those people are annoying for sure. If only they would emulate the wealthy, get jobs, be productive and take some pride in themselves then they could be prosperous and happy and our streets would be a lot safer."

Megalo also served on the Texas Board of Education having been elected five years in a row. Megalo decided to run for election because he wanted to change the curriculum that Texas students utilized. According to Megalo, textbooks used in public schools, especially history, social studies and science books, all had a liberal bias and he simply wanted to bring balance to the textbooks by making changes so that the textbooks would reflect conservative views. During Megalo's time on the Board therefore he worked assiduously to put a conservative stamp on textbooks that would be used in Texas schools. Megalo knew that changes made in Texas would affect other states as well.

Megalo told governor Ricky Sonny Bob, "Sonny, the Texas textbook market is large. We have almost five million students. Textbooks we use often move to the top of the market, decreasing costs for school districts in other states and leading them to buy the same books. What the Board is about to do will have far reaching consequences and will influence the education of young people not only in Texas but across our great nation."

Because the Board had a conservative majority Megalo's motions always passed. The Board approved Megalo's amendment giving the National Rifle Association credit for achieving civil rights in the U.S. and placing blame on the Black Panthers for the Birmingham bombings. Off the record, the Board discussed the fact that Martin Luther King Jr. had too many streets named after him in cities across the nation and that even though they couldn't do anything about it at least they could complain about it to each other while they drank their Hazelnut House Blend Coffee.

The Board also passed Megalo's amendment that the separation of church and state is a constitutional myth and that "our children should be taught that our country was founded on Christian beliefs." The Board approved Megalo's motion to emphasize that during WW II the U.S. government not only placed Japanese in internment camps but also Italians and Germans as well. According to Megalo, this fact would counter the idea that racism played a role in the placing of Japanese into internment camps. Megalo made a motion that Senator McCarthy should be presented as a standup guy and an American patriot who protected our country from numerous Communist infiltrators, although he never nailed comedienne Lucille Ball.

When Megalo moved that Thomas Jefferson should be cut from a list of figures whose writings influenced American society significantly and that he should be replaced with John Calvin and Thomas Aquinas the Board clapped and cheered as they approved his motion.

One Board member shouted out, "Out with Tommy J. and in with Tommy Q."

The Board also passed a motion that Darwin's evolutionary theory would be taught alongside creationism with both views being given equal weight and that teachers should emphasize that Adam and Eve were literal persons.

A religion professor criticizing this viewpoint commented, "I find it ironic that extreme literalists actually end up believing in myths because they are so devoted to their ideological system."

In the end the Board approved over one hundred curriculum changes without consulting any professional historians, scientists, or sociologists because Megalo assured the Board that he had expertise in all these areas.

"We are so thankful to God that He sent Megalo the brilliant to guide us through this very difficult process," said Tru Bleever to other members of the Board.

Although professional scholars from around the country criticized the Boards' actions claiming that many of the changes made were inaccurate, Megalo responded by stating that "the only concern of the Board is to promote the conservative agenda and to put liberals on the run. I have spent my life defending my conservative Lord Jesus Christ in this liberal, Godless world and I will never quit the battle."

## Commercial Break

"I can't believe our series has come to an end," Natu the Narrator remarked. "Megalo and I were talking this morning and were both in agreement that we could go on for weeks and weeks discussing Megalo's life. But, alas, we have to end things here. It's time for the vote folks. You can either call in or text your vote to 'M-e-g-a-l-o' and we will record your vote and announce the winning contribution after the votes are tallied in just a few minutes after we return from commercial break. Sit back and enjoy this five-minute commercial from one of our great sponsors, Colonel Bootupurass from Strike First Torture Training and Weapons Manufacturers. Before Colonel Bootupurass comes to share products the folks at Premillennial Motors wanted me to thank you for your overwhelming response to the Rapture 1000. Mary Natha informed me just today that they sold more vehicles this past week than in the past six months. So, if you loved the Rapture 1000 you will certainly enjoy the product we have for you this week."

Hello people. My name is Colonel Bootupurass and I am here today to show you that you need three things to survive in the world today and in the future. You need Jesus, the knowledge of how to torture infidels who have infiltrated our country, and smart weapons. At Strike First Torture Training and Weapons Manufacturers we guarantee not only to make you into a master Waterboarder we will teach you to use the rack as well. Oh, yes, we have brought back that medieval torture device and updated it making it a certainty that you will garner a confession from any terrorist. Think about it, you probably have Muslim terrorists in your neighborhood waiting to strike. Is there a mosque in your neighborhood? Do you look up in the sky only to see a star and a crescent moon staring down at you from that nearby building? Then, please don't wait. Come train with us then go to the mosque, find out where the terrorists live and one by one drag them from their homes and into that secret room in your home and interrogate them. You can find out where in the mosque Muslims are hiding their weapons. You can discover what terrorist acts Muslims are about to carry out in your neighborhood and beyond. Waterboard the hell out of them. Put them on the rack. Torturing is an art that must be learned. We will teach you how to torture with precision so that you can find out anything from anybody.

If you think your son or daughter is having premarital sex then you can use it on them as well. I guarantee it will work because I have used it on my own kids. I saved my daughter from an unwanted pregnancy of this I am certain. And even though she still has nightmares it was damn well worth the price. We also have a huge supply of weapons on hand in case a neighborhood war between evangelicals and Muslims does break out. One of my favorite guns is the Hand Held Savior. This small device fits in the palm of your hand so you can conceal it easily. If a terrorist strikes you don't want to have to reach down and grab a weapon from an ankle holster. No, the Hand Held Savior is already in the palm of your hand so that when you spot a terrorist or if you see a terrorist about to fire upon you all you have to do is raise your arm and point your index finger and the Hand Held Savior will shoot hundreds of tiny bullets that will kill the Muslim terrorist on impact. The Hand Held Savior is very accurate and easy to use. If you can point your finger you can shoot it. If you call 1-888-TOR-TURE today or visit our web site at StrikeFirst.com we will be happy to answer any of your questions and set up a training appointment and a weapons demonstration for you. Usually, it will take at least a month to complete our torture and weapons training program. For a cost of only $500 we will teach you how to survive in this era of terrorism. Consider giving us a call today. This is Colonel Bootupurass signing off. Good night friends!

# Epilogue:

# Where's Megalo

During the commercial break Megalo walked back to his office to rest for a minute because he felt especially tired. He was sweating profusely. As he leaned back in his office chair, Megalo grabbed his chest and slumped forward. Megalo had a massive heart attack and died instantly. Natu came to get Megalo so he could return to the stage for the big finale but instead Natu found Megalo without a pulse. Natu called 911 and the medics arrived but could not resuscitate Megalo. An anxious crowd knew something had happened but did not know that Megalo had died. After the commercial break a distraught Natu returned to stage and informed the audience that Megalo had just died. The stunned crowd gasped in unison and many in the audience cried aloud. Natu broke down but composed himself enough to announce that it just did not seem right to reveal the results of the audience vote.

The great and wonderful Megalo Maniac had not lived to hear the final results and no one else except Natu would ever know the final results either.

One woman in the audience commented to a friend, "How utterly disappointing that someone so great did not ever get the chance to see what his followers deemed his greatest accomplishment."

Indeed, Megalo died knowing his legacy would be great but not knowing what he could name as his greatest accomplishment. What a pity.

Megalo's funeral could not be adequately described with mere words. He had asked to be buried in a red, white, and blue coffin with a huge white cross atop. On one side of the church hung a giant banner with a picture of the *Ultimater* on it. On the other side of the church attendees saw a huge American flag hanging. At the front of the church a huge Christian flag hung. Megalo's two favorite flags were the white Christian flag with its signature red cross atop a blue background and the American flag with its familiar stars and stripes. Side by side in his office two smaller versions of these flags stood and sometimes when Megalo would pray in his office he would wrap the American flag with the Christian flag and pray earnestly that the Lord would destroy the evil and recent idea of separation of church and state and wrap the nation's government in the Christian religion once again as in the days of old.

A massive picture of Megalo holding his trademark Bible appeared up on the screen above his coffin. The funeral company in charge of the service had taken care of many Southwide Baptist Confederation funerals. The Kountry Kathedral Kompany carried out their duties carefully and with great solemnity. All the KKK employees wore white pants and shirts and white gloves to symbolize their purity. One of Megalo's favorite Southern Gospel groups called Absolute Assurance sang, "God Made Heaven Just For Me." They also sang a song Megalo wrote against his opponents called, "Without a Doubt, I'm In, You're Out." Another gospel group that Sue B. liked called the Doctrinaires sang "The Old Narrow Boundary," and "Are You Washed in the Beliefs of Our Church?"

Megalo's many friends spoke about his greatness, his unwavering commitment to Christ, his unbending dedication to seek the truth, his loving and gentle nature toward all persons, especially his enemies. Never had any individual in the Southwide Confederation received the number and quality of encomiums as Megalo Maniac. Sue B. grieved but felt a sense of pride at the same time.

After the lengthy funeral Megalo's friends met together at his palatial estate and discussed how happy Megalo must be sitting in heaven with Jesus reaping his rewards for exemplary service.

"I'll bet he and Jesus are sitting together on the steps of Megalo's mansion right now and laughing and having a great time," said Uncle Anthony.

Yet unbeknownst to his friends Megalo simply slept and he would just keep on sleeping forever. He never awoke to the paradise he expected. Oh, and that's not to suggest that everyone who has lived will sleep forever after they die. But Megalo did sleep. And he just kept on sleeping.

A hundred years after his death the Southwide Baptist Confederation had dwindled to a small acorn due to doctrinal infighting, the embracing of retrogressive practices, and its general irrelevance to the lives of most people in the world. Megalo slept through the decline of the Confederation although when alive he claimed that the Confederation was God's last and only hope to save a godless world. Megalo could not see that in his day the best days of the Confederation lay in the past. Megalo and his pals contributed significantly to the demise of the Confederation although in their day they were rulers of a great kingdom. In the SBC, the politicians had always won the day but in the end egoism and self-righteous partisan politics disguised as piety and altruism destroyed the Confederation. The self-serving politicians thought they were saving the Confederation but they couldn't see that the organization was not worth saving. They failed to see too that they were ruling a kingdom of dinosaurs. Yes, even in Megalo's era the Southwide Baptist Confederation had already become a toothless Tyrannosaurus Rex aimlessly hunting for food completely unaware that a giant asteroid would soon make him extinct. When the Southwide Baptist Confederation began its slow decline the leaders could never pinpoint the problems because they were not capable of true reflection either personally or corporately. The leaders blamed the decline on pastors who didn't work hard enough at saving people, prayerless churches, apathetic parishioners, attacks by liberals upon the denomination, and so on. How difficult it is for a person to look in the mirror and say, "I am the problem."

Megalo's legacy died when the Southwide Baptist Confederation died. And to add insult to injury, Megalo would never receive divine approval for his ideas and his actions as he thought he would. Had God really paid any attention to Megalo's doings or had God been working to inspire persons to feed the hungry, to give water to the thirsty, and to comfort the hurting? Megalo, God's great defender, missed God altogether. If God exists as a being, a spirit, a presence, or a force, would a "God For Others" stand in the hall of the proud and the powerful or be found stooped low on the margins taking care of the oppressed?

Really, Megalo had slept his whole life away. Even though Megalo claimed he needed only five hours of sleep a night to function he never was awake. He never considered that he might be wrong because he thought he could discern the mind of God. Megalo believed that he knew God; thus Megalo became God. Life became all about Megalo. Megalo advocated what could be called the Priesthood of the Will of God. That is, when a person believes he or she has cultivated such a close relationship with God that the person can know with absolutely certainty what God wants him or her to do in practically every situation in life. Megalo believed he followed God's will almost perfectly. Because he knew the mind and will of God Megalo believed he served as a conduit through which God spoke to other lowly humans whose only role was to listen to and heed Megalo's voice. Megalo heard his own voice and mistook it for the voice of God. He never joined the company of the awakened ones and he never would. The awakened ones are the ones at the edges of life who question, probe, explore, inquire, search, and are not afraid to dissent. The awakened ones question a corrupt establishment even at great personal cost. Awakened ones reflect upon their own actions and seek honestly to address their flaws while embracing and celebrating their strengths. These are actions that human beings must do while it is still daylight because the night comes all too soon and we cannot be certain that after we die we will awaken. But if we do, perhaps it will be for the purpose of further exploration. As we go through life we must act upon conviction without certain proof that we have obtained the truth. Uncertainty, though, should not paralyze but move us forward all the more quickly. Only sleep causes us to cease our questioning. There will be time enough for sleep. Today is the day to be awake. Wake up and live.

www.ingramcontent.com/pod-product-compliance
Lightning Source LLC
Chambersburg PA
CBHW051512260626
47162CB00008B/2942